GOLD RUSH ORPHAN

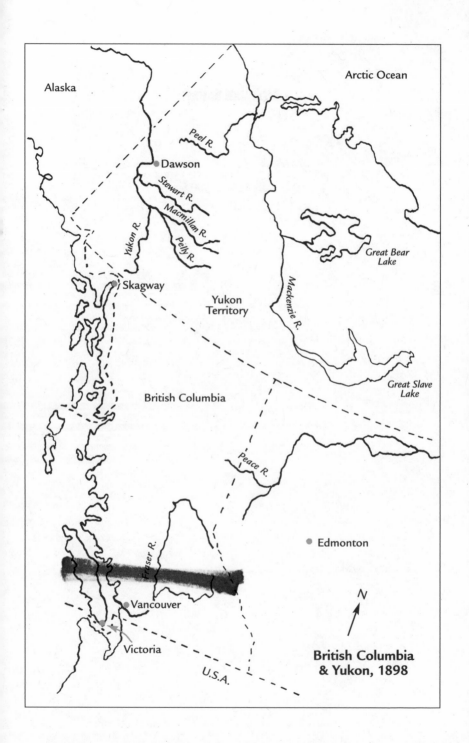

British Columbia & Yukon, 1898

GOLD RUSH ORPHAN

Sandy Frances Duncan

RONSDALE PRESS

GOLD RUSH ORPHAN
Copyright © 2004 Sandy Frances Duncan

RONSDALE PRESS
3350 West 21st Avenue
Vancouver, B.C., Canada V6S 1G7
www.ronsdalepress.com

Typesetting: Julie Cochrane, in Minion 12 pt on 16
Cover Design: Rand Berthaudin
Author Photo: C.T. Humphrey
Paper: Ancient Forest Friendly Rolland "Enviro" — 100% post-consumer
    waste, totally chlorine-free and acid-free

Ronsdale Press wishes to thank the Canada Council for the Arts, the Government of Canada through the Book Publishing Industry Development Program (BPIDP), and the Province of British Columbia through the British Columbia Arts Council for their support of its publishing program.

National Library of Canada Cataloguing in Publication

Duncan, Sandy Frances, (date)
    Gold rush orphan / Sandy Frances Duncan.

ISBN 1-55380-012-5

I. Klondike River Valley (Yukon) — Gold discoveries — Juvenile fiction.
I. Title.

PS8557.U5375G64 2004   jC813'.54   C2003-906868-4

Printed in Canada by Hignell Printing, Winnipeg, Manitoba

For my grandson,
James Llewellyn Maxwell,
with gratitude to my
mother's father, who was
James Allen Fraser

Acknowledgements

The writer wishes to thank her family and the many friends who helped, suggested, and generally put up with her during the years of researching and writing this book. Any errors are hers.

This book was written with financial support from the Canada Council for the Arts and from the British Columbia Arts Council, for which the writer is very grateful.

I

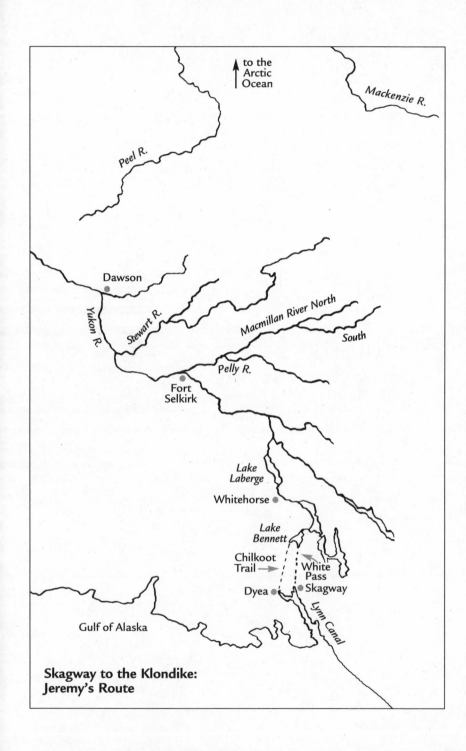

to the
Arctic
Ocean

Mackenzie R.

Peel R.

Dawson

Yukon R.

Stewart R.

Macmillan River North

South

Pelly R.

Fort
Selkirk

Lake
Laberge

Whitehorse

Lake
Bennett

Chilkoot
Trail

White
Pass

Dyea

Skagway

Gulf of Alaska

Lynn Canal

**Skagway to the Klondike:
Jeremy's Route**

1

How it all Began

[On February 7th, 1898, James A. Fraser of Vancouver, British Columbia, began a new journal in which, for the next eight and a half months, he would write a daily entry about his trip to Yukon.]

Monday February 7th 1898

Arose at 3 a.m. went down to office & worked till 8:30, went home to breakfast & said goodbye to family. To dock at 1:30 expecting to sail any moment. Hung around dock till 4:30 when we left on Steamer Danube for Dyea, 4 men & self, with 11 dogs, 2 horses & about 4 tons supplies & outfit for Yukon. Reached Nanaimo 9:30, lay there till midnight. Morning showery, afternoon fine but cold.

Tuesday 8th Feb 98

Steamer collided with buoy in harbor & in getting free ran aground and lay there 2 hours. Anchor toppled over on deck & killed a dog or two. Raining hard all day. Was very rough on horses & dogs which are tied on forward deck without any shelter. Large crowd aboard, more than steamer can properly accommodate. Wrote some letters. Many seasick.

Wednesday 9th Feb 1898

Had rough passage across Queen Charlotte Sound, steamer tossed around a good deal, many sick. Found an old acquaintance aboard in J.R. Perry who is going up to Dyea for Col. Domville's Co. lumbering. Recalled some interesting reminiscences of twenty years ago. Passed wreck of Corona about 10:30 p.m. was very dark. Raining hard & blowing & could not land, lay to for some time.

Sat 12th Feb 1898

Cold & stormy all day. Reached Skagway about 8 p.m. Went ashore, saw customs officials, got release for horses & dogs & feed, tent &c. Watched landing of freight & baggage. Slept on board steamer.

Sunday 13th Feb 1898

Was up early & got our stock & baggage ashore. Went to Skagway Hotel to sleep & took meals in Eating House. Attended Reverend Mr. Dickey's Sunday School in p.m. No general regard for Sunday here. Carpenters, blacksmiths etc. working. Stores, saloons, gambling dens all open full swing.

Jeremy looked over the side of the long wharf at the snowy tidal flats. Behind him, the over-crowded steamer from Vancouver unloaded passengers, dogs, horses, crates, sleds, rocking chairs, bicycles and hundred-pound sacks of beans. Jeremy was jostled and shoved and elbowed in the back as people streamed by, but he paid no attention. In front of him was Skagway and, through those mountains behind, that was where Klondike must be.

The sun found a break in the clouds and glinted off the snowy peaks that rose to left and right. It highlighted the buildings and tents ahead while shadowing the spaces between them. Jeremy breathed in deeply. The cold air prickled his nostrils, and he exhaled through his mouth, watching his breath glitter. He smiled to himself, then included a nearby man with a sack on his back and three pack-laden dogs. The man looked surprised.

Jeremy slung his knapsack and half-empty bag over his shoulder. Should he have sold so many newspapers on the *Danube?* He'd get a better price here. But more papers would arrive on tomorrow's steamer, and he'd made fifteen dollars.

Past the high tide line, stacked in the trampled, muddy snow were caches of bales and barrels and boxes, some stamped with their owners' names, others marked by upright sticks flying coloured strips of cloth in the off-shore breeze. People, dogs, and horses laboured up the wharf from the steamer, deposited their loads, and returned for more. The piles were growing enormous. Jeremy was glad he'd travelled light.

It felt good to stretch his legs. Three days on the boat and the deck so crowded he could only shuffle. The shipping company had over-booked three people for each berth, but Jeremy had found room under a bench in the lounge. Close to the door. Good thing, he'd had to throw up so much. One whole day he'd spent hanging over the railing. And now land again, though it seemed to be tossing as much as the boat.

At the end of the wharf, Jeremy crossed the frozen rutted road. Streets radiated in three directions, full of people and animals. Broadway, in front of him, was lined for blocks with new wooden buildings fronted by boardwalks. Some of the buildings had signs — GOLDEN NUGGET HOTEL, TAYLOR'S MERCHANDISE & FEED — and a number flew American flags.

Oh yeah, Skagway was in Alaska, that was the United States, but somehow he'd figured it would be the same as Vancouver or Victoria. He'd never paid attention to flags. He wouldn't now, he decided, as he climbed up onto the boardwalk.

The walk teemed with people and the road with pack-laden horses, oxen, dogs, wagons and sleds. Skinny dogs were everywhere, skulking at the edge of the boardwalk, darting between horses' legs, barking, fighting, or just shivering. Men clomped into and out of the nearest saloon. Jeremy parked his knapsack by the door and displayed his papers. "*Vancouver World!* Latest News! Read all about it!" he yelled.

"How much, Sonny?"

"Fifteen cents." Jeremy watched the man dig the coins out of his pocket. He handed him a paper. The man winked and whispered, "Better charge thirty cents like everyone else or they'll run you out of town."

Thirty cents! Six times the cost of a paper in Vancouver! Jeremy had thought he was pushing his luck to triple the price. At this rate he'd get rich in no time, even before seeing Klondike. "*Vancouver World!*" he yelled again. "Read the latest news!"

The saloon door burst open and a blur of men rushed out, shouting, "You go that way, I'll go this way, don't worry, we'll catch him!" This was thrown at a bewildered man who hesitated while three others ran off.

"Someone in there stole my wallet," the man told passersby who'd slowed to observe the commotion.

"Did you see who did it?" a man asked.

"No, but a chap said he saw and he's gone after him." The robbed man shook his head. "How will I get to the goldfields if I don't get my money back?"

Bystanders craned their necks to look up the road. Someone said, "Lot of money goes missing since Smith's come to town."

"Who's Smith?" The robbed man looked about thirty. He had a handlebar moustache and was wearing a new red and black mackinaw over a white shirt, new wool pants, and new boots.

"Thinks he runs the town. Came here last summer from Colorado. Has a saloon down the block — Jeff's Place. You'd best stay clear of him." The informant spat into the road, just missing a dog. His clothes were worn and mud-spattered. He had a gun in a holster. Jeremy shifted his papers to his other arm.

"Watch out Smith don't charge you with maligning his character," another man butted in. He had a gun too. "We'd a had a lynching as well as two murders if it hadn't been for Smith!"

"Murders!" Jeremy blurted.

The last speaker, whose waxed moustache set off his three-piece suit, flicked his eyes to Jeremy. "Couple a weeks ago. The deputy marshal and another man. The marshal's wife was having a baby right at that very minute. Poor little tyke got born to no father." He shook his head. "But Smith stopped any lynching."

"Yeah — protecting a thug like himself!" The muddy man spat again. "That's what I think of Smith! Smooth-talking opportunist!" He stomped off down the boardwalk. The scattered dogs instantly regrouped. The other man sneered, then turned into the saloon.

The crowd drifted away, four men and one woman with newspapers. Jeremy had only five papers left. The robbed man paced up and down in front of the saloon. Dogs darted at his ankles or slunk onto the road. The three men who had chased after the thief returned. "No luck, pardner," one of them drawled. "We looked everywhere. He's clean gone, probably halfway to Klondike by now."

"Maybe the Canadians'll nab him at the summit," another man added. He was better dressed than the other two and Jeremy thought he looked like a minister though he also had a gun in a holster. He put his arm around the robbed man's dejected shoulders and steered him into the saloon saying, "Come on boys, let's buy this fellow a drink while he figures out what to do."

Jeremy glanced around, then felt his pocket to make sure his money was safe. "*Vancouver World!*" he yelled and a terrier-sort-of dog barked.

Within half an hour he had sold the remaining papers. He

couldn't have stood there any longer, he was so cold, despite the thick jacket and boots he'd bought at a secondhand shop in Vancouver. The sun had dropped behind the mountains an hour ago and now the dark was deep, even though it was only five o'clock. Jeremy was also hungry.

He picked up his knapsack and headed toward a sign that read *SKAGWAY HOTEL Clean Beds DINING ROOM Home Cooking.* In the foyer he took off his mittens and rubbed his hands. Red-fringed gaslights hung from the ceiling over groups of plush armchairs and settees. It'll cost too much, Jeremy thought, but he walked to the desk anyway. "How much for a room?" he asked, trying to make his voice low and deep.

"Ten dollars," the stout woman answered. "But we don't rent rooms to minors. Anyway, we're already full for tonight."

Miners, Jeremy heard. Wasn't everyone going to Klondike to mine? "Thanks anyway," he said.

On the way out, he read the menu posted by the dining room. *Steak flambé avec champignons $5.00. Saumon avec sauce des oeufs frappé $4.00.* This was where he'd eat when he came back from Klondike. *Flambé, frappé, champignons.* He'd have those each night when he was rich, whatever they were.

Outside, the cold struck him anew. Dogs shivered everywhere, including the terrier-sort that had hung around the saloon. Jeremy pulled on his mittens and tugged his soft peaked cap low over his ears. Food and a place to sleep. You know how to do this, he told himself. You've done it lots since people in Vancouver haven't been buying papers or wanting jobs done. Just because it's a strange town . . .

He started walking. A block closer to the Klondike he saw *EAT-ING HOUSE meals $2.00.* That's more like it, though things sure are expensive here. He actually was hungry for the first time since he'd got on the *Danube.*

Jeremy resisted opening the door because he knew that once

he'd eaten he'd be too sleepy to find a bed. At the corner he turned left, walked six blocks to the outskirts of town and turned down a rutted lane, scouting possibilities. The terrier dog followed him, he could see it when he turned his head. A chicken coop, that'd be good, warmed by hens, and maybe free eggs for breakfast. The door was padlocked.

Farther down, a stable. Horses gave off a lot of warmth, and there'd be straw to sleep in. The door was padlocked. More chicken coops, more stables, all padlocked. Never seen so many locks, Jeremy thought. Locks and dogs.

Behind a barn, he found some loose siding and pulled at it. Nails popped. He could pry the boards out far enough to climb in. Satisfied, he walked back to the EATING HOUSE, still followed by the dirty, skinny, brown terrier. Dogs shivered by the door. The terrier nudged closer, hoping, like the rest of them, to slink in. "No," Jeremy muttered and half-kicked at them all as he scuttled through.

Steamy warmth surrounded tables lined with men and women bent over plates. He sat down, stuffed his cap and mittens in his pockets and unbuttoned his coat. His stomach cramped. He hoped it was from hunger, not the nausea of seasickness. He glanced around for the waiter. "You got to go to the counter to get food," the man seated next to him said. "They don't serve you at table. I'll watch your coat."

"It's okay." Jeremy gathered it up. "Thanks."

At the back of the building, he picked up a plate and held it out to a man in a white apron who ladled baked beans and beef stew out of large pots, then placed a baking powder biscuit on top. "Two dollars and help yourself to coffee."

Jeremy paid. He took his plate and a fork. The chair he'd first sat in was still empty. He sat down and ate as fast as everyone else. He loaded a cup with coffee from a pot on the table, added sugar and canned milk, drank it, then poured more. The man across the table still had half a biscuit on his plate. "If you're not eating that, can I have it?" Jeremy asked. The man looked surprised, but nodded.

Jeremy buttoned his jacket, put on cap and mittens, and picked up the biscuit. Outside, the terrier wagged its tail. Jeremy gave him the biscuit. Henry? Mr. Hammond called all his dogs Henry. In the three years Jeremy had been the Hammonds' apprentice, there'd been four Henrys. No, Mr. Hammond beat his dogs as much as he'd beaten Jeremy. Well then, he could call the dog H. No, Hank! After the gardener at the Orphanage! Hank was a nice man and he'd told Jeremy *Hank* was a nickname for Henry.

"Come on, Hank," Jeremy tried. He retraced his steps and Hank came along. Even in the dark, people and animals continued to pack mounds of supplies toward Klondike. Jeremy walked close to the buildings; the muddy, slushy road was so crowded.

At the barn, he pulled aside the loose boards, boosted Hank in, and wiggled through. The boards clattered back into place behind him. By feel he located a pile of straw and what might be empty feed bags. Not the first time he'd slept in a barn; would there ever be a last time? He lay down and covered himself and the dog up. Hank stank. Jeremy turned away.

He'd got to Skagway; now how was he going to get to Klondike?

Jeremy dreamed of fireworks. Too cold for July First so it had to be Hallowe'en. He awakened — pitch dark — barn — Skagway — not fireworks: gunfire. Far away, dogs barked frantically. Hank shivered and inched closer to Jeremy who'd turned toward him in sleep. Jeremy sat up, thought better of it, and burrowed back under the feed bags. Hank growled in his throat. The shots didn't sound too close, but Jeremy didn't know about guns. He'd seen more guns today, he realized, than in all his life. And murders! They'd had murders here! Jeremy shivered and sweated as he lay on the straw, his arm around Hank, even if the dog did smell. But sleep was a long time returning.

2

Tuesday Feb. 15th

McLeod, Patterson & Self took horses, dogs & camp outfit & went out between 2 & 3 miles & camped. Wintemute & Rimmer out to camp later. Rigging up sleds & harness &c. 10 to 15 below zero, strong wind. Put pockets in my pants, coat & jersey. Expected clearance from Customs having paid Bond Commission ($56.00) but was disappointed.

When Jeremy awoke the next morning, it was still dark. He folded up the feed bags and kicked the straw around so whoever came to feed the animals would not suspect an overnight guest. He picked up his knapsack, pushed Hank through the boards, crawled through himself and, after using the nearest outhouse, headed to the EATING HOUSE. Jeremy collected a bowl of oatmeal and a plate of ham and eggs with two baking powder biscuits — he grabbed another when the cook turned away — paid his two dollars and sat down. "When does the next steamer arrive?" he asked.

"One's due at noon," a burly man answered. Someone else added, "One docked last night. It's leaving soon."

When he'd finished eating, Jeremy gave Hank a biscuit and started down to the wharf. The wind hit him in the face. It moaned around buildings and swirled snow down the streets. Jeremy pulled his collar up and tucked in his chin. Already he was cold. Hank trotted by his side.

Copies of the *Vancouver World* were stacked by the steamer's gangplank. Jeremy found a ship's mate, paid him three dollars and signed J. Britain on a receipt. Then he counted out one hundred copies and shoved them in his bag. Turning his back to the wind and whitecapped swell pounding up Lynn Canal, he ran to his spot in front of the saloon. Business sounded good inside even this early and the door was surrounded by dogs. Hank joined them.

Between customers, Jeremy jogged up and down, trying to keep warm. If he sold one hundred papers a day, he'd make twenty-seven dollars profit. That would be one hundred sixty-two dollars a week, over eight thousand dollars a year. What a good thing he'd come here! In Vancouver, in the best of times, he'd only made two dollars a day, which was twelve dollars a week, six hundred a year. Maybe he should just stay in Skagway and get rich from news-papers.

Rich! Should he buy a bicycle or a camera first? If he bought a bicycle he could deliver papers and charge more. But he'd be too rich to have to work. Maybe he'd buy one of those new motor cars he'd seen pictures of. He'd have to order it from the East. Maybe he'd have the first motor car in Vancouver. If he bought the car he could go to Victoria and drive up to the Home and lean on that horn they said cars had that went ka-BOW-ka. Wouldn't Matron have a fit! If he had a car he could look for Cowlick Sunday, his best friend ever. Too bad they lost touch after the Home. But maybe Cowlick's going to Klondike too, maybe he'll show up here, they could team up and get rich together . . .

Jeremy picked up his knapsack and bag of papers and left to

find an outhouse. Hank didn't follow him; some dogs had found garbage down the block. Jeremy sort of missed him. He went into a building with a FINE EATS sign above the door to warm up, and ordered coffee and a sweet roll. Gradually he stopped shivering. But the wind hit him again the minute he left the building. There were so many people everywhere and new ones arriving every day. Should he get two hundred papers tomorrow?

He decided to change his location to the TELEGRAPH OFFICE, as the dogs had, because it had an overhanging roof and faced away from the wind. Hank wagged his tail. Some of the others did too. For a while business was brisk enough to help him ignore the cold, but then his fingers and feet became numb and his cheeks tingled, so he stepped inside to warm up again.

A jostling crowd lined the counter sending telegrams — *Anywhere in the World Five Dollars* the sign read. Most people wore clothes so new they'd squeak if he touched them. Jeremy blew on his fingers.

"My wallet! Someone's taken my wallet!" a man shouted.

The crowd stilled. A man pushed out the door. It banged behind him. "Stop him!" a lady yelled.

"We'll get the thief!" Three men elbowed others aside and crashed out.

They're the men from the saloon robbery, Jeremy realized. They'll run off in different directions and come back saying they couldn't catch him. What if it's a set-up and they take the wallets themselves?

The minister-looking man put his arm around the robbed man's shoulders. "They'll catch your thief if anyone can. Let me buy you a drink. Jake," he turned to the telegraph man behind the counter, "when they come back with this fellow's wallet, tell them where we are."

"Sure thing, Reverend Bowers," Jake said.

A scam? Jeremy remembered what the man had said yesterday:

lot of money's gone missing since Smith came to town. He decided that, first thing, he'd sew his money into his underwear. Why didn't they make long johns with pockets?

Warmer now, he went back outside. Yes, here came the three men. When they saw each other they smiled in a way that reminded Jeremy of Matron's phrase, "the cat that swallowed the canary." But as the men turned toward the Telegraph Office their faces grew downcast and they shook their heads. They stormed into the building and instantly came out. A nice blast of warm air as they pushed by Jeremy again and started across the street. The last man slowed and stared at Jeremy. Jeremy looked away. *"Vancouver World!"* he yelled.

The man moved back into his line of vision. Jeremy looked the other way. "Get the latest news!"

The man moved again. "How long you been in town, boy?" He took off his glove, brushed his jacket aside and put his hand on his hip. He had a gun in a holster. A gun with a brown, carved stock. His hairy hand had a long scar across the knuckles. Most of the dogs slunk away. But not Hank.

"Why?" Jeremy told his knees to stand straight and his brain to work.

"Because this here's a company town, that's why. And we like to know who's in it. Yer either in or out of it." Scarknuckle's voice was horribly soft. He kicked Hank in the ribs. The dog squealed and limped off, its tail clamped between its legs.

"Hey! You didn't have to do that!"

"Yes, I did." The man slitted his eyes menacingly and moved his hand closer to his gun.

"What company runs the town?" Jeremy clutched his papers to his chest.

"Heard of Soapy Smith?" Jeremy shook his head. "Planning on staying long?" Jeremy shrugged. "You better meet him. He don't take kindly to strangers selling papers. He'll want to make an arrangement."

"What sort of arrangement?" Jeremy's voice seemed to be working better than his knees. He pulled off his mitten and shoved his hand in his pocket, checking his money. Scarknuckle smiled knowingly. Jeremy felt himself blush.

"Well, well, what good timing. There goes Smith now." Scarknuckle jerked his head toward a man in a cowboy hat on a grey horse cantering down the road. He put his hand on Jeremy's shoulder and squeezed his fingers. "Let's go see what he says, Sonny."

He hauled Jeremy down Broadway and propelled him through the door of JEFF'S PLACE. So-called Soapy Smith was just sitting down at a table with two men. The bartender was pouring a drink. At the slam of the door, Smith turned around. "Well, well, Yeah Mow, what do we have here?"

"New paper boy in town. Thought he'd better meet you."

Jeremy tried to twist away from Scarknuckle's — Yeah Mow's — hand, but the fingers clamped more tightly under his clavicle. "Let go of me!"

"Say please," said Smith.

"Please," Jeremy muttered.

"Louder."

"Please!"

Smith looked Jeremy up and down while the bartender brought him a drink, which he sipped before putting it down. "You can probably let him go, Yeah Mow." His tone was mocking. "But guard the door in case he decides he doesn't like our company." The men laughed as Jeremy pulled away and rubbed his shoulder.

Smith lifted up his cowboy hat and resettled it. He had black hair and a trimmed black beard and moustache. He wore a well-cut three-piece suit with a gold watch chain draped across his vest, a white shirt and tie. Another man was small and slight, looked young, and held a white handkerchief to his mouth. The last man was older, with a flat-brimmed hat over bushy grey sideburns. He cut and recut a pack of cards.

Yeah Mow pulled up a chair and sat down. He emptied his glass. The bartender poured him another drink.

"Well boy, what do you think of our town?" Smith asked.

"It's fine," Jeremy ventured cautiously.

"Fine? Just fine? Is that all? This is the finest town on the continent! We're all real partial to it, aren't we, boys?" The *boys* all grinned and nodded.

Jeremy cast about for something more to say. "It's got a lot of dogs."

Yeah Mow guffawed and banged the table with his open hand. The others laughed too, and the young one coughed into his handkerchief. "Tell him about the doggies, Soapy!"

Smith shook his head and looked sorrowful. "People ship up dogs because they hear dogs are wanted in Klondike, and they figure they can make some money. It's true dogs are worth lots here, but only big dogs that can work. People ship up lap dogs and tiny mongrels and they just wander about unwanted. We must have over a thousand dogs in Skagway." Smith shook his head again, took a drink. "It's more than I can stand, seeing these poor scrawny beasts starve or freeze to death so I started an adopt-a-dog program. Got over a hundred placed so far."

"Mr. Smith's done a real good community service," the man with the sideburns said. He smiled and opened his eyes wide. "You can save a dog too. A dog'd be your friend."

I already have a dog friend, Jeremy thought, but said nothing.

"Now George, don't bother the boy. He's new in town. Let him get settled first."

Jeremy felt really confused. Weren't these men planning something awful for him? An arrangement, Scarknuckle had said? Why were they talking about dogs? They kept staring at him. He felt like a cat to their dogs.

"You are getting settled, aren't you?" Smith was saying.

"What?"

Smith slammed his glass down, sat upright and glared. "My, my, boys, this young man has no manners. Say, I beg your pardon."

"I beg your pardon. Sir."

The cougher came to a pause and pulled his handkerchief away from his mouth. "Watch your manners around Mr. Smith. He is a gentleman of a powerful Southern family."

Southern what? Jeremy wondered. But maybe that explained his strange accent, a sort of drawl.

"Answer the question, boy!" Yeah Mow yelled.

"I don't remember the question," Jeremy blurted. He was beginning to feel dizzy with his coat and cap on and the bartender stoking the stove which already threw an immense heat.

"Are you getting settled?" Smith asked. "Are you planning to stay?"

"Yes. I don't know."

"Come on, boy. Yes, you don't know?"

Jeremy cleared his throat and addressed Smith, but kept his eyes on the rest. "Look, Sir, I'm just a boy selling newspapers. Give me a clear question and I'll answer back clear as I can. Then let me get out to my job."

"Oh, he's a straight talker," George said to Smith, then to Jeremy, "Play cards, boy?"

"No."

"We can teach you." Jeremy didn't like George's sly smile.

The door opened with a blast of cold air that Jeremy was thankful for, and in walked Reverend Bowers. He glanced at Jeremy. Smith stood up, also keeping his eyes on Jeremy.

"Gibbs is having trouble with the game at Clancy's," the Reverend said to Smith. "You'd better come."

"Hear that boys?" Smith took down a rifle from the wall. As he followed Yeah Mow and George out the door, Smith added, "Syd, make a proposition to our young friend on my behalf."

Syd's attempt to speak led to another coughing fit. Jeremy put his hand on the doorknob and looked at the bartender. "He can find me later. I'll just be selling papers."

The bartender shook his head, frowning. "You heard Soapy. Give Syd a minute."

"Why's he called Soapy?" Jeremy asked.

"He sells his own soap." The bartender's laugh was unpleasant. Jeremy wished he hadn't asked.

Syd finally raised his head. His white face shone with perspiration. He wiped his lips and sipped his drink. "You heard how good Mr. Smith is, looking after dogs. He looks after his friends too. You want to work in this town, you got to be his friend. Otherwise he can be downright unfriendly. Fifty percent is all it costs to be friends."

"Fifty percent of what?" Jeremy asked.

"Of whatever you make. Just like everybody else in town."

"You mean you want me to pay him?"

"Well, you can pay me or Yeah Mow or the Rev or George or even Frank here." He jerked his head toward the bartender. "Frank, you want to show our friend how unfriendly we can be to help him make up his mind?" Syd smiled. His face was so thin and drawn that Jeremy thought of a grinning skull.

Frank came around the bar. Jeremy twisted the doorknob but he couldn't pull the door open before Frank grabbed the front of his jacket and slammed him against it. "What's your name?"

"Sam Moss."

Frank slapped Jeremy across the mouth. "That's not the name you signed for the papers!" He slapped one cheek then the other. Jeremy could feel his lip begin to bleed. His cheeks stung and he fought back tears. What had he signed? Jeremy or J? "Jim," he faltered, bracing himself.

Frank twisted his jacket more tightly and banged him against the door again. Jeremy could feel his brains rattling. Syd said, "Let me do the arithmetic for you, Jim. You took one hundred papers. You've been selling them for thirty cents. Fifty per cent of thirty dollars is fifteen dollars. That's how much friendship costs today."

"I haven't sold all the papers," Jeremy stammered.

"You've sold enough."

"I have to go get the money."

Frank slapped Jeremy again. The back of his head hit the door-frame. "In your pocket, Jim," Syd said. "See what good friends we are. We know the things about you that friends know." His tone changed. "Help him get it out, Frank!"

"I'll do it," Jeremy said quickly. "Let go of me."

Frank lifted him off his feet and shook him before letting go. Jeremy stumbled and nearly fell down. He drew out his money and leaned into the wall while counting it. Slowly he handed fifteen dollars to Frank.

"That's right friendly of you, Jim," Syd said. "Mr. Smith will be pleased and he will look after you. No one will bother you now."

"No one was bothering me before," Jeremy muttered.

"What'd you say, Jim?" Frank grabbed his coat again. Jeremy cowered and covered his head with his arms. "Nothing."

"Better watch it, Jim," Syd added mildly. "Mr. Smith don't like lip. Now, Frank, open the door nicely for our friend. We'll see you tomorrow, Jim, won't we? Friends see each other every day, don't they, Frank?" Jeremy stumbled out the door to a burst of laughter that started Syd's cough again.

Jeremy's sore face stung in the cold air. He sucked on his swollen lip, trying hard not to cry. He didn't know which was worse, the beating, the humiliation, or having to hand over his money. Half of it! Every day! It'd take him twice as long to get rich! Maybe every day they'd demand more!

3

Friday 18th Feb 1898

Went to town to pay dockage & load teams. Rest picked up camp & went to foot of cañon (4 to 5 miles) where the carters left stuff & left Rimmer there with one tent. Rest of us went on with 2 horse & 2 dog team loads about 2 miles over very rough trail & camped. Cold & windy. Took us till 10 o'clock to pitch camp & get supper. Had Rimmer (being an American citizen) sworn in as convoy for our stuff through Alaska.

Jeremy became aware that he was stumbling down Broadway, blocks from JEFF'S PLACE. He still had his knapsack and newspaper bag, he discovered when he banged them against a post. His heart was drumming and he was gasping for breath. He was furious. His hands were fists and he wanted to plow that Smith, that Frank, that Syd. Crash, pow, bam. But he was also scared. They could really hurt him if he didn't pay every day. They could kill him.

He was walking automatically, stumbling over his boots and ridges of ice, trembling with cold and shock. They'd played with him, jeered at him, they'd do it every chance they could. They'd take his money, beat him up and laugh at him. If they could make him hand over half his earnings so easily, they'd find ways to get all his money, make him play cards or steal his wallet . . .

Now he was crying, he couldn't help it. He leaned against the nearest building and tried to swallow his sobs.

"Boy, what's the trouble?" It was a kind voice and made Jeremy's shoulders shake harder, made him swallow more.

"I'm all right," he muttered, and made go away motions with his hand.

"You don't look it." A hand touched his shoulder. Jeremy winced. "Sometimes it helps to talk, even to a stranger."

Jeremy shuddered and gulped. He wanted to talk, he wanted to tell on Soapy Smith and his gang and the way they'd beaten him up, but what if this man was another of them? He sniffed hard, rubbed his nose and wiped his eyes on his sleeve. He said the first thing that came to his mind. "I lost my dog."

The hand drew back. Jeremy turned around. "You lost your dog and you're crying? A big boy like you?" The blue eyes were incredulous. "There are dogs everywhere! Just whistle and you'll have a dog!"

Jeremy wished he'd thought of something better, but he was in it now. "It's a special dog. It's been in my family for years. I was going to sell it and make a lot of money."

"Boy, you have to do better than that." The man's tone was stern. "Dogs that have been in families for years are not called *it*. Dogs that have been in families for years are not sold for money. Do you want to try again?"

"Maybe I should tell Smith," Jeremy ventured.

"Go tell Smith, whoever he is. You can also tell Fraser, who's standing before you."

"You don't know Soapy Smith?" Jeremy tried to keep his voice flat, casual.

"No. But I recommend that if you have someone to talk to, do so."

This Fraser was losing interest, Jeremy could tell. He'd be off in a minute. Maybe he wasn't part of the gang. His parka looked new, as did his boots. Hadn't he seen him on the *Danube?* When the anchor had fallen over and killed two dogs? Wasn't this the man who'd complained to the Captain about the animals' accommodations?

Jeremy took a deep breath. It caught in his throat. He hawked and spat into the icy mud. Fraser jerked his lip in disgust. "Mr. Fraser, Sir, I said the first thing that came into my head, because I didn't know if you were — but I remember you from the steamer and — please Sir, I'd like to tell you. I don't know where to turn." Mr. Fraser blew on his mitts. Jeremy breathed deeply. "We could go somewhere warm while I tell you, Sir, if you want."

"You are blue with cold." Mr. Fraser pulled a watch out of his vest pocket. "I can spare a half hour, so lead me to a warm place that is not a saloon."

Jeremy looked around. The FINE EATS where he'd had the sweet roll this morning was only a block away. He led Mr. Fraser there. Warmth blasted out the door as he opened it. They sat at a table close to the stove and took off their mitts, hats, and coats. Mr. Fraser was bald on top of a greying dark fringe. He was also clean-shaven except for a neat moustache. He had fine lines on his face so he was getting old.

After the waitress had brought their coffee and pie and they'd each had a sip and a bite, Mr. Fraser said, "All right, boy, give it a go."

Jeremy licked his split lip where the hot coffee had stung. "Well Sir, I'm to meet my father in Dawson City — he's struck it big and needs help in his mine — and I ran into this gang here, Soapy Smith's, and they stole all my money so how am I to get to Dawson? You caught me at a weak moment, Sir." Jeremy allowed the derision he now felt for his earlier crying to show.

"You had enough money to get there?"

"Yes Sir."

"And these hoodlums have taken it from you?"

"Yes Sir. Well, a lot of it, Sir." Jeremy didn't want to get in any deeper than he had to. He leaned across the table. "Sir, they've got scams going on — "

"Who?" Mr. Fraser asked.

"Soapy Smith's gang, Sir. Haven't you heard of them?"

"No." Mr. Fraser didn't seem to talk any more than he had to. His face didn't give much away either. Jeremy decided to practise that. He wouldn't be caught sobbing again.

"Sir, watch your wallet."

"I always do," said Mr. Fraser.

"I mean, especially. I've heard of two stolen wallets since yesterday. The same men offer to help the robbed man, but I think they steal the wallets themselves. There were two murders a while ago. And I heard gunshots last night. And one of the men kicked the dog that was following me. I haven't seen it since."

Mr. Fraser nodded. He sipped his coffee. "There's more to your upset than this. Tell me the rest."

"If I stay in town — to earn money to get to my father in Dawson — they want half of everything I make each day. I've been selling newspapers," Jeremy explained.

"What in particular were you crying about?" Mr. Fraser asked, after a moment.

"I'm trapped. If I stay, I'll have to pay them or they might kill me, yet how can I leave if they take my money? I never planned to stay in Skagway," Jeremy added.

"Write your family to send you money."

Jeremy shook his head. "There's only my father. I could telegraph him, but he's at his mine."

"Telegraph him? There's no telegraph in Skagway."

"There's an office. Haven't you seen it?" Jeremy sipped his coffee, then winced.

Mr. Fraser looked at him. "There is no telegraph wire within five hundred miles of Skagway — or the Yukon — yet."

"There's the telegraph office," Jeremy repeated, and then realized the truth. "Is that another scam — five dollars anywhere in the world? Some of the people receive telegrams too!"

Mr. Fraser tightened his lips and shook his head. "Go talk to the Reverend Mr. Dickey. He's a minister."

"No! A man said Smith built the church! Besides, there's a Reverend Bowers in his gang!"

Mr. Fraser's eyes snapped. "Reverend Dickey built his own church! He's an honest man, a fine man, a fine minister!"

"I'm sure he is, Sir," Jeremy said uncertainly, "But what could he do? Soapy Smith runs the town. Everybody knows it." The scene in JEFF'S PLACE flooded back. Jeremy felt Frank's blows again, heard the jeering of Smith and Syd. He shuddered and covered his burning cheeks with his hands.

Mr. Fraser took another tack. "You could hire on with a crew going to Dawson."

"That's a great idea! Do you need an extra hand?"

"Perhaps, but my outfit's not going to Dawson."

"Oh." Jeremy's dejection was as profound as his previous momentary elation. He felt safe with Mr. Fraser. "I could help you as far as you're going. At least I'd be out of Skagway."

"My crew's established. We're leaving as soon as the paperwork's done — I hope today." Mr. Fraser's tone was kindly. "But there are a lot of other outfits, just look around you."

"How can I tell who's not a gang member?" Jeremy muttered.

"You managed with me," Mr. Fraser pointed out.

"I remembered you from the *Danube*. The next man might say he wasn't in the gang but he could be and they'd beat me up for trying to leave." Jeremy licked his lip and moved his hands on his cheeks. He winced.

"What's your name?"

Jeremy paused. *Sam Moss?* No. "Jeremy Britain."

"How old are you?"

"Sixteen." Mr. Fraser just looked at him. "Well, nearly."

"Nearly fifteen?" Mr. Fraser's eyebrows were raised.

"Nearly," Jeremy said. "But I'm really strong and I'm used to hard work and not much food and sleeping out."

"Nearly fourteen?" Mr. Fraser continued in the same flat tone.

"No!" Then Jeremy realized the trap. "I'll be fifteen in October!"

"So fourteen," Mr. Fraser stated.

"And nearly a half," Jeremy added.

"Do you have a rig?"

"A rig?"

"Gear. Enough for a year in Klondike."

"No, my father —"

"The Mounties aren't letting anyone over the border without enough supplies to last a year."

Jeremy sighed. His shoulders slumped. Maybe he should just go back to Vancouver. Try to get rich there.

"I must go to the Bond Commissioner's to see about clearance." Jeremy looked up. Mr. Fraser was tucking his watch back in his pocket. "What will you do?"

"Don't worry about me, Sir. I'll be fine."

"My boy, I am sure you will be. You seem a resourceful young man." Mr. Fraser stood up and pulled on his coat and hat. "However, I will inquire about the situation. You, in the meantime, plan how to outfit yourself. I understand you can buy complete rigs for the price of a ticket to Vancouver from people too discouraged to continue. I'll return when I've finished my business. If you decide to go elsewhere, leave a message at the counter." He pulled on his mitts, cocked a salute, and left.

Jeremy felt heartened. This Mr. Fraser sure knew how to do things. He hadn't laughed at him. He hadn't even seemed to mind that he was only fourteen. That salute was like he was an adult too. Jeremy looked around, then pulled out his money and, hunkering over so no one could see, counted it.

Seventy-three dollars. Plus his lucky hundred dollar bill that he'd stitched inside his pants. He'd found it blown against the corner of the Rainier Hotel at Cordova and Carrall the day before his birthday, October thirtieth. There was no one around. Of course, if anyone had run up shouting that he'd lost a hundred dollar bill, Jeremy would have returned it immediately, he liked to think. But there had been no one around. One hundred dollars was more money than he'd ever seen. It was his omen that he was going to be rich. He'd spend it now if it meant he could go into Klondike with Mr. Fraser.

Jeremy had just decided to leave the restaurant and look for Hank when Mr. Fraser returned. "Did you get the clearance?" Jeremy asked.

"No. They're way behind in their paperwork. Perhaps tomorrow." Mr. Fraser sounded irritated, but resigned. "They say there are thirty thousand people headed to Klondike and half that many leaving it. Now, I've decided that, if you can get a rig, you can come with my crew as far as Lake Bennett. There you can find someone going all the way to Dawson."

"Oh thank you, Sir!" Jeremy was surprised at how great his relief was.

Mr. Fraser looked stern. "It will be hard work. If you can't afford a horse or dogs, you'll have to carry your gear yourself. And we won't let you slow us down."

"No, Sir. I understand." Jeremy paused to deliberate before adding, "I have one hundred seventy-three dollars."

Mr. Fraser frowned at him. "You told me the thieves took all your money."

"Well, I didn't mean *all*," Jeremy backtracked. "It was just a way of saying it."

"How much did they take?"

"Fifteen dollars. Half of what I made today, and they'll take that everyday."

Mr. Fraser was still frowning. "Is that the truth?"

"Yes, Sir." Jeremy could feel his neck burning as well as his cheeks.

"Lying is worse than a bad habit. It is character-destroying."

"Yes, Sir. I didn't mean to, Sir."

"Exaggeration is a form of lying."

Jeremy wriggled under Mr. Fraser's glare. "I'm sorry, Sir."

"See that you stick to the truth from now on."

With that, Mr. Fraser ushered him out and down the boardwalk toward the wharves. With a joyful yap, Hank detached himself from the pack of dogs and wriggled over, keeping a wary eye on Mr. Fraser.

"Hank!" Jeremy bent down and patted him.

"Is this your family dog?" Mr. Fraser asked.

"No, but he seems to like me."

In front of the wharf they came across a dejected man slumped against bales and bags and boxes. On top was a sign: *complete rig for sale.* "How much do you want?" Jeremy asked.

"Seventy dollars. Fifty for a ticket home and an extra twenty. Whole outfit cost me five hundred in Victoria, but I just want out of this hellhole!"

Jeremy counted out his money. "Just a minute." Mr. Fraser had been poking and prodding. "This isn't a complete rig."

"No, it isn't. You are discerning. Half's already at White Pass City. Marked *Magnus.* Got it that far and got fleeced in a card game. Think I'd better go home."

"Do you have a horse or dogs?" Jeremy handed him the money.

"Did have, but I gambled them too. Well, better luck to you." They watched him hurry to the steamship office.

"I bet it was Soapy Smith's gang," Jeremy commented. "I bet the game was rigged. They offered to teach me cards. Maybe they'd have put me in their gang."

"Gambling and drinking are not good activities," Mr. Fraser admonished.

This topic was too close to the *lying* lecture. Jeremy patted Hank. "What do we do now?"

"Load up your new sled and we'll get packers to bring up the rest tomorrow. I have to collect an oven, so I can't help you."

Jeremy looked at the mound of stuff he now owned. "Maybe I should stay here," he worried. "What if someone steals it?"

Mr. Fraser smiled. "Unlikely. There are only so many stoves and pickaxes one wants to carry." He crossed the road to the KLONDIKE OUTFITTERS.

Jeremy stuffed a bundle marked *evaporated potatoes* into his knapsack and another that he hoped contained blankets into his newspaper bag. He loaded a tent on the sled and boxes on top of it, but that didn't seem to make much of a dint in his pile of acquisitions. Then he and Hank crossed to the store and he sold his remaining newspapers.

Mr. Fraser reappeared, carrying an odd metal contraption. "Don't let that dog follow us."

"Why? He's a nice dog and he likes me!"

"He's too small and thin. He can't work. He's not in good condition. The trip will kill him."

Jeremy nearly blurted, I'm small and thin, maybe I shouldn't come! But he just looked at Mr. Fraser.

"Look, boy, it's no kindness to take animals somewhere they're not suited. They don't know where they're going so they can't make the choice to go. We do, and can. No small, half-starved dog, and that's final." Mr. Fraser's face was stern.

Jeremy dropped down and hugged Hank. He'd only known the dog a day and half and a night, but . . .

"What if he follows?" he whispered.

I doubt he'll follow far." Mr. Fraser's tone softened. "Now let's get going. The horse is cold."

4

—

Sat. 19th Feb 1898

Left dogs in Camp & took the 2 horses & made 3 trips with stuff from where Rimmer was camped. Hired some help & got all up except 10 sacks of Fish & 4 Bls. Hay. Got some bad falls & hurt myself. Got good wood & brush & pitched tent for horses & dogs & made all comfortable

On the outskirts of Skagway, State Street merged into Brackett's wagon road, wide enough for Jeremy and Mr. Fraser to walk side by side. Jeremy pulled his sled and Mr. Fraser led a black horse which hauled a sled — a rectangular box on runners with leather traces to the horse-collar — containing the stove he'd just bought. In front of them laboured six large dogs hitched single file to another loaded sled. Hank stuck to Jeremy's side. The sky was dark, but snow and fog drifting around the large firs and cedars that lined the road provided an eerie glow. Laden people and pack animals — dogs, horses, mules, oxen, even a team of long-haired goats — passed them or plodded ahead and behind. A man and woman on bicycles overtook them and swung into the crowd ahead. The road was fairly level and Jeremy's sled bounced over the frozen ruts.

Jeremy worried about Hank. The little terrier pranced beside him on tiptoe, as if trying to keep his feet out of contact with the icy road. His tongue lolled and his sides heaved. Jeremy'd said, "Go back!" numerous times, but Hank ignored him.

Then Jeremy worried that one of Soapy Smith's gang would loom out of the dimness and grab his shoulder. "Where do you think you're going? You ain't going nowhere!" He kept his eyes open, but none of the travellers paid any attention to him. Then he worried about Hank again.

He glanced at the man trudging silently beside him. Not tall, maybe five eight, about three inches taller than Jeremy, a solid, business-type man. When Jeremy had sold papers on the corner of Dupont and Carrall Streets, this was the sort of man who'd bought them. Solid men in their forties wearing stiff white collars and gold watch chains, men who went home to their families in two-storey houses on Georgia Street, men who belonged to the Vancouver Club. The sort of man he'd be when he got rich.

He felt the thrill of his original excitement which he'd lost in the run-in with Smith's gang. Klondike! He was really on his way! He had a rig and everything! And a friend! Well, maybe a friend. Then he worried about Hank again.

A mile and a half farther on, Jeremy saw lights shining through the walls of tents on the edge of the road. He smelled the smoke which rose from stove pipes and mingled with the fog. Dogs leapt up and rushed toward them, barking. The sled dogs answered. Hank crouched beside Jeremy's leg, but barked bravely also. The horse jerked its head up. A hunger pang cramped Jeremy's stomach. He drew his sled up to the line of the tent's lamplight on the snow, dropped the handle and rubbed his shoulder. Mr. Fraser halted the horse where the light shone most brightly and began unhitching.

An arm pushed open the tent flap and a bearded man appeared, still pulling on his mackinaw. He headed toward the dogs.

"Quiet!" he shouted at them, then, to Mr. Fraser, "How'd it go, James? Did you get the papers?"

"No! Red tape, Rimmer, red tape. Possibly tomorrow." Mr. Fraser led the horse into another tent. It must serve as the stable, Jeremy decided.

Hank lay down on the snow, shivering and panting. Jeremy dropped his sled handle and picked up the furry bundle. He couldn't let Hank suffer. He'd have to stay in Skagway too, to look after the dog.

Rimmer unhitched the sled dogs. They immediately rushed toward the others, snarling, whining, sorting out their places in the pack. Rimmer ducked into the tent and came out with an armful of frozen fish which he tossed on the ground. Hank wriggled out of Jeremy's arms. The growling and snapping deepened, and then there was blessed quiet as all the dogs chowed down.

Rimmer turned and saw Jeremy. "Oh," he let out, then stared, frowning. "That furry excuse for a canine yours?"

Jeremy had known there'd be other men; Mr. Fraser had mentioned his crew. But he hadn't really thought about it. Would these men beat him as Mr. Hammond had? His inclination was to fade away, as if around a street corner, and watch until he knew what was up and who was who. But there were no familiar street corners. He dropped his gaze to the dogs, to Hank.

Rimmer was still staring at him when Mr. Fraser crunched across the snow. "Ah yes, Rimmer. This is Jeremy Britain. After hearing his story, I said he could team up with us over the summit. His father's sent for him to come to Dawson. He can go on with another crew from Lake Bennett or before."

"Is that *doggie* coming too?" Rimmer sneered.

"No. It's a Skagway dog," Mr. Fraser said.

Jeremy worried again. What was Hank going to do? Where was he going to go?

Rimmer jerked his head. "Is that all the boy's gear?"

"No. Half's in Skagway, half's in White Pass City. At least, that's what the man who sold it to him said."

What if it wasn't there? Jeremy worried. Might the Mounties not let him through to Klondike? And what about Hank?

"Well, welcome aboard, Jeremy." Rimmer's tone was cautiously friendly, but his eyes were still sizing him up.

"Where shall I put my tent?" Jeremy asked.

"Don't bother. There's enough room for tonight, and we're moving on in the morning." Rimmer turned to Mr. Fraser. "Ben cooked, and the food's still warm. You go on in. I'll feed the horses and put the dogs in the stable tent."

"Hank too?" Jeremy inquired. "Just for tonight?"

Rimmer rolled his eyes, but Jeremy hoped he might look after Hank.

Jeremy followed Mr. Fraser into the tent. Sitting on cots and crates were three more men sipping mugs of coffee. A pot simmered on the stove next to a coffee pot. Jeremy pulled off his cap and mittens as Mr. Fraser introduced him to Ben Wintemute, Bob Patterson and Mac MacLeod. Jeremy nodded his head at them while Mr. Fraser repeated what he'd told Rimmer. Ben was the slightest and youngest looking, maybe in his early twenties. He was clean-shaven beneath long dark curly hair. Bob Patterson was stocky, with blonde, thinning hair and a red handlebar moustache. He seemed pleasant, and about Mr. Fraser's age. Mac was a bit younger, maybe in his thirties, like Rimmer. He was broad through the shoulders and dark-haired with a few days' growth of beard.

"Help yourself to food." Ben's look included Jeremy. "We rigged up another sled while you were gone, James," he continued. Mr. Fraser passed a graniteware plate and spoon to Jeremy.

They ladled beans and bacon out of the pot. Mr. Fraser sat on the cot beside Ben, and Jeremy sat on the other cot beside Mac.

Jeremy had his loaded fork halfway to his mouth when Mr.

Fraser intoned, "For what we are about to receive — " Jeremy hadn't expected to hear grace said in a tent on the way to a gold rush. He closed his eyes and waited for Mr. Fraser to finish.

"Your father's got a claim, eh?" Bob asked after they'd had a few mouthfuls. "What creek's he on?"

Jeremy chewed and swallowed. If he were not convinced that Mr. Fraser would send him back to Skagway and Soapy's gang, he would own up to his lie and end the deception right now. Then he realized that they'd never find out he was lying because he'd part from them long before he had to produce a father, so he elaborated his tale. "He's on Bonanza," he said. It was the only name he knew.

"Bonanza! Bob enthused. "He's one of the lucky ones! Those claims were all staked by last summer!"

"How's it panning out?" Mac asked.

"Oh it's good! He got a hundred-dollar pan." Jeremy had heard that expression on the steamship and wondered what it meant.

"A hundred dollars!" Mac sounded incredulous. Ben whistled in astonishment and Jeremy wondered if he should have made it only a fifty-dollar pan. "A ten-cent-pan used to be good." Mac was shaking his head.

"That's Klondike for us, isn't it, boys?" Ben grinned and rubbed his hands together. "I could run over the summit right now if we didn't have to cart all this gear!" Jeremy glanced at Mr. Fraser then quickly dropped his gaze. Mr. Fraser was looking at him.

Ben stood up and clapped Jeremy on the shoulder. "You're the lucky one, having a fortune like that to step into! May we get so lucky." He refilled his coffee cup.

Rimmer came in, saw Ben with the pot in his hand, picked up a cup, tossed the dregs out the tent flap and held out the cup. "How about you, James?" Ben asked Mr. Fraser.

"Yes please." He put his plate on the floor and took the cup. Ben held the pot toward Jeremy with an inquiring gaze and Jeremy nodded. He put his plate on the floor also and Ben handed him a cup. Mac picked up the dishes, placed them in a pail of water on the stove and began washing.

Mr. Fraser cleared his throat. "First, Jeremy needs to know our camp rules and then we must discuss tomorrow." He looked at Jeremy. "We rest on Sunday. Those who observe the Sabbath do so." Jeremy nodded. Resting wouldn't be too hard. "We take turns cooking and look after all our personal needs ourselves."

"I don't know how to cook," Jeremy admitted.

"You can assist the others until you learn."

"Some of us are not very good at it," Ben laughed and nudged Mac. Jeremy felt relieved.

"We act all the time as if there were ladies present," Mr. Fraser went on, "that is, no swearing, especially no taking the Lord's name in vain, and no spitting. We maintain a tidy person and camp. Everything shipshape. We do not beat the animals unduly, and we bathe once a week."

"Once a week!" Jeremy blurted. His last bath — well, it must be over a month since he'd skimmed these trousers off the table at St. James' rummage sale. They were good worsted and he'd paid ten cents for a bath in their honour. He'd washed his hair too.

"Proper hygiene prevents disease," Mr. Fraser lectured. "If one of us gets sick, all of us are held back. The same with the animals, so they get fed first."

Jeremy stopped listening. There were a lot of rules. It sounded like the Orphans' Home again, or the Hammonds' where he'd been apprenticed until he'd run away. For the last half year, he'd lived on the streets. He bet Mr. Fraser didn't know — none of these men knew — what it was like living on the streets, selling newspapers when he was lucky, scrounging through garbage when he was not . . . Jeremy ground his teeth. Enough. He was getting to Klondike. He was going to be rich. If he had to follow rules to do that, he would.

When he tuned back to the conversation, it sounded as if Mr.

Fraser planned to go to Skagway alone tomorrow while the others loaded up to carry on to Porcupine Hill. Jeremy worried about finding a packhorse or dogs. And about Hank. Should he go back to town too? The thought of Smith's gang made him shiver.

"Mr. Fraser, should I go to Skagway to take Hank back?"

"I'll take him. If you do, he'll just follow you again."

"If you come across a horse for sale tomorrow, would you buy him for me? I'll give you the money."

"I'll try, but don't hold out hope. There were a lot of horses for sale in the fall when the trail was too muddy to get through, but once it froze, they were snapped up."

"How about dogs?"

"Or an ox," Ben added.

"Or a goat or a sheep or cow," laughed Bob. "The only animal I haven't seen packing is a pig."

"They brought in camels for that Cariboo gold strike in the '60s," Mac stated, "but their smell scared the horses so bad they stampeded."

"There're still some camels roaming around the Interior," added Bob. "I know a couple of fellows go hunting every year. They want camel trophies so much they pass up good moose."

"How about a camel then?" Jeremy finished and all the men laughed.

Mac threw the dishwater out the flap and scooped up a full pail of snow which he put on the stove. He pulled out his watch. "Ten o'clock, boys. Time to hit the sack."

"Yessir," Ben saluted. Jeremy thought he might like him. He seemed to make everything fun.

Mr. Fraser stood up. "Jeremy, you can bunk with Ben and me in the other tent. Get your bedding."

Jeremy stood up too, thinking of his load of mystery boxes. "There might be some on the sled."

"What did you use for bedding last night?"

"Straw, Sir." Jeremy heard the silence around him. He heard what he'd said. He wished he hadn't said it, but if they knew how he'd been living . . .

5

———

Monday 21st Feb 1898
Blowing hard & hard frost. Mac & I went ahead with two horse loads. I left 3 bags fish about 5 miles from camp & we took balance up to the ford, about 13 miles from summit. Had hard trip. Trail drifted & sliding. Ben & Bob went back to Porcupine with dogs & brought up 12 sacks fish left there. Tried to go to Bateman Camp near town for 4 bales hay loaned them but found too much water on ice & turned back.

Jeremy was running down Water Street, chased by a man who said he was his father, but Jeremy knew he was a killer. No matter how fast he ran, the man ran faster. When the hand grabbed his shoulder, Jeremy screamed. Even with his eyes open he couldn't see a thing.

"Time to get up."

Jeremy sat up. He still couldn't see anything, but he felt cold air on his face and smelled the tent's oiled canvas. A lantern flared. Mr. Fraser, fully clothed, placed it on a crate and went outside. Ben sat on his cot lacing his boots. Jeremy climbed out of his sleeping bag, reluctant to leave its warmth but grateful to leave the nightmare. He pulled on his trousers, cap, mackinaw shirt and jacket, buttoned everything but his fly, then laced up his boots.

He opened the tent flap and stepped outside to pee. Mac was doing the same. "Going to be a cold one," he said.

"What time is it?" Jeremy asked.

"Three-thirty. We got to get moving. Takes a while to load up." He shook, buttoned and disappeared.

Being awakened at three-thirty reminded Jeremy of the Hammonds' farm and he made a sour face as he buttoned. Rimmer strode by to the horse tent with a bucket and Ben came out to pee. "Hate mornings," he mumbled. "Breakfast's in the other tent. Pack up your gear first."

Last night Jeremy had had to go through three cartons and a canvas sack before he'd found the sleeping bag. Then he hadn't cared what state he'd left everything in and now he looked at the jumbled mess of gear. What were all these things? A box with a red cross contained packages and bottles, one marked poison, and some bandages: a medicine box? There was enough flour to start a bakery. A striped knitted tuque. He pulled it on over his ears and settled his cap on top. Netting. Netting? He pulled out gumboots and leather boots — too big. Why carry things that didn't fit? Still, he crammed them back into boxes and crates and despaired when he remembered that this wasn't even all of Magnus' rig.

The other tent smelled of bacon, coffee and baking powder biscuits. Everyone was eating. Jeremy piled food on a plate and filled his cup. By his second cup of coffee, he felt brighter and, judging by the increase in conversation, so did everyone else. Ben said, "Well, boys, time to start humping this stuff up the mountain," as he picked up the dishes and hastily washed them. Mr. Fraser left the tent. Bob and Mac began packing sleeping bags and boxes.

Outside, Jeremy picked up his sled handle, ready to start, then wondered if he should wait for the others. Were they to travel alone or together? He found Mr. Fraser in their tent dismantling the canvas sleeping cots. "Shall I do something?" he asked.

"Carry things outside and pile them by the sleds."

Jeremy did so, and by the time the tent was empty Ben had appeared. Jeremy tried to help them take down the tent, but he kept having to dash out of their way and, after taking an inadvertent rope-lash across the legs, stood back and watched.

All around them, other crews packed up too. Bob and Mac flattened, folded and roped the tents together, and Rimmer hitched the horses and dogs to the sleds. He entered the stable tent and re-emerged with Hank in his arms. "Your dog died in the night."

Jeremy gasped. He touched the wiry fur covering Hank's small frame, then looked at Rimmer. "How? Why?"

"Dunno."

Mr. Fraser came over. "I told you he was sick. You could see it in his coat. Well, that disposes of that problem." He saw Jeremy's devastated expression and said, more kindly, "You gave that dog a last few good days. It was going to die anyway."

"Did the other dogs kill him?" Jeremy asked.

"No," said Rimmer. "There are no marks. I just hope the others don't get whatever made this one sick." He walked to the edge of the forest and placed Hank in a snowy hollow. Jeremy chewed his lip. It stung and began to bleed.

Bob and Mr. Fraser took down the stable tent, and the other three men loaded the sleds. Mr. Fraser started back to Skagway to see about clearance, and the rest faced north. Nobody said anything more about Hank. Jeremy felt empty. Every time he made friends he lost them — Hank, Cowlick, Catherine first of all . . .

Rimmer and Bob led the dogs, Ben and Mac the horses, and Jeremy pulled his sled. The trail still followed the wagon road. Although the terrain was icy and rutted from the feet of thousands of animals and people, the road was wide and reasonably level. It was busier than Cordova Street at noon.

As the morning grew lighter, Jeremy saw people with every possible vehicle. There were home-made sleds like theirs pulled by horses, mules, oxen, dogs, men and women; horses, dogs and peo-

ple back-packing; dogs harnessed to small travois; a family pushing barrows on skis instead of wheels; and even more men and
women on bicycles. Hank might have been trampled to death.

Jeremy wanted to get to White Pass City, wherever that was; he
hoped that the rest of Magnus' goods really were there and had
not been stolen. The trouble with having things, you had to worry
about losing them. Since he'd left the orphanage, all he'd had were
the clothes on his back and his slowly accumulating money. But
when he got rich he'd buy all sorts of things, a bicycle, a camera,
red plush upholstered furniture, so many things he'd have to buy
a house to store them in. Then he'd need a lock and key.

People hauling sleds had their ropes across their chests. He
stopped to adjust his rope like that, and transferred the wooden
handle to his left hand. He felt like a horse or dog in harness, but
it was easier than using just his hands. He hurried to catch up.

Rimmer and Bob were talking; Mac and Ben were silent. Bob
seemed the next eldest to Mr. Fraser. Mac and Rimmer were
maybe in their thirties, but it was hard to tell. Between the ages of
twenty-five and sixty, adults looked pretty much the same, just —
adult. Jeremy wondered what sort of work they'd done before.
Rimmer — whose first name was Joseph, he'd seen it on a box —
and Mac looked more outdoorsy than the other three. Maybe they
were loggers or miners. Bob could be a businessman like Mr.
Fraser. Ben could be a bank clerk.

This was the first time Jeremy had ever been out of a city, except
for the Hammonds' farm. Stanley Park in Vancouver was the closest he'd been to trees like these. They lined each side of the road,
so huge and close together there was hardly any room to squeeze
between. Their tops were shrouded in mist. He dropped his gaze
to the road.

He trudged on like everyone else, shifting the sled handle between his hands, until they came to a crowd milling around a
snowy collection of tents and humped-up lumps. A hand-

scrawled sign attached to one tent proclaimed: WHITE PASS CITY EATS. Behind the tents were a few ramshackle buildings, one with a sign: WHITE PASS HOTEL. Jeremy noticed the mountains had closed in all around. Beyond the "city" he could see a single dark line of travellers winding worm-like out of sight.

"End of the road," said Rimmer. "Now the fun begins."

"Where's the rest of my stuff?" Jeremy unhitched himself from his sled, hurried over to the nearest cache and brushed off the snow.

"What are you doing?" a woman asked sharply. "That's my pile!"

Jeremy backed away. "I'm looking for mine. Have you seen one marked *Magnus?*" She was young and pretty and wore a shiny red dress under a black coat with a fur collar.

"No," she sniffed. "Don't you know where you left it?"

Jeremy brushed snow off three separate caches before he found the right one. So Mr. Magnus hadn't lied. He hurried back through the crowd. Ben, Bob, Mac and Rimmer were helping the Indian carters unload their sleds. "Did the rest of my gear come on that load too?"

"Yes," Bob replied. "You owe thirty-five dollars."

"Thirty-five dollars!"

"Seven cent pound," the man answered.

"But the road was easy!"

"Twelve cent pound from here. Dollar pound over a mountain." Jeremy clicked his tongue in disgust.

A boy about Jeremy's age plopped a huge crate down in the snow. "My uncle Tagish Charley," he said to no one in particular. "He find first gold. Start all this," he grinned and waved his hand indicating the tent city and the crowd.

Did he mean that gives them the right to fleece everyone? Jeremy sneered to himself. Behind the nearest tent he made sure no one was watching then pulled up his trouser leg and the leg of his long john. He unplucked the thread that held his hundred dollar bill secure. This would leave him only sixty-eight dollars. Did he have to get poor before he got rich? He walked back.

"Can you make change?" he asked as he reluctantly held out his money. The man just looked at him as he drew out a thick roll of bills from his pocket and peeled off an American fifty and a Canadian ten and five. Jeremy took them.

Rimmer broke up a bale of hay for the horses and Mac gave the dogs each a frozen fish. Bob and Ben piled up the gear from the carters' sleds; Jeremy hauled over boxes from the Magnus cache. On his third trip he noticed two men on horseback threading through the constant flow of people and animals. They looked like — they were! Yeah Mow and George! Skagway had come to him! They were talking to each other, but in a minute they'd see him.

He ducked behind a pack-laden mule and walked alongside, pressing his face into the mule's shoulder. His knees were weak enough to buckle. The man leading the mule gave him a peculiar look. At the corner of a tent, Jeremy veered off, ran behind it, plunked his box down and sat on it. His heart thrummed. He waited as long as he could then got up, peered around the other corner. No sign of them. He crept along the wall and peered around the front corner. There they were — the backs of them. They hadn't seen him. But it was only a matter of time. And he'd thought he was safe, out of Skagway.

He picked up his box and, trying to keep his eye on the disappearing horses, crossed to the new cache. Mr. Fraser had just arrived and was talking to the rest. "Did you see those riders?" Jeremy interrupted, shuddering. "They're Soapy Smith's gang! The ones that beat me up! They're here too!"

Mr. Fraser frowned. "Control yourself."

Jeremy set down his box. Bob put a hand on his shoulder. "If they're as nasty as you say, they're after bigger fish than you. You're just small fry to them." Jeremy wasn't sure whether this observation was as kind as Bob's tone intended it to be.

"I want to get as far away as possible, as fast as possible!"

"We're going to," Mr. Fraser said. "But we'll do it in an orderly fashion."

Rimmer built a fire and put on the pot of last night's beans to heat for lunch. Bob and Mac pitched a tent, Ben and Mr. Fraser reloaded the sleds, adding more gear, and Jeremy shuttled back and forth until all of his cache was moved. When he sat down and Rimmer handed him a plate, he realized he was starved. He waited, along with the rest while Mr. Fraser said grace, then no one said anything until all had finished eating.

Mr. Fraser reiterated the plan. "Rimmer will camp here tonight to keep an eye on our gear and also to get sworn in to convey our stuff through the States so we don't have to pay that thirty per cent duty. There's an official in the hotel who will do it. The rest of us will take loads through and camp at the other end. We'll continue in this way until we have everything moved. Jeremy, can you put more stuff on your sled?"

"I guess so." It hadn't been very hard this morning. "You couldn't find me a horse or dog?"

"None that would stand up to work." Mr. Fraser shook his head. "Those that are alive are in a deplorable state."

Like Hank, Jeremy thought.

When they were loaded up, Rimmer gave everyone a handful of refrozen beans to put in their pockets so they could munch them along the way. The group started through the tent city. Jeremy inserted himself between the horses, Blackie, led by Mr. Fraser, and Sue, the chestnut mare, led by Mac. Ben and Bob walked ahead with the dogs.

Eight miles from Skagway was as far as Brackett had taken his road. Now they had to funnel into the trail Jeremy had seen earlier. This created a bottleneck as everyone waited for those in front to form a single line. Jeremy looked around nervously. Any delay would allow the gang more time to find him.

Mr. Fraser turned and saw Jeremy's darting eyes and twitching cheek muscles. "I talked to a Mr. Frank Reid this morning. He's forming a committee to get your Smith and his cohorts — whom he agrees are the hoodlums you claim — out of town. He said the citizens of Skagway are fed up. Apparently there is a story going around — and he didn't know if it is only a story — that the gang dynamited a snowpatch to close the trail and set up crooked card and shell games for everyone who had to wait. Creating their own captive audience, so to speak."

"Like Magnus' card game," Jeremy agreed. "Whose stuff I have." He looked around again. "Maybe that's what those two came here for! They're going to do it again!"

Mr. Fraser shook his head. "Too chancy. With a rumour going around, any next time would warrant a full investigation. And Smith will have heard the rumour."

"But the marshal was murdered so there's no one to investigate! Anyway it'll be too late for us! We'll be killed in a snowfall!" Jeremy's intestines churned and his teeth chattered.

Mr. Fraser frowned at him. "I shouldn't have told you! Keep a curb on your imagination, boy, and don't trouble trouble till trouble troubles you." Mr. Fraser turned forward again. "Ah, here we go."

Jeremy followed close upon Blackie's rump, hoping the horse wouldn't kick. Mr. Fraser hadn't been reassuring. Maybe Yeah Mow and George had pushed ahead and were right now looking for a good dynamite spot. Maybe they were going to dynamite a tree to fall across the trail — right across him. He looked from one side to the other; if any of these huge trees fell . . . He wished he were standing on a street corner selling papers. He knew what was safe and what was dangerous in downtown Vancouver.

Nothing was safe about this trail. It twisted around trees and boulders, only occasionally widening enough to allow those returning to pass. Underfoot, roots and rocks stalled the sleds. Jeremy often had to yank his sled free from snags or walk backwards to guide it around tight switchbacks. The first time a branch let loose its snowy overload down his neck, he screamed, convinced it was an avalanche. Mac, behind him, yelled, "It's only snow!" in a disgusted tone, so Jeremy felt embarrassed as well as afraid. The snow melted down his back and his neck grew chilled and chafed against his collar. The dusky dark made travelling more dangerous; Jeremy's only comfort was that he wouldn't get lost; all he could do was follow the rump of Mr. Fraser's horse or be run over by Sue from behind. Jeremy reluctantly conceded that Mr. Fraser had been right, Hank could not have made it up this trail. Though he could have ridden on the sled.

When the black worm — the line of packers against the snow — curved around a half-frozen pond or gigantic boulder, Jeremy could see how far it stretched. He felt insignificant, as if he only existed as one segment of the worm's body.

Mostly Jeremy didn't think; he just trudged on, trying to put one foot safely in front of the other on the icy, treacherous ground. Except for the occasional curse at a pack animal or rock, the trail was silent; men and women channeled their energy into their tasks.

Then the worm stopped. Everybody, every animal, just stood, unable to go forward or back. Jeremy was sure the Smith gang had dynamited a tree. "What's happened?" he whispered, not wanting confirmation. Word passed down the worm, "Horse fell at the swamp." People perched on their rigs or boulders, some lit their pipes, some stepped behind trees to relieve themselves, a kind few found food for their animals. Jeremy munched his frozen beans, shivering as his sweaty long johns grew clammy. Bob's, Ben's and Rimmer's dogs flopped down in their traces. Each wore four booties. Jeremy turned around and asked Mac about them.

"So the ice won't cut their paws or the snow ball up. Lame dogs could hold us back."

There were eleven, all big. Jeremy didn't know much about dogs, but recognized a Labrador and a collie. Two of the Hammonds' Henrys had been a Lab and a collie. Jeremy had particularly liked the collie.

One man ahead, with a packtrain of goats, set up his camera and flashpowder. Jeremy looked behind as if studying a photograph of snow-covered boulders ten feet tall, deadfalls as thick in diameter, frozen swampy patches in between, and the trail packed tight with bodies. If he'd seen a photograph of this in Vancouver, would he have come? He faced front again just as the flash powder caught. Would he be in the photograph?

The worm started wriggling forward again. Each person put out his pipe or gathered up his hay and stepped back into line before someone behind squeezed him out.

As Mr. Fraser started forward, Jeremy realized that, when they got to wherever they were going, they would have to turn around and do this again, and again, and again, until all their gear was moved.

6

Tuesday 22nd Feb 1898

Mac & I made two trips to where I left fish yesterday. Boys with dogs made one trip. Strong wind & cold.

Wed. 23rd

I made one trip & got my left shoulder badly hurt by being thrown on ice & did not make another trip. Mac made 12 trips. Dogs ditto. Cold & very windy.

Thursday 24th

Mac & boys with dogs made one trip from camp & then picked up yesterday's loads. I went to town with my horse. Was thrown on ice on left side & hurt same shoulder again & having previously sprained left foot & right knee I was almost crippled. Paid Brooks for teaming loads to Porcupine on 18th. Left town 3:35 & came to Bateman Camp & got the 4 bales hay & reached camp 7:30. Water on ice in two places over my sled. Wind blew very hard & was cold.

Saturday 26th Feb 1898

Blowing hard & drifting. Mac & I started for summit with horse loads & Bob with dogs. Ben stayed to help Rimmer at camp. Mac's horse & load went over side of first hill & fell considerable distance but was not materially hurt. My load came over side on top of me in narrowest part of pass above ford. Horse did not fall over but I hurt my sore shoulder, knee & foot so that I was almost disabled – only made one trip. Boy came along selling newspapers. Bought Victoria Colonist Feb 19th, 25¢.

Within a week, Jeremy had made so many trips over the trail that he was intimate with every inch of it. Here was the fallen tree with its treacherous roots that his sled stuck on every time, here was the two-log bridge thick with pounded-down snow, growing more greasy and dangerous with each passing foot, here the trail curved around a swamp that, depending on the temperature, was either icy or wet, and here was the stretch that everyone called Dead Horse Gulch. As many as three thousand horses had died here last fall, people said. They'd slipped off the trail unable to save themselves, as Sue miraculously had the other day, and plunged down the rock face to their deaths. Others had drowned in the swamps, and others had died of starvation, overwork and beatings. Why, just now Jeremy had seen a man suddenly turn on his horse. Shrieking, he beat its head with his fists, then swung a pickaxe. The horse screamed and Jeremy turned away. The horse died quickly, which was the only good thing, but the man kept on beating its bloody carcass and packload until he was exhausted, then he collapsed in the snow and sobbed like a baby. The rest of the worm just shuffled on by, including Jeremy. And he wasn't the only person Jeremy had seen letting loose his frustration on the animals.

At least Mr. Fraser's crew didn't mistreat their animals. The dogs and horses were unharnessed and fed before the people. Every night forty-four dog booties hung on a line over the stove to dry, reminding Jeremy of the babies' booties in the Home. The dog-booties were fur-lined. Mr. Fraser had made them, Ben told Jeremy. All the dogs knew that when their booties were tied on they were supposed to work. Along with the men, Jeremy now took his turn at animal duty. This also involved oiling the horses' hooves each morning, so the snow wouldn't ball up.

He was beginning to distinguish between the dogs. The collie's name was Collie and the hairy Labrador was Prince. Captain looked like a German shepherd except for his short nose and Leo must have had some bulldog ancestor. Tom, Frank, Harry and Bill definitely had husky blood. Jeremy thought maybe Collie was his favourite, though he wouldn't let the other dogs know that, and when he thought of favourites he felt a twinge for Hank.

Some people said the trail was easier than in the fall or summer, now its swamps and creeks were frozen and its boulders levelled beneath fifteen feet of snow. It was bad enough, he thought, when he allowed himself to think. Once he'd caught himself whimpering. He was so tired and sore that he hadn't even known he was crying until he couldn't see because of the tears frozen to his eyelashes. He'd given himself a good talking-to in a Mr. Fraser voice then counted each step to one thousand for punishment. But mostly he just slogged on silently, one foot in front of the other, one foot . . . like everyone else, from dark before dawn to dark after dusk, until he slid into his cot for a few hours. Some nights he was so tired and sore that his muscles jerked as if they couldn't forget the trail, and sleep was long in coming.

It was the repetition that built monotony. Once over the White Pass would have been bearable. Once up the last mile above the tree line, once seeing the Union Jack at the top, once digging snow off his gear pile to add more boxes and bags, once looking back at the folds of mountains framing the way he'd climbed the Pass . . . but no, it wasn't just once. He'd lost track of how many times he'd done it, seventeen or thirty. Up to the top, then down again with an empty sled; the first part of the way he could slide on it. That was his only rest. Too soon, he was back at the bottom again, loading it again, starting up again.

So when Mr. Fraser announced that the next day was Sunday —

he kept track of the days by writing in a little black notebook each night — their day of rest, Jeremy, and everyone else, was grateful.

No one climbed out of bed until the tent walls glowed in the faint sunlight. Even then, Mr. Fraser didn't. Twice he'd fallen so badly that any movement made him wince. But he could still give orders. As Jeremy untied his sleeping bag, Mr. Fraser said, "You have the first bath, then wash your clothes." Jeremy sat up and pulled on his trousers. Mr. Fraser added, "On second thought, melt extra snow to wash your clothes. They won't get clean in your bath water."

It was Rimmer's day to cook. He had bacon and rehydrated potatoes frying and biscuits in the oven that attached to the stovepipe. Jeremy poured a cup of coffee, added milk powder and sugar. "Where's the bathtub?" he asked.

Bob looked up from the pages of the *Victoria Colonist* he was reading. "Don't tell me you are going to honour us by subjecting your body to soap and water?"

Jeremy blushed. "I'm not that dirty," he muttered. "Sweat cleans."

"Boy, you are so dirty, your dirt has dirt. The 'bathtub' is that pail. Fill it with snow now and put it by the stove to melt." He turned back to the paper, shaking his head. "Too bad we don't have twelve pails."

Jeremy scowled at Rimmer smirking into the frying pan. Mac entered, poured coffee, and Rimmer said, in a flat tone, "Jeremy's going to have a bath."

"Really?" Mac looked astonished. "I hope it won't hurt."

Jeremy clicked his tongue on the roof of his mouth, picked up his coffee, and went outside. He examined his hands. His fingernails were clean because he bit them, but the rest — the palms, the backs — were grimy. He set his mug down on the chopping block, spat on his index finger and rubbed at the base of his thumb. Dirt streaked, then rolled away. He went back inside the tent, collected the pail and packed snow into it.

When they'd sat down to breakfast, Ben said, "Hear we're going to have a white man among us again." He chuckled.

"How many pails of water is it going to take him to get clean?" Rimmer mused.

"Minimum twelve," Bob said promptly.

"I'm not that dirty," Jeremy reiterated but the men ignored him.

"Twenty-four," Ben wagered.

"Sixteen, if he's frugal," said Mac. "If it weren't Sunday, we could bet on it."

Jeremy felt like a racehorse.

"It'll take him all day to melt enough snow for water," Rimmer commented, then asked, wide-eyed, "Wait! Is there enough soap to get him clean?"

Bob got up to pour more coffee. "Last look-see we had a case and a half. This bath should lighten our load." They all laughed.

"Does he know how to bathe?" Mac inquired. "Doesn't look like he's had much practice. Maybe we should help." More laughter.

"Tsxhh — ohh, that's mean!" Jeremy stood up, fetched a clean plate and cup, and loaded a breakfast to take to Mr. Fraser.

Outside, he stood on trembling legs, blinking, until he could see clearly again. They were so mean. He wasn't that dirty. It was like at the Orphans' Home, when boys ganged up on a smaller one, or a new one. But these were grown men! It was like that man with his horse, hitting something defenceless. Like Mr. Hammond. Like Soapy Smith's gang, ganging up on him, though these men hadn't beaten him. Okay, he'd have a bath. Then he'd leave them at Lake Bennett, wherever that was. Till then, he wouldn't talk to them! Let them tease him, he didn't care!

By the time he handed the plate and mug to Mr. Fraser, its contents were lukewarm.

The pail of snow melted into a tenth of a pail of water. He filled it up again and waited, again and waited. Rimmer was right; it would take all day to melt enough snow. Where was he to have his bath? The men were in the tents. Bob was lying on his cot reading bits of the *Victoria Colonist*, Mr. Fraser in the other tent, also reading bits of the paper, Rimmer, Bob, Ben, and Mac in and out of either tent, pursuing their various tasks, and grinning each time they passed him. Damned if he'd have a bath in front of the men, too embarrassing. Besides, they might really try to help him. If he set up his own tent he could have privacy — perhaps they'd been waiting for him to do that. Perhaps they were tired of having him around all the time.

Finally he lugged two full pails of water and a bar of soap to the stable tent. Once they discovered he wasn't bearing food or harnesses, the dogs and horses looked at him curiously. He started to get undressed, then realized he had nothing to change into so he had to go out again and rummage through Magnus' gear until he found new long johns, socks, and a shirt. When he got back, a dog — or dogs — had drunk half of each pail of water. What was left was nearly as cool as the air. "Damn," he muttered, then remembered the rule about not swearing.

Jeremy stripped off his jacket and shirt, and pulled down the top of his long johns. It was so cold. Did he have to do this?

Taking a deep breath, he plunged his head into a pail, grabbed the soap, lathered his hair, neck and face, then rinsed. He'd forgotten a towel. Blindly, he reached for his old shirt and dried his face. The drips hitting his bare chest made him shiver more. When he'd finished his top half, he put the new shirt on and stripped his lower half, which he washed as quickly as possible. The water was pretty disgusting, he had to admit, but he'd never tell the men. He wouldn't even tell the dogs, which were sitting in a circle, studying him.

"I'm not your entertainment!" Collie, Prince and Leo wagged their tails. Collie wagged harder. "Oh well, if you think a bath's a good thing . . ." He scratched Collie's ears and neck.

Jeremy pulled on the new grey wool long johns, and wiggled his toes into the thick socks. He buttoned the shirt — heavy red wool — and, as he warmed up, he had to admit that clean clothes on a clean body did feel nice. He pulled on his trousers, wondering if Magnus had provided another pair. These were stiff with grime.

By the time he'd washed his dirty clothes, thrown out the water, and returned the pails to the kitchen tent, he was ready for a nap. He steeled himself for more ribbing, but all Bob said was, "Smell like a rose, I bet. String up another line near the stove to hang your laundry on." He did so, then crossed to the other tent and flopped down on his cot. Mr. Fraser was snoring, the newspaper fallen across his face. The sound lulled Jeremy to sleep.

When he awoke, it was dusk. He was alone in the tent. He'd been dreaming that he was hauling a load up the mountain and, when he turned around, his sled contained not gear, but Soapy, Yeah Mow, George, Frank and Syd. They were laughing at him, and he realized he was naked. He felt furious and scared.

Outside, lights shone through the walls of other tents. Not everyone rested on Sunday; people, horses and dogs continued their ceaseless relays. Jeremy stopped by his pile of gear and contemplated it. It had not, unfortunately, shrunk since yesterday. Was there anything he didn't need? People were shucking off unnecessary items; the trail-sides were littered with pots, frying pans, rocking chairs, tables; there were three bicycles on this side of the ford. The first time he'd seen them, Jeremy wondered which of the four bicyclists he'd seen had given up, and thought he'd take a bicycle, but by now he scorned the contraptions as just more things to carry.

He could chuck out his cooking gear and tent since he wasn't using them — but where was Lake Bennett and might he need them after? He could definitely get rid of the two pairs of too large boots and one frying pan. What about this funny slope-sided pan without a handle? Maybe keep the Red Cross box? He put it aside. But all this netting?

Mac passed by to feed the animals and Jeremy held it up. "What do I need this for?"

"Mosquitoes," said Mac.

"Mosquitoes!" he guffawed. "It's winter! I'm going to chuck it out!"

"You do, you'll be sorry come bug season." Mac ducked into the stable tent. When he came out, Jeremy held up the slope-sided dish. "Gold pan," said Mac. Jeremy put it with the netting and Red Cross box. He would only ditch the boots and frying pan.

When Jeremy approached the other tent, something smelled delicious. He entered, sniffing.

"Here's the rose in the bouquet." Bob looked up from the dog harness he was mending. "In honour of all our clean bodies, Rimmer has baked an apple pie."

"Apple pie!" Jeremy pushed aside his earlier resolve never to speak to them again. If they were going to make pies, he'd contribute all his flour.

"And beef stew," Rimmer said. "Amazing what they can do with this new evaporation process. Meat, vegetables, fruit, really light to carry and all you do is soak them overnight." He grinned and shook his head. "Remember when we had to pack tin cans into the bush?"

"Or live on dried fish and pemmican," Mr. Fraser added. He was lying on one of the cots. "That was the fare on the Boundary Survey. Forty-ninth parallel by fish."

"Too bad they can't evaporate flour or oatmeal," Bob commented.

"Technically, it is already dehydrated," Mr. Fraser corrected.

"Is it suppertime yet?" Jeremy asked.

"I could eat," said Ben, looking up from his book. "What do you say, Rimmer?"

He poked the stew with a fork. "Soon as Mac gets in from feeding the animals."

"Jeremy, you'll be interested in this." Mr. Fraser folded his section of newspaper and read, *"The Thugs of Skagway. Washington, February 14. Secretary Bliss is in receipt of a letter from Governor Brady, of Alaska, descriptive of the lawless condition of affairs at Skagway and Dyea. It was referred to a cabinet meeting to-day, when Alaskan affairs were under discussion, and was considered sufficient justification by the members for the despatch of the additional military force already authorized to be sent to Alaskan territory —"*

"Yay!" Jeremy shouted, "they should lock them all up!"

Mr. Fraser continued. *"The following is a copy of the letter. News from Skagway by the steamer now in port is serious. The United States deputy marshal has been shot dead in the discharge of his duties. Another man was killed at the same time and at the same place. Recently the steamers have been carrying great lists of passengers: many of them are gamblers, thugs and lewd women from the western centres and from the cities of the Coast. They have taken in the situation at Skagway and Dyea, and appear to have combined to carry things with a high hand. The best people at these places are powerless because they have no municipal form of government. The United States marshal is powerless because he can appoint only a few deputies, and when they undertake to act they are singled out as targets by this rough element."*

"So it wasn't just you, Jer," Bob added.

"Do you think Smith shot the marshal?" Jeremy asked.

"No," Mr. Fraser said. "According to Mr. Reid, he did something even more clever. He refused to let the mob lynch the culprit, making him, Smith, look like a champion of law and order. Then he diverted the crowd's attention by passing the hat for the marshal's widow and new baby."

"That sounds like laudable citizenry. Are you sure he's up to no good, James?" Rimmer asked.

"No, I'm not. Reid is sure though, and he's been in Skagway since Smith got there."

"I'm sure," Jeremy stated, shivering with remembered fear. "They were really mean to me. Then there's the wallet scam and the phony telegraph office and what Mr. Reid said about blasting the snow and crooked games."

"Well, we're out of it now," Ben soothed.

But if Yeah Mow and George could ride to White Pass City, perhaps they could come to Klondike. Perhaps they'd already tired of Skagway and were moving up. He shivered and his stomach clenched, then he looked around the tent: Bob folding up the mended harness; Rimmer stirring the stew; Ben and Mr. Fraser reading. Don't trouble trouble till trouble troubles you. Jeremy breathed in deeply.

In a minute he collected a plate, knife and fork, and sat down. Then he thought about Rimmer cooking for all of them and Mac feeding the animals, so he stood up, put his utensils down, and brought out five more sets.

"I've been thinking," he said, "that if everybody worked on the trail for a week, nobody would have such a hard time."

"I had the same thought too," agreed Mr. Fraser. "But everyone wants to get to the goldfields first. So they'll stumble and haul and make more difficult trips just to beat someone else. No one stops to think."

"The government would have to legislate it," Bob added.

"The trail's in the States," Rimmer said. "You know how we Americans are about our individual freedoms. Less government the better. Besides, ninety percent going up are Americans. And I get a crew of Canucks." He shook his head, but Jeremy thought he didn't really mean it.

"You know that's so we don't have to pay duty in the States and you don't have to pay duty in Canada," Bob stated.

"I know," said Rimmer. "I was just joking."

"Some government regulation is good." Mr. Fraser, grimacing, struggled to sit up. "The rule to bring a ton of supplies will save a lot of lives before the year is out, you mark my words."

"I'm not debating it, James. I'm just saying it's one way our countries are different." Jeremy thought they'd had this conversation before.

Ben looked up from his book. "This whole gold rush is mass hysteria. Thirty thousand — maybe fifty thousand — men spend their life savings on gear, leave their families — "

"Some have brought them," Rimmer interrupted.

"— and run out to the wilderness, the coldest, harshest wilderness in the world! Bank clerks who've never been out of a city! I had to show a bank clerk from San Francisco how to bridle a horse, let alone load it!" His tone calmed a bit. "I think even we're hysterical but at least you know the bush!"

"You may be right, Ben, but Klondike gold is getting the world out of this awful economic depression," Mr. Fraser said. "You may be right too, Jeremy. I wouldn't have fallen if the trail were better. But it would take a team of engineers and dynamiters to make it so, and I'm the duffer who slipped."

The short silence was broken by Mac's entry. As he took off his jacket, Jeremy picked up his plate, and crossed to the stove.

"The dogs aren't as thirsty as usual," Mac mused.

Jeremy studied the canvas floor.

"It's Sunday. They didn't exert themselves." Mr. Fraser winced as he slowly swung his legs to the ground.

"Come and get it," Rimmer said, and Jeremy shoved his plate forward to catch a huge scoop of beef stew, carrots and potatoes.

After that came the apple pie. Jeremy thought it was the best pie he'd ever had, and said so. Then he heard himself offering to wash the dishes.

As he lay in bed, drifting to sleep, he wondered about *lewd women*. What was a *lewd woman*? Was that pretty girl in the red dress a *lewd woman*?

7

Tuesday 1st March 1898

All started out early & made one trip to summit from camp & then the horses made one from ford to summit & returned to camp about 1:30. After dinner we packed up & moved camp to summit & camped in Canadian Territory (B.C.) beside Mounted Police station where they are collecting duty, Capt. Strickland in charge. Arrived about 6:30 & were somewhat later getting camp in order. I was very tired & sore. A lovely day & magnificent clear night.

When Jeremy had hauled his last load into Canada, he allowed himself the luxury of sitting, just sitting, on his sled. He looked back at the way he had come so many times, the mountains filing one after another twenty miles down to Skagway, the worm slowly and blackly still inching up the snow, and he vowed that he would never, ever, in the whole rest of his life, come this way again. But he had done it, he had made the summit, not like others who'd quit, strewing their gear on the trail — the bicyclists for instance — or those who'd died of typhoid or meningitis. He grinned and shook his fist; maybe now he was finally safe from Smith and his gang!

He caught sight of the Union Jack, and remembered the

American flags in Skagway on his first day — was that nearly a month ago? He wasn't going to think about flags, what were they but bits of cloth, but still, this flag looked like home, though that was silly; he didn't mean the Home. Like the Legislature in Victoria or City Hall in Vancouver. Maybe he meant familiar, like a friend he hadn't known he'd had.

For weeks it had been snowing here; the roof of the Northwest Mounted Police cabin was at trail level, and all but this afternoon's caches were buried. Mr. Fraser's crew had marked theirs with a shovel flying Jeremy's old shirt — it had disintegrated after its wash — and each time they added a load, they moved the shovel up another foot or so, depending on how much snow had accumulated since their previous trip. They estimated that their first cache was now under fifteen or twenty feet of snow.

There was that photographer again, the one with the goat team. He'd added a banner to his sled. Slowly sounding out the unfamiliar words, Jeremy deciphered, *Have you seen these views of Alaska? Photographs sent to all parts of the world. E.A. Hegg.* He was taking a photograph exactly the way Jeremy was looking down the cut. It would be fun to have a photograph — not that he was ever likely to forget this. It would be fun to be a photographer — maybe when he got rich and bought a camera — was Mr. Hegg selling photographs? Was that the girl in the red dress? Jeremy got up and joined the gathering crowd.

The photographer had pictures of every stage of the trail. The GOLDEN NUGGET on Broadway Street. Around the end of the swamp. The ford. The tents at White Pass City. An oxen team. Dead Horse Gulch, with swollen-stomached dead horses. And the photograph Jeremy was in when they were stopped on Porcupine Hill. He looked for his image — yes, there he was, behind Blackie's rump. He appeared fuzzy; he'd just moved when the flash went off. Photographed, the trail was even more formidable than he remembered.

He angled around the crowd until he was near the girl. She really couldn't be much older than he was. He blushed to think he'd wondered if she were *lewd,* which must be something *not nice.* He wanted to smile at her but she turned to someone else who was saying something. A large male someone else. Probably her father.

"How much for a photograph?" Jeremy heard a missionary sort of woman in a beaver bonnet ask.

"Five dollars," Mr. Hegg replied.

People started digging into their pockets. Should he? He'd only have sixty-three dollars left. But a photograph wasn't much to carry. The pretty girl now had her arm through her father's and was laughing up at him. Jeremy bought a copy of the photograph on the trail.

As he walked back to his sled, he stared at his image: straight dark hair hanging in his eyes — he pushed it aside now — and had his nose grown? It looked so big that he took off his mitt and felt it. The others in the photograph had beards. He rubbed his cheeks and upper lip before pulling on his mitt. He guessed overall he looked sort of ordinary — like just any boy to that girl.

This was the second photograph he'd seen of himself. The first had been one of all the orphans lined up outside the Home. He'd been six and Matron had scolded him for fidgeting; they'd had to stand still for a very long time. He didn't have a copy of that photograph.

The crew was setting up camp beside the Mountie cabin. Jeremy stored his photograph in a box of tea and wandered over.

Since the men's teasing about his bath, he'd been bothered. Mr. Fraser had said he could come with his crew until Lake Bennett, wherever that was, but maybe that was too far. Maybe they'd had enough of him. He wanted to get one of the men alone. It turned out to be Bob, which was good. Jeremy figured he was the least likely of the men to hit him.

"I have my own tent," Jeremy blurted, feeling stiff. "I can set it up over here."

"If you want." Bob didn't seem interested.

"I mean," Jeremy floundered, "I have a stove too."

"So?"

"I mean I can look after myself. I don't need to depend on you." He glared at Bob. "Bother you, I mean."

Bob looked puzzled. "You've been with us now for how long and I haven't noticed anyone bothered. But set up your own tent, if you want."

"I can get on by myself." Jeremy was getting himself deeper into where he didn't want to be, but he didn't know how to get himself out.

"I'm sure you can."

"I can leave," he said, feeling desperate.

"Of course you can. If we're too slow for you, just go right ahead." Bob was getting huffy.

"No, no, I didn't mean that," Jeremy said.

"Well, what do you mean?" At last he had Bob's full attention, but now he didn't want it. He wished he hadn't brought the topic up, but it felt as if the topic had brought itself up.

"You're trying to tell me something," Bob said. "You're not doing it very well. Do you want your own tent? Do you want to go on ahead? What is it?"

"I don't want to be a bother," Jeremy whispered. Then he glared again.

"No one's bothered," Bob said, "except me, right now."

"Should I set up my own tent?"

"Suit yourself, but it's just more work."

Jeremy thought that probably meant he could continue to bunk in with Ben and Mr. Fraser. "I won't set up my own tent then," he challenged, halfway between a statement and a question.

"Fine," Bob said. "Set up this tent then," and he stalked away shaking his head.

But Jeremy felt a little glad that probably no one seemed to mind that he was around.

Next morning, as they dug their caches out from under all the snow and assembled their gear for the Mounties' inspection, the clouds broke into wisps that quickly blew away, and the snow sparkled in the sun. Jeremy squinted against a bright grittiness bombarding his pupils. Ben strode over. "Let me blacken your eyes."

Jeremy threw down his shovel and cocked his fists. "No you don't!"

Ben guffawed, then slapped his knee. He pointed at Jeremy, and shook his head. Each time he tried to say something, he laughed even more until he doubled over, holding his stomach. Jeremy felt confused and foolish.

Finally Ben wiped his eyes and put his hand on Jeremy's shoulder. "With this," he started to say, and chortled again. "Charcoal." He was holding a piece of burnt wood. "Against snow blindness. And now I'll have to do my eyes again." Jeremy saw that he'd smeared the black circles from around his eyes all over his cheeks. He tried to laugh too, but still felt scared. It was so like Mr. Hammond who cuffed him "just because" as he passed by.

Jeremy closed his eyes and Ben blackened all around, then he re-did his own. "We'll carve proper snow goggles when we get time, but this will do for now." It did cut the glare, Jeremy noticed.

The whole black-eyed crew, except Mr. Fraser who was still too sore to do much, spent the morning shovelling out the various levels of supplies. Then Mr. Fraser and Rimmer, because he was the American convoy, waited for the Mounties. The rest, including Jeremy, packed up camp. There were many groups of Klondikers doing the same, and, even though the Mounties had devised an efficient system, it still took two hours until they got around to Jeremy's crew. Finally they were free to carry on, walking all together for the first time.

It felt so good to have the White Pass to their backs that everyone was giddy. Ben began to sing, "I know where the flies go in the wintertime/each year in September up the wall they climb/lay their eggs and fly away/come back on the first of May/hatch their eggs and then they say/I've travelled far and — eaten all the peaches down in Georgeeea!" The last line had to be said very fast. Ben had a fine voice, and started in again, conducting with his free hand, until finally everyone was singing.

When Jeremy joined in, Ben looked surprised, and beckoned him up. Jeremy thought he should have kept his mouth closed; his voice was too high. But Ben was looking pleased. "Oh, you have a true alto," Ben said, putting his arm around his shoulder. "Carry the upper notes and blend in as you will."

In a rumbling baritone, Mr. Fraser started, "Onward Christian Soldiers/marching as to war/with the cross of Jesus/going on before." Jeremy thought of waging war on the ground until they freed the gold it held, although he didn't have the slightest idea about mining, he realized. He picked a higher key and joined in. Ben started *Clementine* and they sang through all the verses of the poor girl with her apple-box shoes, then *I'm the Very Model of a Modern Major General,* and *PollyWolly Doodle all the Day.*

By now, every group on the trail within earshot was singing. *Amazing Grace* rolled up from behind them, and *Shenandoah* drifted down from in front. They sang *Rock of Ages* and *Abide with Me* and *Annie Laurie* and *There's a Long, Long Trail A-Winding.*

Suddenly they were twelve miles closer to Lake Bennett. Jeremy thought he could go on another twelve miles singing, but Mr. Fraser had been limping and it was dark, and yes, he was tired when they stopped. They made camp near some other tents, unharnessed and fed the animals, ate re-heated beans, and went to bed. Jeremy silently sang himself to sleep.

8

—

Thursday 3rd

A perfect day. Clear, bright & not cold. Sent Rimmer to Skagway to report as Convoy having passed our stuff into Canada. Rest went back to summit for loads. They were late starting & did not get in with loads until 9 p.m. I was busy baking, cooking &c.

Friday 4th March 1898

Rest went back to summit for loads & I baked & cooked &c. Fixed up my snowshoes & used them getting wood & making place for the horses. Rest arrived about 6:30 with loads all wet & tired & I was wet & sore, & very tired also. Began to snow early in a.m. & stormed all day. Tent was a little flat & leaned badly so that beds & everything nearby was wet.

Sat 5th March

Still snowing & very disagreeable. All hands tired so decided not to move but fixed up tent & things. Mac & Bob got wood & Ben repaired outside things while I baked & cooked. Rimmer returned about 2:30 p.m., having left one sleigh in cañon (about 4 miles back) & bringing two with him. Mac & Bob took Sue & went back for it, Ben made dog shelter, Rimmer hurt his back & quite lame.

Monday 7th March 1898
Snowing & stormy. Horses went through to Lake Bennett & the
dogs to within about 3 miles. Were very late returning, the dogs
getting in about 9:30 & the horses about 11 p.m. To bed 12:30.

Jeremy thought of the part of the trail from camp back to the
summit as the singing trail, because each time he went over it,
bringing more gear, he heard the songs they'd sung on the first
trip from the summit and sang them in his mind. Without the
others, he didn't want to sing out loud. Back and forth, as it had
been before, but now he went uphill with an empty sled and
downhill with a full one so it was easier. Also, the snow was different here, more granular, not so wet and slippery. The air was
even different, though he didn't register that until his third trip. It
felt as if the land were kinder, he thought one day, and then
thought, how strange to think of the land as a something. But it
seemed freer, he decided, not so towering or clinging. Freer and
drier, in spite of the snow.

Because the way was easier, he could make more trips in a day.
Everyone was pushing himself so Jeremy, without thinking about
it, pushed himself too, and they moved the cache from the summit in two days. He asked Mr. Fraser, who kept track of such
things, how long it had taken them to get to the summit.

"Eleven days," he answered.

"Wow! And only two days from there. What a difference!"

"I'd have to compute the sum of the individual man, dog, and
horse trips to know how many actual trips we made to the summit," Mr. Fraser added, looking as if he'd started computing
already.

Of course, Jeremy thought during one supper, we're eating up
our supplies, so after each meal there's less to cart. Not that he
noticed it made any difference.

One day, while Jeremy was loading up to go on, Mac strode back into camp empty-handed. He frowned as he yanked the axe out of the chopping block. Mr. Fraser emerged from the tent where he was baking bread. "What happened?"

"Agh," Mac spluttered. "Don't ask!" He stomped off toward the trees, but within a few paces he slowed and then returned. "Ben went ahead to help Rimmer and Bob get the horses over a rough spot so I had his sled as well as mine. I hit the ice and went head over toenails down a hill before I could let go of them. Smashed up both sleds! Stuff everywhere. Got it stacked but we can't go on until I make more sleds." He slammed the back of the axehead into his gloved hand a couple of times, then he smiled and his eyes regained their usual sparkle. "But don't you worry, James. I'll have them whipped up in a day or two. We won't lose much time."

"Could you salvage any pieces?"

"No. Too cold. That green wood just shattered."

Mr. Fraser shook his head in resigned sympathy and went back into the tent.

"You watch that spot, boy," Mac said to Jeremy. "It's about five miles on, around a bend with a slant like this." He held his hand out at a sharp angle. Jeremy nodded, and Mac stalked off toward the tree line.

He was getting to know these men almost without paying attention. Ben was a smoother-over, a joker, wanting to keep everybody happy. Bob was generally quiet and efficient, and completed tasks with little wasted motion. Rimmer seemed to like the animals almost better than people. He and Mac were special friends, just as Bob and Mr. Fraser were. Odd that he didn't think of Mr. Fraser as James, Jeremy ruminated, but then, he was the boss of this crew, even if the others thought everyone was equal.

Mac's a blower, Jeremy thought, as he finished loading up and started out. Like Mr. Hammond, the Saanich farmer to whom Jeremy had been apprenticed when he'd left the Home. "He blows hot and cold," Mrs. Hammond said when Jeremy had slunk onto the back stoop after his first beating. He'd been so tired from hilling potatoes since dawn that when he'd sat down to milk he'd fallen asleep with his head against the first cow's flank. He was ten — old enough to work, and it hurt cows not to be milked, he knew that. Still, if he'd not been asleep, he could have avoided the beating and waited until Mr. Hammond blew hot. Or cold. Jeremy wasn't sure which was which. But Mrs. Hammond always said, when Jeremy appeared after "an incident," "he blows hot and cold" so Jeremy came to think of it as Mr. Hammond's blowing. In the beginning, Jeremy had learned ways to disappear. Then he'd just taken the beatings. Until last summer, when he'd disappeared for good to Vancouver.

Jeremy had discovered from conversations that Rimmer had met Mac while surveying for the Canadian Pacific Railway and that Bob and Mr. Fraser had both lived in Port Arthur, Ontario. Mac had met Mr. Fraser in Winnipeg in 1881 — that was three years before he, Jeremy, was born — but they'd lost touch and then bumped into each other on Cordova Street a year ago. Jeremy imagined them clasping each other's hand and pumping hard, perhaps their free hand grabbing the other's forearm. *What a surprise, bumping into you after all these years!* Maybe it was then that Mac told Mr. Fraser he'd been surveying in the Yukon with Mr. Ogilvie.

Fancy knowing the man who'd written *The Klondike Official Guide*. William Ogilvie, Dominion Land Surveyor and Explorer. It said so right on the cover of the copy Mr. Fraser read every night. "Must sell like a dime novel," Ben had commented. "Every crew on the trail has a copy." He'd called it the Klondikers' Bible. Jeremy didn't think Mr. Fraser liked that, in spite of his little smile. He didn't take to teasing about the Bible.

Jeremy's foot slipped, snapping his attention back to the trail. The narrow path angled around the side of a steep, overhanging hill. Thousands of footsteps had pounded it into sheer blue ice which some had roughened with pickaxes. The loose chunks, while providing a grip, also increased the hazard. The snow was falling more densely, he now noticed. Below the trail was a drop of twenty feet. At the bottom, Jeremy saw two broken sled runners arching over snow-covered lumps — Mac had marked his cache. Had he come five miles already?

He waited while six men with back packs and sleds, two women in fur-lined, black poke bonnets and a dog team crossed over. Then he followed, keeping one hand on the protruding rocks beside him, his gaze on his shuffling feet. Fresh snow on old ice increased the path's slipperiness. His sled stuck with a suddenness that nearly pulled him over. He slid toward the edge, but there was a raised lip he braced his foot against. He teetered there, hoping the sled wouldn't pick this moment to come unstuck. When he'd regained his balance, he backed away and turned around. Breathing deeply, he yanked up on the handle and the rope. A chunk of ice careened over the edge. The sled's rear end slithered around and gathered speed. He grabbed the handle in both hands and braced his back and heels. The sled came to a halt at a forty-five degree angle to the hill, its last two feet hanging in space. He pulled. Slowly it straightened and regained the trail. Jeremy wiped sweat off his forehead. He could see how easily Mac had been pulled over the side. He could almost feel himself tumbling down the slope, bumping into the sled, perhaps breaking his arm or leg. And Mac had had two sleds. A miracle he hadn't been hurt.

Around the hill the trail widened again. Coming toward him were Ben and the dogs. Jeremy waited until he got closer, then told him what had happened to Mac.

"Oh, hot diggetydang," Ben muttered, peering down. He pulled off his hat and scratched his head as he looked back at the dogs, which had flopped down in their traces, as usual taking any opportunity for a rest. Ben replaced his hat and studied the valleyside. "If we go back to there," he pointed to a rock about fifty paces ahead of Jeremy, "and cut down at an angle, we should be all right." He smiled with resignation. "Saves me going all the way back to camp for the next load."

"I'll give you a hand," Jeremy offered.

Ben ordered the dogs to their feet and turned them around. Jeremy dragged his sled to the rock and pulled it off the trail. With Ben breaking trail at Captain's head and Jeremy braking and steadying the dogsled, they slipped and slid down the slope.

In this direction the wind blew stinging pellets of snow into their faces. Jeremy's eyes teared and he blinked to clear them. Between blinks he licked his chapped lips. At the bottom of the hill they turned around. The dogs seemed to agree, as they lay down again, that the wind at their backs was a relief.

Jeremy dug out the crates and cases and bags and passed them to Ben, who loaded the sled. "If we don't find gold in Klondike," Ben shouted at one point, "we'll be qualified for jobs as cart loaders!" Jeremy smiled as he kicked through the snow for any last goods.

They roused the dogs and trudged back up the slope. In the time they'd been loading, the snow had obliterated their previous track. At the top Ben halted while Jeremy retrieved his sled. Ben said, "I was going to load your stuff on the dogsled and tell you to go back for more, but maybe the dogs could do with a light load. Collie and Prince are not holding up as well as the rest."

Jeremy looked at the dogs.

"Their noses are hot," Ben continued. "And you can feel their ribs. They're just not eating."

"Do you think they have whatever killed Hank? Do you think they caught it from him, as Rimmer said?"

"Hank died weeks ago. I don't know."

"It can't be overwork if the others are fine," Jeremy offered. "And you treat them better than other crews treat their dogs." He patted

Collie, then Prince and Leo. All briefly wagged their tails. "So what is it?"

Ben snapped his fingers at the dogs, and started walking. "I don't know," he repeated. "We'll give them a light day. Yesterday was enough to exhaust anyone. Aren't you fagged?"

Jeremy tugged on his sled and fell into step. The trail widened enough after the rock to allow people to walk two abreast. Yesterday was enough to exhaust anyone. What about all the previous yesterdays? Could he really say how he felt? Did he even want to think about it? He tried for a light tone. "A bit fagged."

"Maybe it was the night the tent leaked that did us in," Ben said.

"Could be." Jeremy slapped his forehead in sudden thought. "Speaking of tents, I haven't put mine up ever! Why am I bothering to cart it?"

Ben gave him a long, strange look. "Because you'll need it going downriver to your father's mine. Have you forgotten we're nearly at Lake Bennett? You'll be leaving us in a day or so."

"Oh. Yes." Jeremy turned away and laughed, but it sounded like a strangled croak. As he switched the sled handle to his other hand, he realized that his father was more real to Ben than to him. He felt — his insides buzzed — bits of all feelings. Should he tell Ben he didn't have a father? That he'd made it up? It would be easier to tell Ben alone than everyone together, especially Mr. Fraser. But did he have to tell?

"Ben," Jeremy asked, after a few more paces, "How did you meet Mr. Fraser?"

"He gave me a summer job when I needed one." Ben looked sideways through the snow at Jeremy. "Office boy in his mining brokerage firm. If he hadn't given me a job I wouldn't have had the money to finish law school."

"When was this?"

"Summer before last — '96. When he first moved to Vancouver." Ben paused so long Jeremy thought he'd finished, but then he continued, with a sneer, "The next winter — last winter — his partner absconded with all the funds, and James had to close down."

"What's absconded?"

"Took off. The partner stole the money."

"Did Mr. Fraser get the money back?"

"No. The villain took off to the States. James was flat broke, with a family to support. That's why he started selling real estate as well as brokering mines." Ben looked at Jeremy. "But don't tell him I told you. He hates it mentioned."

"Maybe that villain's come to Klondike," Jeremy said. "Maybe we'll meet him. We could make him give the money back!"

Ben laughed bitterly. "Dream on."

"Maybe Smith's gang fleeced him in Skagway. That's the sort of guy it should happen to."

"Fat chance. And remember, don't mention it around him."

"Do the others know?"

"Bob does," Ben replied. "He was the bookkeeper."

They lapsed into silence as they passed a group coming back with empty sleds.

Jeremy pulled his sled thoughtfully. Ben had told him a secret. He could tell Ben a secret too. He didn't want to, but he did want to. With each step, with each group of people they passed, with each swish of the sled runners on the path, the desire to tell grew, until finally he blurted, "Ben, I'm going to tell you something too, but I don't want you to tell anyone, all right?"

"Depends what it is," Ben said grudgingly. "I don't like secrets much."

"Please?"

"Well, I won't promise."

"I promised you," Jeremy pointed out.

"Hmm. Well, maybe."

It wasn't a satisfactory reply, but Jeremy could almost taste his desire to continue. The words spat themselves out. "I'm an orphan. I was left at the Orphans' Home in Victoria. Then I was a farmer's apprentice until I ran away. Last summer. I lied about a father in Klondike because I thought Mr. Fraser wouldn't let me come along just because I was scared of Smith's gang."

"Oh." Ben looked at him, digesting this. "Why haven't you told anyone before this?"

Jeremy shrugged. "I mainly forgot about it. Or I thought anything could happen. I just took it day by day."

"And hoped the lie would go away," Ben finished, in a flat tone. Jeremy nodded. "Why tell me now?"

"Because you told me something, and because I want to go wherever you're going. I have no reason to go to Dawson if that's not where you're going."

"Oh good grief!" Ben scowled at him. "We've taken you this far based on a lie! The rest of the men, James especially, are not going to be pleased!"

"I know." Jeremy blinked his gritty eyes.

"What else have you lied about?"

"Nothing. Just — everything about a father."

"You'll have to tell them," Ben stated. "And soon. I can't keep this secret for you, because it's not a secret. It's a lie." He stalked on ahead and Jeremy wished he'd kept his mouth shut.

9

——

Friday 11th March 1898

Stormy in morning but turned out fine. Moved camp to Lake Bennett. Exceedingly bad trail & we were late getting in & pitching tent. Supper late (9:30). Crossed end of Lake Lindeman about midday. Portage 2 mile to Bennett.

Sat 12th March

I had to cook, get wood & some brush, Ben stayed in to help, rest went back for loads. Brought a good deal. Met Major Walsh & Phil, his brother.

The tents on the portage between the icy stretches of Lakes Lindeman and Bennett were covered in snow. So were the saw-pits, lumber piles, and half-built rafts. So were many of the people. It took Jeremy a while to realize what he was looking at through the blowing snow, but then, as he stared all around, his mouth dropped open. "Holy smoke! It's a city! A tent city! Where did all these people come from?"

Bob smiled, and even Rimmer grinned. "Same place we came from, kid," Bob said.

"But there weren't this many people on the trail! There're more people here than Skagway! I bet there're more people here than Vancouver!"

"Some came over Chilkoot Pass from Dyea," Rimmer said, "and you can't tell how many people are in a crowd when you're moving with it, like on the trail."

"Now they've all got here, and here they have to stop till the ice goes out — if they're building a boat, that is," Bob elaborated.

Mac, Ben, and Mr. Fraser pulled up from the ice of Lindeman to join them. "Impressive sight, isn't it?" Mac said.

"Even though you described this," Ben declared, "I didn't believe you. I apologize." He placed his palms together and bowed low.

Mac thumped Ben's shoulder. "Apology accepted if you move up an extra load."

"The Mounties estimate there are ten thousand people here," Mr. Fraser announced.

Jeremy craned his neck to see around a bend. "I hope there's room for us."

"Oh sure, and you can have your pick of crews to go down to Dawson with," Mac replied.

Jeremy caught Ben's eyes locked on him. He looked away. Lake Bennett. Somehow he'd believed that they'd never really get here. Or had he just wished that? Maybe he should blurt out right now that he didn't have a father anywhere, let alone one with a gold mine. If the men didn't want him along after that, after he apologized, he could probably team up with some others. Probably. He mentally squared his shoulders, turned to look at the men and opened his mouth, but Mr. Fraser said, "Enough gawking. We need to set up camp and bring forward the rest of our gear."

Ben looked at Jeremy purposefully. Jeremy frowned and looked away. Okay, okay. He wished he'd said nothing to Ben. He'd confess when they had all their stuff here. When they were ready to move on. If he couldn't think of another plan by then.

They headed east along the lake and pitched the tents in the first empty spot, then built a fire in the tent stove and ate beans and biscuits for lunch as usual, washed down with mugs of chicken soup made from concentrate.

Rimmer was recounting a conversation he'd had with a crew who'd come in over the Dyea trail. It was a shorter route, but so much steeper and rockier that even pack animals couldn't make it. People had to cart all their gear on their backs. But there were steps carved up the Chilkoot Pass, and some enterprising soul had built an aerial tramway so those who could afford it — and there weren't many who could at a dollar a pound — skipped up the Pass only once. "Not the crew I talked to though," Rimmer said. "They humped all their gear, just like us."

"Without animals to help," Mr. Fraser pointed out. "That's why we decided to take the Skagway Trail, remember."

Rimmer walked to the tent flap, scooped up a handful of snow and rubbed his plate clean. "We concluded that whichever route you took, you wished you'd taken the other one." He tucked the plate in the crate of kitchen supplies. "Ready to get on with it again?"

With another meaningful glance at Jeremy, Ben led the parade outside. He stated, "The absolutely worst thing — "

Jeremy gasped and closed his eyes. He knew he should never have told Ben!

"— about this adventure," Ben continued, "is having to repeat each part of it four or five times. Once is interesting. But after that —"

"Hear, hear," everyone agreed, Jeremy the most fervently, with relief. Even Sue chose that moment to shake her head and snort so she looked as if she were agreeing too.

On the trail, Jeremy remembered what Bob had said, and asked Mac, who was closest, "When does the ice go out?"

"Depends. Usually sometime in May."

"May! But it's only March!" *I don't want to wait here for two months,* he nearly blurted, but strangled the words into a cough. After a minute he asked, "Are you going to build a boat?"

"Not here."

"Where?"

"Wherever we get to when there's no ice." Mac was walking more quickly than Jeremy or the mare Mac was leading were comfortable with.

"Where are you going?"

Mac looked sideways at him and strode even faster. "Klondike's a big area." He clamped his lips shut and looked as if he'd next say, "Children should be seen and not heard." Jeremy fell behind.

He hadn't thought to ask where they were going before this. He'd assumed they were going to Bonanza or wherever everyone else was going. He was suddenly curious. What if they knew of another place with gold, a place with fewer people? That would be one more reason to stick with them, one more reason to own up about his lie. He'd heard people say that claims on the best gold-bearing creeks were already staked. If so, what were these ten thousand people on the shores of Lake Bennett going to do for gold? If Mr. Fraser's crew knew something no one else did, well then, if he were they, he wouldn't tell either, for fear the person would blab it all over Dawson. So if he cleared up the lie about meeting his father in Dawson, they could tell him where they were going.

Maybe Mr. William Ogilvie had told Mac where some gold was when they were surveying up here twelve years ago. Maybe he'd written it in his *Klondike Official Guide.* No, if he'd done that everyone would know and Mac wouldn't have to keep it secret.

By the time they'd come to the rough part of the trail, Jeremy had decided that for now he wouldn't ask any more questions. He didn't want to be told curiosity killed the cat; he'd heard enough of that from Matron.

The next day was more of the same. Jeremy had lost count of how many times he'd regretted buying Magnus' gear. The caches seemed to grow each time he turned his back, as if the minute he started off with a load, the stuff left behind reproduced. With each move to a new cache point, the boxes and bags and cartons became frailer. The sled's over-turning — how many times had that happened? — didn't help the goods either. He'd lightened his load as much as he could, like everyone else, discarding things beside the trail. Except for his unused tent. He could throw that out too after he straightened out the Dawson business. If the men allowed him to continue with them.

When he got back with his last load for the day he found Mr. Fraser and Bob in conversation with two men. One sat ramrod stiff on a crate by the stove. He had greying hair and a trimmed beard topped by a short, bristly moustache. He was slim and well-groomed despite wearing trail gear. Jeremy was suddenly conscious of how wet and grimy his clothes were.

The other man was younger, with brown hair and flowing ends to his moustache. He smiled as if he did that a lot. Mr. Fraser introduced Jeremy to Major Walsh and his brother, Philip. "The Major is the new Commissioner of the Provisional Yukon District. He's going down to Dawson the minute the ice goes out. He's willing to take you with him."

"Oh no, I can't," Jeremy blurted. "But thank you. That's very kind of you, Sir."

"Yes, it is," said Mr. Fraser, glaring.

"You don't want to keep your father waiting any longer than you have to," Bob threw in.

"No, Sir." Jeremy gave automatic responses while his brain whirred. But the whirring wasn't producing anything useful. He picked up the coffee pot and asked, "Would you like a refill?"

"No thanks." Major Walsh stood up. "We'll push off. Some of my men are helping Reverend Doctor Grant collect logs for his new church. I'll check in on you again. Good to get caught up, Fraser. Good to meet you, Patterson." He nodded.

The minute the Walshes were out of the tent, Mr. Fraser and

Bob turned on Jeremy. "No? What was that 'no' about?" Bob asked, at the same time that Mr. Fraser said, "Do you know who that man is? Do you know what an historic opportunity you have?"

Jeremy shook his head. "The new Commissioner of the Yukon?" he ventured.

"He's the man who single-handedly calmed the Sioux when they came into Canada after massacring Custer! When he was in the North West Mounted Police! Walsh was the only one Sitting Bull would trust! He convinced him to go back to the States!" Mr. Fraser was shaking his head and looking disgusted. "What do they teach you in school these days?" Jeremy just bit his lip.

"And you said 'no!' Now explain yourself!" Mr. Fraser's eyes glittered like shot. His cheeks were mottled.

"I was just startled," Jeremy muttered. Mr. Fraser's anger made his innards churn.

Bob didn't seem so angry, more surprised. He said, "This is a perfect opportunity for you to get to Dawson safely."

"Yes, Sir. It's very kind of him, Sir. And very kind of you to arrange it."

"Give over with the Sirs." Bob smiled, but his eyes were solemn. "Sometimes I wonder just how keen you are to get to your father."

"Yes, Sir — Bob." Jeremy darted a glance at Mr. Fraser who was staring at the floor, as if he were somewhere else, back wherever he'd known Major Walsh. Then Jeremy had the inspiration he'd been waiting for. It was so obvious he completely forgot Ben, and remembered only his month of wiggling out of tight spots about "his father." He backed up to the crate Philip Walsh had deserted and sat.

"It's like this! The ice won't go off the lake till May, Mac said, maybe the end of May. That's over two months from now. What would I do here for two months? And I'm not expected in Dawson just yet." Bob was watching him intently. Mr. Fraser looked up again. "My father's found his mine and got it working. All I'd have to do is help him. I'd like to prove myself capable before I join him. I've learned a lot from all of you."

He paused, realizing that that was true. "But I've got more to learn and so I'd like to come with you, wherever you're going — at least till the ice goes out. Then I could join up with Major Walsh and have an historic opportunity."

"Absolutely not," Mr. Fraser said, but it sounded automatic.

Bob frowned, chewing the inside of his lip. He got up and put a stick of wood in the stove.

Mac, Rimmer and Ben entered the tent's thick silence. "What's going on?" Ben asked. Jeremy brushed past them.

Outside, he stood looking over the dusky grey expanse of the frozen lake. He could hear the mutter of voices inside the tent as Bob and Mr. Fraser explained. I messed that one, Jeremy thought, disgusted with himself. He imagined Ben sneering, telling on him right at this moment. That's that, he thought. End of the road with them. Damn Ben. If he didn't know, it probably would have worked. Then he thought, if they wouldn't have let me come with them, I wouldn't have to explain. Oh well, he thought, I don't care anyway. I'll go with Walsh. He's probably more interesting anyway, all that Sitting Bull stuff.

But the lie seemed now to stretch all the way down the ice to Dawson. Telling Ben didn't seem to have shrunk it, but rather hardened its edges so that he had to look at it in its entirety. If he didn't say anything and went with Major Walsh, his mythical father would continue to be given life by others' belief in him. Walsh might be the sort of man who'd insist on personally hand-delivering him to his "father." Jeremy knew that sort of man. They sat on the Board that ran the Orphans' Home — men like Mr. Spencer and Mr. Cartwright, men who made the rules.

He could hear Mac's voice raised now; were they having an argument? He moved farther down the lakeshore. Sounds of chopping and the crack of falling timber came from the tree line.

In front of the tent next to Mr. Fraser's crew was a sign announcing LAUNDRY. Beyond it, another sign read SALOON. Lanterns lit edges of a saw-pit where two men still laboured, panting and cursing. The man on top pushed down on the two-handled saw; the man underneath pulled, trying to keep his face out of the dribble of sawdust. That didn't look like fun; Jeremy thought he'd rather keep on walking than have to build a boat.

A hand clamped down on his shoulder and he gasped. Ben stuck his face close to his. "You have to tell them! Now! They can't make an honest decision if you don't."

"You didn't tell them?" Jeremy couldn't believe it. He'd taken it for granted Ben would tell. Everyone at the orphanage told on everyone else. *Tattle-tale-tit, your tongue shall be split and every little puppy dog shall have a little bit.*

Ben was saying, "No, of course I didn't tell! That's your job! And whatever did you go and compound the lie for now?" Ben crossed his arms and stared at him.

Jeremy felt his eyes fill with tears. He turned away. It wasn't true that he didn't care, he realized. He wanted to go on with them and he wanted them to like him. "I don't know," he mumbled. "I just saw a way and took it. It just came to me."

"If you want any chance of sticking with us, you have to own up." Ben's tone was as cold and hard as the icy droplets of his breath.

Jeremy blinked his frozen eyelashes. He stared across the dark lake. It had stopped snowing. He stared at the soft lights from the many tents. He was cold. He clenched his teeth to keep them from clattering. Why didn't he just go back to Vancouver and forget Klondike? Forget these men? He could go to New York and never see them again. But . . .

He turned back. Ben was still there, his arms still crossed. "What do you care that I lied?"

"I don't know, but I do care."

Jeremy looked at the lake again. He sighed. "All right. If they decide I can come, I'll tell them."

"That's blackmail!" Ben grabbed his shoulder again and whirled him around.

"Ow!" Jeremy pulled away. "If they won't let me come, I won't have to tell them I lied because it won't matter. What's blackmail?"

"Ohhh!" Ben turned and strode back to the tent. Jeremy waited a moment while he realized his heart was not going to calm down, then he tiptoed into the yellow lantern glow around the tent.

Mac was saying, "The deal was that he could come with us to Bennett. I don't want him coming any farther!"

"He's pulled his own weight." Mr. Fraser's voice. "He hasn't slowed us down."

"I don't want anyone but us to know where we're going!" Mac sounded angry. "Turn him over to Walsh."

"Right." A low growl from Rimmer. "You have sons, James. You're too soft on boys."

"He's a hard worker," Bob acknowledged. "We might want another body when we get to McHenry's —"

"It's our duty to look after those weaker," Jeremy heard Mr. Fraser say.

"You've done your duty by asking Walsh to take him," Mac countered. "Your obligation is to us, your partners."

Mr. Fraser lowered his voice and Jeremy had to strain. ". . . get into serious trouble."

"All the more reason to turn the responsibility over to Walsh." Rimmer had not dropped his voice.

"I would not want any of my sons wandering around out here without a guardian," Mr. Fraser emphasized.

"Walsh can be his guardian. You wouldn't want your sons held up from meeting their father if you'd sent for them," Mac argued. "I vote he doesn't come."

"Me too," echoed Rimmer.

"He comes." Mr. Fraser added, "Bob? Ben?"

The pause seemed long to Jeremy before Bob finally said, "I don't have strong feelings one way or the other, though I have got used to having him around. I sympathize with his desire to prove himself. Maybe we're all doing that, one way or another. He can come, I guess."

Jeremy could feel all the men's eyes on Ben. He imagined him squirming. Please say yes, he thought to him. Then, please say no. Ben said, "We've got a way to go before we turn off. How about if he comes with us until the ice goes out or we hit the Pelly? There'll be others to take him to Dawson at that point."

Yay, Jeremy thought. Then, oh no.

"Oh, all right, let your mascot come," Mac sneered. "But no farther than the Pelly, mind! I don't want anyone but us to know where we're going! Now let's get on with supper."

Jeremy backed away into the shadows then walked quickly to the lakeshore. He'd said he'd confess. They'd give him the beating of his life, he bet. He could run away. He couldn't run away, he'd freeze. He walked along the shore, turned back to the tents.

Ben was standing in front of the tent, arms crossed. Jeremy nodded and sighed. "Just tell them what you told me," Ben said. "They'll be shocked and angry, but they won't eat you."

"Wanna bet?" Jeremy muttered. As he pulled open the tent flap he thought this must be how a murderer feels when he sees the hangman.

"I've deceived you all, and I've come to apologize." No one paid attention. Jeremy realized he'd only shouted the words in his mind. He cleared his throat and repeated himself aloud.

Mr. Fraser turned from the stove, spoon in hand. Rimmer stilled, his arm half into his coat sleeve. Mac put down his coffee mug and stood up. Bob cocked his head quizzically. Behind Jeremy, Ben entered the tent. The rustling flap sounded loud.

"I do not have a father with a gold mine or a father anywhere.

I am an orphan." He turned to Mr. Fraser. "I told you I had to meet my father because I didn't think you'd let me come if I was just scared of Soapy Smith's gang." He flicked his eyes to the other men. "I kept the lie going because I didn't know how not to, and because somehow I never thought we'd get here or when we did get here, I'd just leave and not have to tell. But I want to come with you," he blinked hard, sniffed and tried to steady his voice. "I'm sorry I lied. I won't do it again. Ever. If you don't want me to come now you know this, I'll go with Major Walsh and tell him I lied. I won't ever lie again." A sob overtook him and he turned away, swallowing hard. He wiped his eyes. "I'm sorry."

Inwardly he flinched; they could all beat him up at once. Oh, what did he care? A beating wouldn't hurt much worse that this confession.

Mr. Fraser's face had paled; it now mottled with red. He put down the spoon. Rimmer looked disgusted as he finished pushing his arm into his coat. Mac's face was flinty behind a sneer. Bob looked sad and thoughtful as he gave Jeremy a little smile. Ben took a step closer.

"What other lies do you have to confess?" Mr. Fraser asked.

"None, Sir. I tried to lie about my age, but you caught me. I am fourteen."

"Are you sure?"

"Yes Sir."

"And you've learned your lesson?"

"Yes Sir."

"We had reluctantly agreed to let you come with us, at least for a month. We will have to re-consider that decision."

Jeremy swallowed and nodded.

"You will eat and sleep with the animals tonight so that you will remember that your actions have consequences for others. You will hear our decision in the morning. Is that clear?"

"Yes Sir."

Jeremy took his sleeping bag and folding canvas cot from the cache and set them up in the stable tent. The dogs thumped their tails on the floor, but Jeremy didn't feel welcome. He unlaced his boots, climbed into his sleeping bag and sobbed. If confession was supposed to be good for the soul, why did he just feel ashamed? A hot nose nudged his hand: Collie. Jeremy put his arm around the furry neck and sobbed some more.

Later, a bobbing lantern approached: Ben with a plate of food. As he handed it to him, he said, "That was hard to do, Jer, we all know that. Try to get some sleep."

Jeremy doubted that he would. He dreaded the long night ahead.

II

10

Friday 18th March 1898
Up at 4 a.m. Struck camp & got loaded up about 8:30 when we
discovered wind was fair so we rigged up sails on all rigs [sleds]
but found we could not work them as the wind increased rapidly
to almost a gale & would upset or blow out our rigs & after losing
nearly 4 hours on them we had to abandon them. Had very heavy
loads after picking up those brought forward yesterday, each
horse having over 3000 lbs. & the dogs nearly 2500 lbs. Prince
too sick & sore to put in harness. Made about 10 miles & struck
a good camping ground & stable for horses. Stormy all day.

The morning after his confession, Jeremy took as long as possible to feed the horses and dogs. He stroked Collie, whose
nose was still hot and his fur dry. Prince's nose, if possible, was
even hotter. Slowly, he folded up his cot and sleeping bag, picked
up his supper plate and fork and crossed the snow to the main
tent. Drawing a deep breath, he entered.

"Good morning." Mr. Fraser's tone was neutral.

"Good morning." Jeremy glanced from face to face to see if the
men's decision showed. Mac scowled at his plate, Bob eyed him

over the rim of his coffee cup, Ben raised his eyebrow and gave a quick grin, and Rimmer had his hand over his face.

"We have two questions," Mr. Fraser said. "The first is, whatever made you think you could get away with your last egregious lie when you had already told Ben the truth?"

Jeremy looked at the tent wall. Ice that had formed in the night now dripped in the heat of the stove. "I don't know, Mr. Fraser. It just came to me and I guess I forgot I'd told Ben. I guess it was an old habit."

Mr Fraser nodded, considering. "Our second question is, what made you decide to tell the truth?"

"It seemed to matter to you." Jeremy added, "I wanted to right from the beginning, but I thought maybe I wouldn't have to."

"On the basis of those answers, you may continue with us." Jeremy sighed in relief and smiled, but Mr. Fraser still looked stern. "However, because of old habits, I have drawn up a contract for you to sign." He produced three pieces of paper. "Do you know what a contract is?"

"I think so," Jeremy said dubiously.

"A contract is an agreement between two parties — in this case, you and the rest of us. Breaking a contract is a serious offence under the law. Do you understand?" Jeremy nodded. "This contract binds you to tell the truth, only the truth, and all of the truth, as long as you are in our company. It is to help you break old habits, and to give us the assurance that you will. Do you understand?" Again, Jeremy nodded. "There is one copy for you, one copy for us, and an extra copy, so you must sign three times." He handed Jeremy a pen and inkpot.

Jeremy took the documents, inked the pen and leaned over a crate. Mr. Fraser shouted, "No! No! No!" so loudly Jeremy jumped. "Don't ever sign a contract without reading it!" His tone moderated. "Good heavens boy, you could be signing away your rights to all the gold you'll ever find in your whole life!"

"Oh," Jeremy said. He held the contract under the lamp to read.

He recognized *not to lie, tell the truth* and his name, so he figured it said what Mr. Fraser said it said. He signed it, thinking that he was happy to if they needed this paper to let him continue with them.

Mr. Fraser handed him his copy and, as Jeremy folded it and stuffed it into his pocket, stated, "Now we will say no more about this."

Hauling load after load down Lake Bennett, Jeremy thought about the questions, especially the first one, why continue the lie after telling Ben the truth? He couldn't come up with a better reason than the one he'd given, but he kept remembering his rush of enthusiasm when he'd had the inspiration. As if he were suddenly bigger and stronger because he'd had an idea.

Then Collie staggered in his harness and collapsed. The other dogs milled about, howling or whining.

"Collie!" Jeremy shouted. He dropped his sled handle, knelt, took off his mitt and stroked the dog's head. Mr. Fraser felt for Collie's pulse. The other men strode over, and Prince, riding on Mr. Fraser's sled, raised his head.

"Is he going to be all right?" Jeremy asked.

"No. He's dead." Mr. Fraser stood up.

"Unharness him, James," Mac instructed.

Jeremy felt his eyes sting, and blinked against tears. It wasn't right he got to go with the crew and Collie didn't.

As Mr. Fraser removed the dog's body from the traces and reorganized the team. Captain licked Collie's snout and made a noise deep in his throat.

Do the dogs know Collie's dead, Jeremy wondered. Do they feel sad like me? Do the horses? Rimmer led them over to redistribute the dogs' load.

Mr. Fraser removed Collie's booties and put them in his pocket. Gazing at the cooling carcass, he said, "Your work is over, good dog. Rest in peace."

"But he won't, of course," Mac pointed out. "The minute people aren't around, the ravens will arrive. They're the best-fed beasts on the trail."

Jeremy looked up at the sky. Ravens eat Collie! He knew he couldn't stay to protect Collie. He knew he couldn't bury him. His chest and stomach surged with sadness and anger.

The men lightened the dogs' load and increased the horses', and then Mac had to whack their haunches to get them moving. Jeremy picked up his sled handle and, looking back at Collie, departed down the ice.

Rest in peace, good dog, he thought. Had the dog really come over to comfort him last night? Had Collie wanted comfort? Had he known last night he was going to die? His nose had been hot; should Jeremy have done something?

Of course it wasn't fair that Collie died. *Fair doesn't run the world, boy!* Jeremy could hear Mr. Hammond's favourite phrase. The farmer used it when he killed the chickens and butchered the pigs. *What's fair got to do with food, boy?* He used it when he drowned the runty kittens, and sometimes when his beating was so severe he flayed Jeremy's skin raw. *What's fair got to do with survival, boy? Them as won't learn won't survive.*

Collie wasn't the first dead dog he'd seen. There'd been Hank of course. Had ravens eaten him? Dogs' carcasses were constant along the trail, worn out by overwork, mistreatment, or illness. But Collie was a nice dog, a loving dog, like Hank. Neither asked for much; neither should have died.

Horses died too, and people. Reverend Dr. Grant had told Mr. Fraser that he'd treated over forty cases of meningitis on the Skagway Trail before he'd got to Lake Bennett, and most of the ill didn't recover. People tried to bury human corpses, but it was too hard to dig graves in the frozen ground, so dogs and horses were abandoned. Of course Jeremy knew that when the ice went out Collie'd have the deepest grave — the bottom of the lake — what was left of him after the ravens and wolves passed by.

And now, Prince was too sick to work. Mac had suggested shooting him, but Mr. Fraser said maybe he just needed a rest, and so the dog was strapped in a blanket on the top of the loaded sled, looking as if he didn't care what happened to him. Jeremy was glad they were giving him a chance — but why not Collie too?

He asked Ben, when the parallel ruts they were following converged.

"Collie didn't seem as sick as Prince," Ben said. "I guess we were wrong."

"What did he die of?"

"I don't know."

"He was nice to me last night." Jeremy's voice was low. He didn't think Ben heard.

"He was a good dog with a lot of heart. Just not up to Klondike."

They slogged on and Jeremy thought about the next camp they'd make without Collie. Maybe without Prince too. Well, he vowed, he'd never forget Collie.

"Too bad those sails we rigged up didn't work," Ben said. "It was better riding on the runners than pulling."

"Until the sleds fell over." Jeremy made an effort to put Collie's death further back in his mind. "The sails would have worked if it hadn't been blowing a gale. If we made those steering things and folded the canvas in half . . ."

"Rudders." Ben stated. "They might work better. But the ice is so cracked and bumpy we can't glide." Ben pulled his sled over a thick ridge. "This isn't like skating on the duck pond of my youth!"

He started to hum *Tales of the Vienna Woods*. Then he switched to *Greensleeves*. Jeremy made himself join in. He couldn't remember all the words and it was a complicated tune so they practised. After the fifth rendition, Mac yelled, "Give over! Even Sue is wincing! Sing something else!"

"You just don't appreciate art!" Ben yelled back.

"If Art were singing, Mac might appreciate him!" Bob contributed.

Jeremy giggled, then whispered to Ben, "Do you know that new song, *A Bicycle Built for Two?* Let's sing it just for them."

The second verse sputtered into "Oof!" when Jeremy's sled arm was wrenched so hard he lost his balance. He scrambled to save himself but fell forward, knocking his breath out.

"You all right?" Ben asked. Gasping for air, Jeremy nodded. He sat up, rubbed his shoulder and looked back at his sled. Its nose was jammed in a ridge of ice and its tail waved to the sky. "It's not broken and neither are you, but you'll have to scrape those runners. I'll see you later," Ben said as he headed off.

Jeremy stood up. The runners had swollen to double thickness with melting, then freezing slush. He tried to work it off with his hands but it was too solid and only made his mitts wet. He kicked at it, but his boots slithered along the ice. There was nothing sharp nearby so, with resignation, he walked the quarter mile to the shoreline, scuffed around in the snow-covered bank until he found a rock, and walked back. By the time he'd chipped the ice off the runners, readjusted his load, and yanked the sled over the ridge, the rest of the crew were black specks far up the lake.

Although most people had stayed at the head of Lake Bennett to build boats while waiting for the ice to go out, others continued on sleds, and so, while Jeremy worked, a thin but constant procession overtook him. As he started forward, he heard, "Ho there, boy, aren't you part of Fraser's crew? Where's the rest?"

It was Mr. and Mrs. Robinson. Jeremy fell into step. They'd camped beside them in the Pass and once more before Lake Bennett. The Robinsons, a couple in their twenties, had sold their dry goods store in Chicago to finance this "opportunity of a lifetime." They'd joined up with Mr. and Mrs. Black from England, who were going to meet their grown son in Dawson, and Ole and

Sven Larson, brothers from Sweden. Emma, the Robinson's two-year-old all bundled up in furs, rode in a sled.

While Jeremy explained his delay, he noted that something seemed different about the Robinson's outfit. Finally he exclaimed, "What happened to your dogs? Didn't you have four teams?"

"That we did, lad," said Mr. Black. Both he and his wife were small and quick, with very bad teeth. "But we ran out of fish and had to shoot one dog to feed the rest."

"Then we procured some horsemeat," Mrs. Robinson took over. She was billowy and nearly as tall as her husband, who was nearly as tall as the Swedes. "But it must have been poisoned, for eight dogs died the next day."

"Not poisoned," Mr. Robinson corrected. "Just too long dead."

"Poisoned." Mrs. Robinson insisted. "There are people up here who will do anything to keep others from getting to the gold-fields!"

She was about to go on, but Mrs. Black cut her off. "Don't worry. Our dogs can feast tonight." She turned to Jeremy. "We found a nice fresh carcass a while back. The Lord doth indeed provide," she finished with a wink.

Jeremy looked at the loaded sleds and cold shards of realization pricked his stomach. Down the side of one, partly obscured by a tarp, hung two hind legs and a tail, the fur the same gold colour as Collie's.

"That's our dog, Collie," he blurted. Then he clamped his lips shut against a sudden roil of nausea as he had an image of the Robinson's dogs feasting on poor old Collie who, just last night —

"The Lord giveth and the Lord taketh away," Mrs. Black expanded her previous paraphrase.

"The other way around, in this case," Mr. Black laughed.

It's just the thought, Jeremy told himself sternly. They have to feed their dogs. And something would have eaten Collie. Ravens,

Mac said, or wolves, and dogs are like wolves. Still, it took a few minutes for his stomach to settle down. Finally he said, "At least dogs eat meat. It's really hard on our horses. There's no food for them."

"You're lucky they've lasted so long," Ole commented. His nose was crooked; perhaps it had been broken. "Most horses gave up long ago. If they made it over the Pass they didn't make it to Bennett." Between the Swedish, British and American accents, Jeremy's ear was switching as much as a railway yard.

"We've been lucky," Jeremy said, then added, with a novel feeling of loyalty, "Of course, Mr. Fraser and the rest insist that the animals be well taken care of."

"More than I can say for some," sniffed Mrs. Robinson. "The horsemeat they've been serving in those so-called restaurants along the trail is definitely tainted. I talked to a man yesterday who nearly didn't survive."

"It won't happen in our establishment, Mrs. Robinson," Mrs. Black stated. Then, to Jeremy, "That's what we've decided to open in Dawson City. Everyone needs some good home cooking. We'll call it *The British-American Dining Establishment*. It will keep us out of trouble while the men go find the gold, isn't that right, Mr. Black?"

"Indeed yes, Mrs. Black." Mr. Black winked at Jeremy.

"You come right in for a meal," Mrs. Robinson said to Jeremy. "We'll put some meat on your bones."

"Sure, but I might not be in Dawson." Jeremy peered up ahead to see if he could spot any of his crew yet.

"Oh, I thought you were meeting your father with the rich mine." Mr. Robinson sounded surprised. "Course I guess you'll be out on the diggings before the women get the Dining Establishment open."

Jeremy sighed. His "father" again. I'll never see these people again, he thought. I can just agree with Mr. Robinson that I'll be out at the mine, and drop the topic. But then he thought of the contract he'd signed. Did it mean he wasn't to lie when he was physically in the men's presence, as he was not now, or did it mean he was not to lie during the time he was attached to their crew? He sighed again, and decided to play it safe.

"I don't have a father. He's not in Dawson or anywhere. I just made that up." This time confessing wasn't as hard. "So I'm going with Mr. Fraser's crew, and they're not going to Dawson."

"Oh? Where are they going?" Sven wanted to know.

"I don't know."

Sven looked at him. So did Ole, Mr. Black and Mr. Robinson. So did the women. Even Emma watched. All watched with so much interest that Jeremy's heart drummed.

"Everyone's going to Dawson," Ole stated. He had narrow eyes, Jeremy noticed.

"Everyone's going to Klondike," Jeremy stammered, echoing Mac. "Klondike's a big place."

Mr. Robinson and Mr. Black looked at each other, then away. "Sure is." Mr. Robinson tried to keep his tone light. "That's why everyone goes to Dawson first. Only place to register claims."

"But you have to find something worth a claim first," Ole pointed out.

"So I guess we will get to Dawson after all," Jeremy said, trying to laugh. "So I will eat at your British-American Establishment. I just haven't thought about getting there. One day at a time, Mr. Fraser says. We probably are going directly to Dawson, I just haven't thought about it." Jeremy knew he was prattling. Why wouldn't his sled get stuck now so he could get out of this? The truth was as hard to deal with as lies. Or maybe not saying the whole truth was the same as a lie. That was part of the contract, telling the whole truth. Then why did telling the whole truth — not that he knew it anyway — to these people seem so dangerous?

"Emma hungry. Emma eat," the child declared. She started to fidget, trying to stand up.

Mrs. Robinson pulled out a package of sandwiches from the

sled. She unwrapped one, broke it in half, and gave it to Emma. "Anyone else?" she offered, shoving the package at Jeremy with a smile. They looked like jam sandwiches. A sudden spurt of saliva made him realize he was hungry. And jam! But he didn't want to be indebted for their food, and, somehow, eating seemed disloyal to Collie.

"No thank you," he said. Mr. Robinson took one, and Ole and Sven. Mr. Black said to his wife, "Where's our lunch then?"

She reached into her pocket and produced sandwiches as well. All this food business had slowed the group to a crawl. Out of politeness, Jeremy had slowed too. Now he shaded his eyes and looked down the lake. "I think that's Rimmer up there, having trouble with the horse. I'll get on and help him." He nodded to them all and walked away as fast as the rough ice and heavy sled allowed.

Of course the blob of man and beast ahead wasn't Rimmer, or anyone else Jeremy knew. He had to keep walking extra fast to get some distance in front of the Robinson crew. His sled jerked and bobbed over the lake surface, the icy air speared his lungs, and his calves grew razor blades between muscle layers as he pushed himself onward. He felt eyes boring into his back, questioning his crew's plans and possible information.

After a while he dared to slow down, but not to stop and eat. Then he remembered he had some beans and a crust of Mr. Fraser's sourdough bread in his pocket so he munched as he carried on. He couldn't get the image of Collie's dangling legs and tail out of his mind and his eyes teared up at the thought of Collie's fate. Poor dog, and only last night . . .

The jagged peaks of the mountains had rounded to crests that no longer loomed so high above him. The valley surrounding Lake Bennett was wide and the dark spruce trees at the end of the lake drew closer. He had to detour around ice ridges, some half as tall as he was, and he remembered how he'd always thought of ice as smooth. It sure hadn't been, so far. Mr. Fraser had told him that, all winter, you could read how the weather had been on the day the lake froze. This was like a photograph in ice, Jeremy thought, of a windy day with towering waves.

The closer he pulled to the end of the lake, the more it seemed that the trees were coming out to meet him, but he knew they weren't doing any of the work. He was.

He saw Bob and Rimmer just into the timberline. They seemed to be tugging and scraping at a sled, but before he could approach, he really had to pee. Judging by the colour of the snow behind the first convenient tree, this was a favoured rest stop. More comfortable, he carried on.

Drenched in sweat, Blackie stood with splayed legs and hanging head, breathing so hard his skinny flanks moved like a bellows. The snow here was soft and granular, slushy from the day's melting. The edge of the sled had sunk down two feet and jammed against a boulder; Rimmer and Bob had been trying to dig it out. "Can I help?" Jeremy asked.

The men straightened and turned. Jeremy noticed how thick and long their beards had grown, Bob's red and Rimmer's black. Rimmer said, "Help us haul her up and maybe we won't have to unload."

They put their hands and backs to it, but it was still too heavy for the three of them. Bob said, "Nothing for it, we unload some."

Tentatively, Jeremy offered, "If two of us pull on the back of the sled while one guides Blackie —"

"Tried that," Rimmer cut him off.

"Blackie's had some rest," Bob said. "Worth another try now we've got two more hands. Anything's better than unloading and reloading."

Rimmer and Bob pulled on the end of the sled while Jeremy took Blackie's bridle and backed him around the boulder. It wasn't like having a horse between wagon poles because the traces to the sled were leather. The weight of the horse could not help; it was a case of keeping the horse out of the way while Bob and Rimmer did the work. Slowly the sled moved back and up and swung away from the boulder. Bob yelled, "Move him forward now."

"Come on, Blackie." Jeremy tugged the other way on his bridle. The horse shook his head and snorted hard to clear his nostrils. He moved one foreleg and wobbled unsteadily. "You can do it, boy," Jeremy whispered.

"Get going, Nag!" Rimmer yelled. "He's half dead! You'll have to whip him, Jer!"

"Come on, Blackie." Jeremy tugged harder. Blackie wobbled all four legs forward. As the traces tightened, Bob and Rimmer pushed on the back of the sled and slowly it regained the trail. Once in forward motion, Blackie continued, unsteadily, head down. Within yards, he was breathing like a bellows again. Bob lurched the sled into the path behind the horse and Jeremy picked up his sled handle and rope.

This was an awful bit of trail: slush on top of deep frozen ruts, deadfalls and boulders. The dark spruce concentrated the warming rays of the sun so that now, mid afternoon, pools of water had formed. By the time they reached the flats of Cariboo Crossing Jeremy's leather boots were soaked. Blackie churned up slush as they sloshed through melted shallows at the end of Nares Lake and along the beach, where the sun and many feet had beaten the snow off sand and rock. The sleds stuck time and time again.

Still, the Robinson party had not caught up with them, in spite of their slowness. Jeremy's worst fear had been that they would camp beside them, offer cups of tea and pump the men about where they were going before he could warn them. Which he did, while they were eating supper.

"You did what?" Mac spat, his eyes narrowing in the lamplight.

"Told them you weren't going to Dawson," Jeremy repeated. "I didn't know they'd be so interested." Bob, Rimmer, Ben, and Mr. Fraser had all stopped eating, and were staring at him as well. He shifted on his crate, his plate momentarily forgotten. "Look, I didn't have to tell you about it! I could just have left it! Stop staring at me! Did you want me to lie?"

"In this case, yes," Mac said. Ben guffawed. Mr. Fraser contemplated both of them.

"No, Jeremy, of course not," he tried to soothe. "It's just — unfortunate. One of those things. And it's right you told us. Forewarned is forearmed." With a glance at the other men, he began eating again.

Mac scowled and muttered something to Rimmer, then he shovelled up a spoonful of beans, still glaring at Jeremy.

"They're feeding Collie to their dogs," Jeremy blurted.

"Who? That crew?" Ben had stopped chewing.

Jeremy nodded, blinking.

"That's what happens," Rimmer said. "If not dogs, then ravens or wolves."

Jeremy was not comforted. Later, he had trouble getting to sleep around his mental image of the dangling Collie. Of course, Collie probably wasn't dangling any more.

11

Monday 21st March 1898

Rose 3:45. Got off 7:30, called at Police Camp a mile down & at head of Tagish Lake. Met Phil Walsh & William Willison (Toronto Globe) & a little further on saw Captain Harris & partner & about 22 miles farther had a long chat with Mr. J.R. Perry, he is putting in a sawmill. Went about 15 miles & camped late, I went ahead to pick out place but did not find one till 5:30 & rest did not arrive till 7. Nearly midnight when I got to bed. Day fine.

Wed 23rd March 1898

Froze hard last night, cold north wind blowing. Started late (10:30) made about 10 miles to island. Animals all very tired. Camped 6:30 but late getting to bed as usual. Prince, the sick dog whom we had hauled on sled, died here.

Sat 26th

Moved camp about 10 miles to where loads were left yesterday. Camped early & fixed up for Sunday &c. Trail soft & bad on river, light snow falling. Discovered bag of flour was stolen from stuff left yesterday.

Sunday 27th March 1898
Very fine, warm day. Lay in camp. Ben baked an apple custard pie
& an omelette of evaporated eggs & we lived high.

The days and weeks were going on with the same regularity —
moving from river to lake, from flat-topped mountain to
rolling hill, from crisis to near-crisis to averted crisis, interspersed
with the monotonous slog through snow, hauling the sled. Jeremy
could not have told one day from the next if Mr. Fraser with his
journal had not announced them. Most nights they set up a new
camp further on, taking only half an hour for that, and another
half hour to make the dogs — now minus Prince — and Blackie
and Sue as comfortable as they could with such scarce feed. Then
an hour to collect kindling, locate a dead tree, buck and split it, get
the stove going and heat the food that someone, usually Mr.
Fraser, had prepared the night before. They took their boots off
with groans of discomfort and examined their feet for damage.
Everyone's feet hurt; there had to be oozing wounds before anyone mentioned it, even to himself.

"You might think your most important body part is your brain
or your heart, but on the trail it's your feet," Bob was fond of saying.

Now it was Sunday again, a day off from work, a day to do only
the essentials, to cook, bake, inspect, wash, mend, repair, and
build. From Mr. Fraser's frown and tight mouth, Jeremy knew he
was displeased that Bob and Rimmer had gone back for a load on
Sunday; he'd said nothing only because he felt sorry for Blackie
out in the cold wind.

After his bath, which Jeremy had perfected into a five minute,
two bucket affair — one for his hair and one for the rest of him
and to heck with washing his clothes every week — he emptied the

buckets, swished snow around in them, refilled them and carried them to the stove. Mac was sitting on a cot mending a dog harness. Ben lay on the other cot, reading a dime novel he'd found discarded at Lake Bennett. Mr. Fraser was kneading bread dough.

Jeremy watched him punch and turn it. It made slurping noises as it rolled away from the side of the metal pan. Mac's needle sissed as he pulled the thick waxed thread through the leather. The fire sizzled and cracked in the stove. Ben punctuated the sounds by turning a page.

"What would you be doing if you were home today with your family?" Jeremy asked Mr. Fraser.

"Going to church."

"What church?"

"Central Presbyterian. Thurlow Street."

"Your whole family?" Mr. Fraser nodded.

"How many children do you have?" Jeremy hadn't thought to wonder before.

"Five boys."

"How old are they?"

"Ross is eleven, Horace is eight, Allen five, Lyall nearly four, and Clarence, the baby, is two."

"Wow," Jeremy said, "it sounds like the boys' side of the orphanage." Mr. Fraser stifled a smile. Ben laughed.

Jeremy opened a bag and pulled out some slices of evaporated apple. No matter how much he ate, he was hungry again in half an hour. "And then what?"

"Dinner."

"What do your boys do after dinner?"

"Sunday afternoon is quiet time. They can think, study their Sunday school lesson, read a book if it's uplifting. Sometimes we all go for a walk. But no running, and no playing. Then we go to church again in the evening."

"Mm," Jeremy agreed. "We went to church twice a day in the

Orphan's Home too. But it wasn't always the same church. Sometimes we went to the Methodist, sometimes the Presbyterian, sometimes the Anglican. But I couldn't tell much difference." He wondered if that was too honest and added, "Except for the Anglican cathedral. They wore long gowns and swung incense."

"Nearly Papist," Mr. Fraser said to the bread dough. He gave it one final knead, covered it with a cloth and set it to rise on top of the little oven that fastened into the stove chimney.

"We had to be quiet too, Sunday afternoons." Jeremy pulled up a crate and sat down. "But we weren't always." He smiled, remembering Cowlick Sunday, the tickling games and arm wrestling. The loser was the one who made a noise. It felt good to be able to talk about the orphanage now that he didn't have to pretend he was meeting his father.

"We had Real Orphans and Home Boys and Home Girls. Home Boys and Home Girls had visitors on Sunday afternoons, they were just there because their families couldn't afford to feed them, but they came to visit them. I was a Real Orphan. So was my best friend."

"Do you know anything about your parents?" Mac asked, putting down the mended harness and picking up another. Mr. Fraser had sat down beside him and was examining the soles of his boots.

"No. They called me the Basket Baby, though I wasn't left in a basket, just on the doorstep. They'd had a Basket Baby before, left in a real basket, but I never knew her."

"Did you like the orphanage?" Ben asked, looking up from his book.

Mr. Fraser said, "It's a good thing there was an orphanage for you."

Jeremy had never thought about whether he'd liked it, nor thought to be grateful. He said, "It was all right. They didn't beat us without a reason. It was better than being an apprentice at the

Hammonds. The food was pretty good. And yeah, I liked Matron and Catherine, she looked after us, and sometimes bought us sourballs and jawbreakers. And Cowlick Sunday and me, well, we did things together."

"I," said Mr. Fraser. "Cowlick Sunday and I."

"I," Jeremy dutifully repeated.

Ben laughed. "Cowlick Sunday. That's quite a name." Jeremy smiled.

"Did you ever wonder about your parents?" Ben asked.

"No." He thought. "Well, not really. I just didn't have any." He was not going to say that every night when he was eight and nine he'd made up a story about an English Lord and Lady who'd met on board ship. They were shipwrecked in a ferocious storm — that must have been when Catherine was reading them *Mr. Midshipman Easy* — and they'd had to fend for themselves on a deserted island, and then, just after he was born, his parents died from the bite of a snake that lived only on this island. He was rescued by passing Indians who took him into their canoe, and he would have grown up with them, but some sailors who had a rowboat from another shipwreck shot everyone but him, and they rowed him to Victoria, but then had to go back to sea so they left him on the Orphanage doorstep. He wasn't going to tell the men that, even if "not really" was a sort of lie.

"How did they know your last name was Britain?" Mr. Fraser asked.

"They didn't. When I was leaving age Matron said I had to have a last name and what would I like. She suggested Smith or Brown; they were common, sturdy names, she said. I remember that, common, sturdy, but I said call me *England* because the map of the world has more red than any other colour, and I'm going to be rich, like England. Then she said *Britain* would be a better last name than England, and I thought, well, all right, Britain is England." He thought he'd said too much, and blushed. "Good thing I didn't take Smith," he added, "that'd make me related to Soapy."

Ben smiled. "Not many people get to name themselves," he said, standing up.

"I didn't get to name my first name. Matron did. She said they had too many boys named Matthew, Mark, Luke, and John so she called me Jeremiah. I changed it to Jeremy. Jeremiah's awful."

"You'd need a long white beard to suit Jeremiah." Ben turned back to his book.

A minute's silence, then Jeremy asked, "What are you reading, Ben?"

Ben looked at the cover. "*The Phantom Tracker or The Prisoner of the Hill Cave.*"

"Is it any good?"

"It's exciting, but completely unbelieveable. The hero, Cimarron Jack, the kingpin of rifle shots, keeps chasing Colorado Jack, otherwise known as The Tiger. You can read it after me, if you want. Trouble is, the ink's run in the last half from lying in the snow, so I might not find out what happens."

Mr. Fraser was frowning at Ben's book. Did he not like Ben reading something unbelievable? Or reading a dime novel on Sunday? Did he think a story was a lie? Was it?

Hastily, in case Mr. Fraser was going to lecture, Jeremy observed, "Cowlick isn't any stranger than the names in that book."

"Was he named because of his hair?" asked Mac.

"Catherine kept trying to stick it down, but it was stronger than her hair goo. He chose Sunday because that's the day you don't have to work." Jeremy could see him, could feel him again, and wished he were here. Maybe he'd come to the gold rush too and they'd meet up, the way Mr. Fraser kept meeting people he knew. Maybe the men would let Cowlick join their crew . . .

Ben got up and put the pails of melted snow on a board supported by two crates, and began washing shirts, socks and long johns. Lines strung between the tent poles close to the stove already supported the others' laundry. "Cimarron Jack — or Colorado Jack — never has to do laundry. I'm beginning to appreciate my mother," he muttered.

Jeremy turned his attention to Mac. "Do you have a family, Mac?"

"No." He ran the traces through his hands, searching for more weaknesses.

Jeremy waited for Mac to elaborate. When he didn't, Jeremy asked, "Why not?"

"My wife died. The baby died too." His tone was flat.

"Oh." Jeremy wished he hadn't asked. He caught Mr. Fraser's eye.

"It's been five years, Mac," Mr. Fraser said to his boot. "You might meet a lady now."

Mac laughed but it sounded more like a grunt. "I'm not likely to meet anyone up here."

"You never know," Bob teased. "Why, just around the next bend you might come upon a beautiful damsel in distress — ." Mac's scowl cut him off.

Jeremy took another handful of apple slices and changed the topic. "Why won't you tell me where you're going?"

Mr. Fraser looked up from the boot he was patching. "Because of what happened with the Robinsons. The less you know, the less you can say."

"I wouldn't have told them!"

"This way you certainly won't," Mr. Fraser said to the bottom of his boot.

Ben, emptying a pail of soapy water, saw Jeremy's wounded look. "There are just too many people here lusting after gold. Lust doesn't go along with thoughtfulness. You've seen how people have treated their animals, driving them past endurance to get to gold. The further we get from civilization, the more they taste gold, and the worse they behave. Whoever stole our bag of flour didn't care if that was all there was between us and starvation. Sometimes I'm convinced that humans are just beasts with a thin veneer of moral behaviour. So this is for your own good, Jeremy."

"And ours!" added Mac.

For your own good was a phrase Jeremy loathed. At both the orphanage and the Hammonds it had frequently preceded a whipping. "Will you ever tell me where you're going?" he whispered.

"We'll see," Mr. Fraser said. Another phrase Jeremy hated. Mac was scowling, Jeremy noted, as he pulled on his jacket. He pushed open the tent flap, picked up the axe and attacked the pile of bucked logs. After splitting and stacking, he felt better and wandered down to the lake edge.

He was so tired of snow. Tired of the look of it, the smell of it, slogging through it. Tired of thin black trees against stark white. Tired of the trees' gunshot-loud cracklings, the ice's booming in the cold.

The dark green spruce fringing the lakeshore was the only colour that relieved the white monotony, Jeremy thought, until he looked at the blue sky. Then he looked back at the leafless tree trunks among the spruce. They were more a cream-grey than white. The still upright dead trees were grey or black. And those round balls of dead twigs some of the trees had on their branches were new-wood brown.

Actually, when he really looked, even snow wasn't all white. It was blue in the shadows of some ice ridges and almost purple between the trees. This sunlight made it sparkle in colours too — dancing bits of yellow, green, rose. Later, if the day stayed clear, the snow would turn orange and red and deep violet in the sunset. But it was still snow. And if someone, say that photographer, Hegg, took a photo, this would all be black and white again.

There was no one else camped here. No one passing by just then. There were just their two tents and the stable tent in the whole land. Some area around his stomach ached, and he longed to be back at the orphanage. He saw Catherine's face bending over him the time he'd fallen out of the tree. He'd been safe there. He'd never been alone and he'd always had Cowlick. Too bad they'd lost touch when they were apprenticed, Cowlick in Sooke, Jeremy in Saanich with the Hammonds. He'd written Cowlick the first Christmas, but Cowlick had never replied. Mr. Fraser's family would be like the orphanage. He bet those boys arm wrestled on silent Sunday afternoons, and got frowned at for giggling.

Jeremy blinked fast and sniffed. He'd felt this way at the Hammonds, and when he ran away to Vancouver. He vowed he'd never feel this way again, and mostly he didn't. But the nights he'd had to sleep on Carrall Street because he hadn't sold enough papers or begged enough money to buy a bed — was that the economic depression Mr. Fraser talked about? — those nights he'd felt this way. As freezing-aching as the windy lake here.

That's what Klondike was going to fix. He was going to get rich. He'd buy a house, maybe near Mr. Fraser's, with plush sofas and electric lighting. He'd buy the best camera and learn how to use it. Then he'd invite Mr. and Mrs. Fraser and their sons over for tea. They'd want to see his photographs.

Right now, he was cold and hungry again. He turned to walk back to the tent, but the stream of smoke from the chimney-pipe heightened his loneliness. They were in there, together, knew where they were going. He was out here, alone, left out of their secret, cold and hungry again.

Well, he'd show them. Let them go wherever they were going, there probably wasn't any gold there anyway. He'd go on to Dawson City and make his fortune alone. Just wait until he bought his house on Georgia Street. He'd meet them at the Vancouver Club. He'd be wearing a straw boater and an embroidered vest. Well, hello there, Ben, hello Mr. Fraser — no, hello, *James*. Wouldn't they be surprised? Ben would say, Good heavens, it's Jeremy Britain! You look as if you've done very well for yourself, Jeremy!

Smiling, he grabbed an armful of split firewood and entered the tent.

"You are going to have to do something about your boots, Jeremy," said Mr. Fraser. "They won't last another week."

Jeremy deposited the wood and looked down. His right boot had split at the seam he'd sewed up two weeks ago. The left required mending now.

"Is there an extra pair in your load?" Ben asked.

"They were too big. I dumped them before the Pass." He wiggled his toes. He'd known for certain he'd never fit Magnus' boots, but now his own were tighter. They'd probably shrunk in all the melting snow.

"Soon we'll switch to gumboots," Ben tried to console.

"Dumped them too." Jeremy picked up the needle and thread that Mac had finished with, sat down, unlaced his boot and began sewing. When he finished, he rubbed grease on all the seams.

Then it was time for lunch, dish washing, more laundry, sorting and repacking the sleds, and preparing dinner.

"Sunday isn't much of a rest," Jeremy announced. "It's just different sort of work."

"We aren't walking," Ben retorted. "We aren't hauling things. The animals can rest."

"Is Sunday a day of 'rest' so we can work harder the other days?"

Mr. Fraser ignored the sneer in Jeremy's voice and his answer was mild. "It may seem that way if you don't go to church or read your Bible."

12

―――

Wed 30th

Rose early. Rest went down river 12 miles with loads & were back about 5 p.m. I baked, cooked beans, apples &c & tried to secure horse feed but did not succeed. Sorry, for our horses are failing fast for want of hay.

Sat. 2nd April 1898

Rest all went back for the load left on Wednesday. Distance too great for tired animals. Mac got back with his load 7:30. Blackie played out & they had to leave him & his load about 10 miles back. All very tired as they had been up since 2:30 a.m. I was up at 1:30 & cooked breakfast &c.

The next morning, Bob and Rimmer were so tired they stayed in camp to rest and Mac went back to get Blackie. That left Jeremy, Ben and Mr. Fraser to start up Lake Laberge. Mr. Fraser hitched Sue to the heaviest sled, but Ben and Jeremy, noting a steady breeze from the south, rigged up sails on four sleds. They lashed the sleds together, one behind the other and, with Ben driving the dogs and Jeremy on the back runners, they launched north.

The ice was smoother here than on Marsh Lake, the breeze continued to blow and their sail train made a quick ten miles. Rather than carry on, they cached their loads in a spruce grove on a point of land and started back for more. Now they walked into the wind, which grew stronger and colder.

"Could snow," Ben yelled. It was hard to hear him, even though Jeremy was walking just behind. Sue plodded on with her head down and ears back. Neither the mare nor the dogs seemed relieved to have no loads; just pushing on was hard enough.

It took them twice as long to get down the lake as it had to go up it. Even at that, they reached camp at the same time as Mac, leading the stumbling Blackie.

Bob came out of the tent when he heard them. He looked from the dogs to the horses and shook his head. Every day Blackie's and Sue's ribs and hipbones stuck out more sharply. Their coats had no lustre and scaly patches replaced hair. Jeremy remembered how proud the crew had been at the summit when they hadn't had to hide their horses' backs from the Mounties' view, as other crews did, because badly loaded packs had rubbed running sores. Klondike was hard on everyone, it seemed, but particularly cruel to horses. And now they were out of proper feed.

Bob and Rimmer had kept the fire going and the cook tent was warm. A pot of something simmered on the stove. Jeremy collapsed on the end of Bob's bed and wished he never had to get up again. But Mr. Fraser frowned; Jeremy knew it meant, look after the animals first. He staggered up and followed Ben and Mr. Fraser back outside. They gave the dogs some beans cooked with bacon ends and each horse a handful of flour and rolled oats. They left the animals hitched up, ready for the next haul.

The pot contained soup concocted from evaporated potatoes, carrots and onions, a bit of bacon and the ever-present beans. After he'd eaten three bowls, Jeremy stopped shivering and began to perk up. Possibly, just possibly, he could make another trip.

The men rested until the fire died down and the stove cooled, then they packed up camp. The wind had veered to the west and was gustier. Ben said the sails wouldn't work. "It's shanks' mare for everybody," he finished.

"Eh?" Jeremy said.

"You walk, boy. On your shanks. That's shanks' mare," Mac answered.

Mr. Fraser had Blackie hitched up to a previously loaded sled. Bob took Sue. Ben, Rimmer and Mac each had a sled with dogs, and Jeremy, as usual, hauled his own.

"Get going, boy!" Mr. Fraser yelled and slapped the reins on Blackie's rump. The horse took a tottery step and Mr. Fraser pushed the sled to start it sliding.

Jeremy was walking alongside. "He sure doesn't look very good." Blackie's flanks heaved with each breath and, in spite of the cold, he was sweating.

"No, he certainly doesn't," Mr. Fraser replied. "He's got a noble spirit though. Always been willing to try anything. If the snow would go and he could get some grass he'd be fine." Mr. Fraser shook his head and looked around. "It could be another month before that happens."

A mile up the lake, Blackie stumbled to a halt and stood with his head hanging between splayed legs. Mr. Fraser sighed and adjusted his parka hood. Jeremy took off his mitts and blew on his fingers. "Maybe if you lighten the load — ?"

"Worth a try, although it's a light load already." Mr. Fraser unlashed a crate and some shovels and picks. Mac rearranged his sled to accommodate the crate and Jeremy and Ben divided the picks and shovels between them.

"That horse can't manage its own weight," said Rimmer, "to say nothing of any load."

"It's not the horse's fault," Mr. Fraser snapped.

"Of course it isn't," Ben soothed, but Jeremy silently agreed that Rimmer's tone blamed poor Blackie.

"Okay, boy, let's give it another try." Mr. Fraser slapped the reins on Blackie's rump. Blackie shook his head and let his breath out in a long sigh.

"James, you're too kind!" Mac admonished. "You'd think this was your sickly old mother and not just a horse! Here, you take the dogs and I'll get this animal moving!"

Jeremy expected Mr. Fraser to refuse, but, with a last pat on Blackie's haunch, he walked over to the dog sled and grabbed the handles. "I've had him since he was a colt," Mr. Fraser muttered, "He's never balked at any job before."

Mac ran at the horse, clapping his hands and yelling, "Get going, you worthless nag! Move it, you lazy lump!" He lashed him hard with the ends of the reins.

Blackie jerked his head up and took a step. He stumbled. "Come on, get going!" Mac whipped him again. Blackie took another few steps. Bob moved Sue alongside Blackie, as if the mare would give him encouragement. Jeremy picked up the handle of his sled as the dog teams moved forward.

Blackie stumbled on for another slow mile. Then he tripped, tottered and fell down. His weight shook the ice. Mac yanked on the bridle and started yelling.

"That's enough!" Mr. Fraser shouted. He halted the dogs and locked the sled brake. "We'll unharness him and get him off the lake. There might be some grass over there." He pointed to a little bay with a sloping shoreline half a mile away. "After a rest he'll paw through that snow."

"If you can get him up," said Mac, yanking again on the bridle.

"Come on, old boy, you can do it. Up you get." Mr. Fraser stroked Blackie's nose. Mac pulled and Rimmer booted his haunch. Blackie stuck out a foreleg, but did not try to stagger up.

"It's no use, James. It's a goner. Best thing is to put it out of its misery fast."

"Come on, boy, up you get." Mr. Fraser continued to stroke the horse's muzzle. Blackie's sides heaved, his eyes dull and half-closed.

"It's no good, James," Rimmer said again. "This animal's not going anywhere." Bob nodded in agreement. Mac unbuckled the bridle. Mr. Fraser paused in his stroking to let Mac slide it off. Then he rubbed Blackie's ears. "Good-bye, old sock," he whispered.

He stood up. "I can't do it," he said to the men. "We've been together ten years." His voice was ragged. He cleared his throat. "I brought him out from Port Arthur —"

"You don't have to do it, James," Rimmer interrupted. "Give me your revolver."

After a deep sigh and a long look at the exhausted horse, Mr. Fraser rummaged in a sack on Blackie's sled and drew forth a large revolver. He handed it to Rimmer. He walked a few paces away and stared at the mountains, his hands clasped behind his back.

Rimmer put the revolver to the horse's head and pulled the trigger. A loud crack. Blackie jerked, shuddered and then lay still. Blood began to ooze in a little line down his forehead.

Where does life go? Jeremy wondered. One minute it's there and the next, where? He remembered the Robinson crew and Collie. Would someone feed Blackie to their dogs?

He turned as the men did. They all looked at Mr. Fraser's back. The crack of the bullet continued to reverberate in the silent whiteness.

Bob strode over to Mr. Fraser and put his hand on his shoulder. "It's the kindest way, James." Mr. Fraser nodded.

Jeremy couldn't hear his reply. Did Mr. Fraser feel the same about Blackie's death as he did about Collie's? About Hank's?

Mac turned back to the horse and pulled off the rest of the harness. "We'll have to redistribute this load," he said.

Mr. Fraser walked back to the group. Jeremy couldn't look at him. Maybe he'd cried — no, he was grown up; he wouldn't do that. Still, he'd had Blackie since he, Jeremy, was only four. That was a long time. Longer than he'd known Hank or Collie.

Jeremy picked up a box and carried it to his sled. He glanced at

Sue. She looked half-asleep in the traces. Did she know Blackie was dead? Did animals care?

The crew slogged on up the lake, each man occupied with his own thoughts. The sky darkened, the wind picked up and it began to snow. Would spring ever get here? Jeremy thought of Victoria in April. Flowers in the gardens and trees in pink bloom. Birds singing everywhere and so warm some days he didn't have to wear a jacket. For a moment he smelled newly mown grass. That brought him back to Lake Laberge and the pellets of snow stinging his cold-chapped face.

By dusk they reached the spruce grove where they'd cached this morning's loads. The snow made setting up camp miserable. Everyone was tired, wet, cold and sombre. Bob had just started a fire with the wood the others had collected when they heard, "Halloo the house!"

Mr. Fraser pulled back the tent flap. Jeremy peered out too. Approaching were two men hauling sleds. "Looks like company," Mr. Fraser said, then he hollered, "welcome!"

The men entered the tent, having brushed as much snow off as they could. "I'm Dunc Lemian," the shorter one said, "and this here's George Sanders. We're on our way out from Dawson."

"Did you find any gold?" Jeremy blurted.

Mr. Fraser scowled at him. "Mind your manners!" He added, "Excuse him please," to the newcomers and introduced the crew. Bob said, "I'm cooking. Will you join us?"

"We wouldn't say no, would we, Dunc?" Sanders said. He had a scar down one cheek, blue eyes beneath bushy black eyebrows and a pleasant smile. He pulled a tuque off his long, springy black hair.

"No indeed. It's been a rotten winter in Dawson. No food. The last steamer didn't get in before freeze-up but all sorts of people did." Dunc was the height of Mr. Fraser and stocky too. He had thinning brown hair and a greying beard. He looked pleasant, Jeremy thought.

"We'll have coffee in a minute," Bob said, "and food pretty soon."

Rimmer and Mac left to feed Sue and the dogs. Jeremy and Mr. Fraser erected the other tent then Jeremy went in search of wood for its stove. The strangers pitched their tent — a more ragged one than theirs, Jeremy noted.

When the chores were done and they all crowded into the cook tent, Bob produced mugs of coffee, then rice, bacon, biscuits and applesauce.

"That's a meal fit for the Queen," Dunc declared, after his second helping. He and George had wolfed it down as if they hadn't seen food for days.

"Sorry to be so greedy," George said. "We've only a handful of beans and flour left."

"Things that bad?" Bob asked.

"Worst they can be." Dunc put his plate on the ground and reached for the coffee pot. "Hasn't been any coffee in Dawson for months."

George held out his mug too. "If anyone's got potatoes or a laying hen, that's a rich man. Eggs cost three dollars each — if you can find one. Miners come in from the creeks with their pockets full of gold and there's no food to buy. And to answer the lad's question, I do have a nugget I found." He drew it out of his pocket and balanced it on his palm. "Someone must have dropped it. I'll keep it as a souvenir of the winter from hell."

"Oh, you didn't mine it?" Jeremy asked, staring at the small, dirty grey rock. It didn't look like the gold he'd seen in OB Allan's jewellery store window. It looked like any dumb rock he'd kick out of the way.

"Is the hard times why you're leaving Klondike?" Bob asked.

"Partly," Dunc said.

George returned the nugget to his pocket and nodded. "Nobody's starved yet, though they're getting mighty thin. Are you going to Dawson?" Jeremy held his breath. Maybe these men could find out where his crew planned to go and then he'd know.

But Mr. Fraser brushed the question aside with a laugh. "Not if it's that bad. There're about ten thousand people at Bennett just waiting for the ice to go out."

"Ten thousand!" Dunc whistled. "We heard reports, but that many?"

George said, "They can't get to Dawson before the ice goes and a steamer might get up river first. Shouldn't be so bad."

"Also, they've got more supplies than those who came last summer," Bob pointed out.

"What's ahead of us?" Rimmer asked.

"Police posts at Hootalinqua and Selkirk," George answered. "Those Mounties are doing a good job keeping track of everybody, making sure everyone checks in."

"Skagway should borrow some Mounties," Jeremy said, "and run out Soapy Smith's gang."

Rimmer frowned at him. "The Americans'll take care of it."

"Oh sure," Jeremy said hastily. He kept forgetting that Rimmer was American. "Was Soapy Smith there when you came up?"

"We didn't come through Skagway," Dunc replied. "We came up-river from Alaska. Who's this Soapy Smith?"

"According to our boy here," Bob jerked his head toward Jeremy, "he's a nasty piece of goods. He's running some crooked games, doing some extortion, sounds like he wants to run the town. Of course, we haven't heard anything since February."

Dunc and George laughed. "That's up to the minute news!" Dunc said. "We haven't heard anything since October!"

"I can't wait to read a newspaper that's not six months old!" George added.

"Where you folks from?" Ben asked.

Dunc said, "New Brunswick."

"Vancouver now," said George, "but Toronto before that and

before Toronto, New Brunswick. Dunc and I were schoolboys together. Bumped into each other in St. Michael and took the last steamer to Dawson. But even by September most good claims were filed."

"What have you been doing since?" Ben asked.

"Hanging around. We visited all the creeks. This gold mining's hard work," Dunc finished.

George winked. "We've been mainly partaking of the pleasures of Dawson and Lousetown. Decided we'd better get out before we lost all our money — Dawson's the most expensive town in the world. We're off to Vancouver to see what's up there."

"It's pulling out of the slump, but not very fast," Mr. Fraser informed them. "Klondike's the best thing for this depression."

"Thought we'd get into bicycles," Dunc said, "or those electric motor cars. Those are the future movers."

"That's what I think too," Jeremy agreed.

George winked again. "Look us up when you've made your fortune here. We'll sell you one."

"Or give him a job," said Bob, "if he doesn't have a fortune." They all laughed. Jeremy assumed they were laughing for the reason he was: not finding gold was a ridiculous notion.

That night, Jeremy lay in his sleeping bag and worried. What if the men wouldn't let him go with them? What if he had to go to Dawson, where there were no food and no gold claims? He certainly wasn't turning back without getting rich.

13

***

Friday April 8

All being tired we did not go after load today but Mac & I went down river to see trail which we found very bad & the river being reported open for 30 miles we decided to build a raft which Mac said could be built in 2 or 3 days including getting out timber.

Sat 9th April 1898

Mac & Rimmer looking up & cutting timber for raft. Ben, Bob & I went back for the loads left behind. I drove the mare & we left camp 2:30 a.m. The day was fine & we got the load down to camp about 5 p.m. Met Captain Newcomb & C. L. Brown of Vancouver who came through with an ox.

Tues, 12th, bought 5 dogs for $25.

The raft was taking longer to build than Mac had predicted. Every evening, Mr. Fraser asked, "How much longer, Mac?"

"Not much. Just another day, two at the most."

On the third evening, Mr. Fraser tightened his lips and muttered something between "hmph," and "pshaw." He was getting exasperated, Jeremy could see.

Of course, Mac's "two or three days" had been optimistic, but Mac was like that. He'd been optimistic about building new sleds, Jeremy remembered. And Mr. Fraser did expect estimates to come out to the exact minute.

Ben responded to the tension with jokes and teasing which made Mac surly and Mr. Fraser stomp off to his cooking or oar-making with more hhmphs. Bob just winked at Jeremy, and Rimmer didn't seem to notice.

The crew would have to stay at the north end of Lake Laberge until the raft was finished. That was enough time to justify construction of a proper latrine pit. The men took turns digging, then hung canvas over ropes tied to trees on three sides.

The work to build a raft was hard, but at least it was different, Jeremy thought. And the snow, the tedious, interminable snow, was finally melting. They could almost see it peeling back under the heat of the sun, which cast light until ten at night. Half the Yukon River, about two hundred yards wide at this point, had an open channel.

Jeremy couldn't say who was more excited to see the end of the snow — him or Sue, the mare. Every minute she wasn't working she had her nose down among the sparse clumps of brown flattened grass.

A grove of spruce close to the river contained a few tall, straight trees a foot in diameter. Mac said they'd make anchor logs for the outside of the raft. Mr. Fraser had calculated that, if they made a twelve-foot wide raft, they'd need fifteen eight-inch logs or twelve ten-inch logs.

"I want the ten-inchers," Jeremy announced.

Bob smiled. "Cutting them's the same amount of work in the end."

"Dragging them isn't — that's a difference of three trips for the dogs."

As Jeremy watched Mac chop, he stomped his cold, wet feet.

Each morning, the soggy ground and melting snow soaked into his boots within minutes, and they were too wet to dry overnight. He tried to endure them but his raw skin grew more painful each day. Why had he chucked out Magnus' gumboots on the Skagway trail, even if they were too big?

Once the crew had removed the branches, they hammered spikes into the logs, fastened the dogs' or Sue's traces to them and guided the animals back to the shore. The five new dogs Mr. Fraser had bought were useful too; they all were at least part husky, although thin. They'd snapped their way into the pack with only a little blood and flying fur.

Captain Newcomb and Mr. Brown had camped beside them. They hauled logs out with their ox, Babe, but since they'd decided to build a boat, they first had to construct a saw-pit to whipsaw lumber. As Jeremy watched the men hoist the first log onto their trestles and take their positions on the saw-handles, he thought they should just build a raft as his crew was doing.

Other than the work and the delay — and Jeremy didn't mind not packing up and moving on — the men had a fine time. Captain Newcomb had been a sea captain out of Halifax and Brown knew someone named Fred whom Mr. Fraser had known in Port Arthur. Saturday night they arrived after dinner — *"halloo the house!"* was the general greeting even though all houses were tents — with a bottle of whisky.

Jeremy looked up from the bucket of salted water where he was soaking his chapped, blistered feet as Bob said, "Well now, is that what I think it is?"

Captain Newcomb held up the bottle. "Brought this along for medicinal reasons of course, then got to thinking you could help us lighten our load." He was tall and thin with a beaked nose.

Bob nodded. "Always glad to help a fellow traveller."

"Indeed." Rimmer produced mugs. "We certainly wouldn't want you fellows to have to manage by yourselves."

Brown shucked off his jacket. "We thought you'd have a neighbourly attitude about this chore." He was stocky with receding blond hair, and accompanied every sentence with a wink.

Newcomb uncorked the bottle and carefully poured into Rimmer's mugs. "How about the boy?"

"He's too young," Mr. Fraser retorted.

"Now, now, it's purely medicinal, Fraser. It'll help his feet. Besides, it's Brown's birthday." Newcomb poured a quarter inch into another mug and Rimmer handed it to Jeremy. He caught Mr. Fraser's scowl of disapproval and looked away.

When everyone had a mug, Bob raised his in a toast to Brown's birthday and Jeremy took a sip. It burned his mouth and nose. He swallowed, then coughed and his eyes watered. The men laughed.

The whisky burned all the way to his stomach. It didn't taste very good. It didn't smell very good either, but it did make him warmer — not that he'd been cold. So this is whisky, he thought, feeling disappointed, what's the big deal? Bracing himself, he took another sip. This time it didn't burn as much, probably because he didn't have any skin left in his throat, he decided, as he waited to feel drunk.

Captain Newcomb explained to Ben and Rimmer how they were going to build their boat and Mac extolled the virtues of a raft to Mr. Brown. But Brown was dubious; the Yukon was a wide river and there'd still be ice floes. "A boat'll be more sturdy in the long run."

"It takes too long to build," Mac stated.

"Even a raft takes too long," Mr. Fraser muttered.

The raft could be finished days earlier and save Mr. Fraser exasperation if he let them work on Sundays. However, Jeremy kept this opinion to himself.

Captain Newcomb knew a lot about ship-building and he was willing to share every detail. Jeremy finished his whisky and looked at the bottle. He didn't think he felt drunk. He looked at the men;

they'd had more to drink than he, but they didn't seem drunk either. No one had passed out, no one was fighting, no one was even slurring.

He put his mug down, removed one foot at a time from the water and dried it. He winced as he pulled his socks over the blisters. He carried the pail to the tent flap and dumped it outside. Would it be polite to offer the men more whisky? It wasn't his crew's bottle but it was in their tent.

Maybe Brown or Newcomb had a spare pair of boots he could buy! He looked at their feet — it wouldn't matter if their boots were too big, anything would be better than this soggy, cracked pair. His feet wouldn't heal in them, they'd just get more chapped and blistered and the crew wouldn't let him come with them, wherever they were going.

Jeremy sat down, picked up his mug and shook the last drops into his mouth.

Still talking about bargeboards and braces, Newcomb reached for the bottle and offered the whisky around. Jeremy held out his mug. He probably had to have two drinks to get drunk. Newcomb wasn't paying attention and poured him the same amount as the men, twice as much as last time. Surely he'd pass out now.

Holding his breath so he wouldn't smell the whisky, he took a gulp and choked. Some went into his nose and he sneezed. The men looked at him. Ben smacked him on the back while he caught his breath. "You're supposed to sip it, not gulp it!" Brown chortled. "Is this your first drink?"

"Ah, well — not exactly," Jeremy lied, "though you could say so," he corrected, then quickly changed the subject. "Do you men have any spare boots I could buy? Mine are wrecked."

"I have some spare moccasins," Mr. Brown said, "But they won't do you much good while the snow's melting."

"You must have some waterproof canvas in your rig," Ben offered. "You could wrap the moccasins in that."

"You should never have thrown out those gumboots," admonished Mr. Fraser unnecessarily.

"They were too big," Jeremy muttered. "I like Ben's idea."

Mr. Brown set his drink down and left. He returned in a few moments with the moccasins. "How much do you want for them?" Jeremy asked.

"Forget it. I have two other pairs. See if they fit."

"Thanks." Jeremy winced as he put them on. He wiggled his toes. "They'll be fine with extra socks. Now I can throw out my boots."

Ben frowned. "Don't you dare. You never know."

The talk turned to whipsawing. Everyone had done it at some time except Ben and Jeremy. It sounded awful; a man could go blind from the sawdust in his eyes, though no one knew anyone who had. Jeremy slipped on Ben's gumboots and limped to his rig in front of the other tent. He had two waterproof canvas bags; of course they were right at the bottom of the box. He got out a heavy pair of socks as well.

Back inside, he put on the extra socks and the moccasins, which fit better now, and stuck his feet into the bags. He pulled the drawstrings out of the top of the bags and laced them around his ankles. Standing up, he shuffled a few steps.

"The height of fashion," Ben observed. "All elegant young men are wearing bags this season." Jeremy made a mock bow.

"Just hope that the snow goes before the waterproofing does," Rimmer cautioned.

"Yeah, if I wear out the bags, I'll have to carry the gold in something else."

Mac guffawed. "You're expecting that much gold? If you had those bags full you could buy your own country! Besides, do you know how much gold weighs? You wouldn't be able to lift those bags! You shoulda hefted George's nugget, then you'd know how much gold weighs! It gets carried in little pokes!" He separated his thumb from his fingers by about three inches.

"If these bags aren't to carry gold, what are they for?" Jeremy shot back. "Why've I carted them all this way?" He took another mouthful of whisky.

"You use them for storing food or carrying water —"

"Or wearing," Ben finished for Mac.

Jeremy looked down and giggled. What if all the businessmen on Granville and Dupont Streets wore bags? He raised his mug to sip, but it banged against his teeth. Whisky sloshed on his chin. Whoops. He looked around to see if anyone else noticed but no one had. Backing up, he sat down on an up-turned crate and glanced at his mug; suddenly he wasn't sure he wanted any more whisky. But the men wouldn't want him to waste it. He drank the last mouthfuls and fought hard against gagging.

Mr. Fraser was saying, "The last newspaper we read said that if they discover that the battleship *Maine* was blown up deliberately then the United States will surely go to war with Spain." Jeremy wanted to giggle again; there seemed to be two Mr. Frasers.

"If that happens, will you join up?" Mac asked Rimmer.

"I don't know. My father lost an eye in the Civil War, he was only a boy at the time." Jeremy shook his head to clear it — that was a mistake. There seemed to be three or four Macs and Rimmers and they blurred into one another.

Newcomb shook his head — or Jeremy's head shook. Newcomb said, "This business with South Africa is troubling too. If Britain has to get firm she could involve all her Dominions. Is there any news?"

"In February President Kruger and the Boers were still rattling their sabres," Mr. Fraser answered. "The only thing for sure is that as long as the Transvaal is unstable, South African gold stocks aren't worth the paper they're printed on, which makes anything from Klondike worth more."

"There isn't much we can do about the rest of the world from here," Bob said. "Our job's to find some of that gold."

"And the sooner we get our raft built, the sooner we can get on with it." Mr. Fraser held up his mug. "A last toast to the Canadian goldfields, boys."

"To the goldfields," the men agreed and drained their mugs. None of them seemed to Jeremy to be behaving any differently. What was wrong with him?

"Thanks for the birthday party," Brown said, standing up. "We'll all sleep well tonight." He laughed.

"Thank you for the party." Bob clapped him on the shoulder.

"Good night," Jeremy mumbled, wondering if he could stand up. He waited until all the men were facing the tent flap, then pushed himself up. His stomach didn't feel very good. He wouldn't throw up, would he? They'd tease him for days.

Swallowing against the sensation, he put his coat over his shoulders and managed to navigate to the other tent. When he lay down, he immediately wished he hadn't, for the tent — or his head — seemed to be spinning into a void. I don't think I like whisky, he thought, as the void claimed his brain.

He awakened in the morning to a flaming thirst. His mouth felt full of wool. For a minute he couldn't remember why this should be, then he thought, oh yes, I got drunk; now I must have a hangover. Just as he thought that, his head began to throb. He would have tried to go back to sleep, but thirst propelled him up.

He drank half a pail of water then sat down on the edge of his cot and put his head in his hands.

Mr. Fraser woke up. "What's wrong with you?"

"I don't think I like whisky," Jeremy mumbled.

"You are too young for spirits. I should have forbidden you." Ben opened one eye. "A hangover's enough of a lesson without a lecture too, James." Then, to Jeremy, "You're just poisoned. It'll wear off." He rolled over and went back to sleep.

Thinking that fresh air might help, Jeremy pulled on his pants and coat and tied up his bags of moccasins. He untied the tent flap and stepped outside. It might be a nice morning, he thought, under other circumstances. The sun held a promise of warmth for later on, but its brightness on the patches of snow made his head pound harder. Squinting, he crossed to the other tent, a plume of smoke indicating that Bob, Rimmer and Mac were up.

The tent smelled of coffee and bacon. Jeremy didn't think he wanted either. "Morning," he mumbled as he picked up his mug. It smelled of whisky; he nearly gagged. He swished it around in the pail of water, then filled it and tried to drink without breathing.

Bob flipped the bacon, which was sizzling very loudly. "How are you this morning?"

"Fine — well, I have a headache."

Bob pulled something out of his pocket. "Take two of these." He tossed it to him. Jeremy caught it.

"What are they?"

"Dr. Wilson's Pink Pills for Pale People. Cleans the blood and strengthens the nerves. I swear by them."

Jeremy opened the box and took out two. He swallowed them with the rest of the water.

"Give them half an hour to work," Bob added as he put the box back in his pocket.

Mr. Fraser entered. Mac said, "James, I know your feelings about working on Sunday, but Bob and Rimmer and I are going to carry on with the raft today. I figure we can be on our way tomorrow if we work today."

Mr. Fraser did not look pleased, but he did not argue. "Newcomb mentioned that Dr. Grant will be preaching at the Police camp tonight. I suppose we can all work on one Sunday if we go down to his service."

After breakfast, which Jeremy declined except for some bread, they trooped outside to examine the raft. It was twelve feet wide by twenty-nine feet long and looked enormous lying on the beach. Its frame was two logs deep and, above the log floor, they'd lashed more logs to make a perimeter another foot high.

"I'm not certain that that railing is a good idea," Mr. Fraser said.

"It'll keep things from being washed overboard." Mac sounded a bit huffy.

"But it adds considerable weight and so we lose buoyancy," Mr. Fraser persisted.

"He's got a point, Mac," Rimmer said. "We can tie things down so they won't go in the drink."

Bob added his opinion. "Then we won't have to cut any more trees to roll it into the water, just use the railings. The whole thing must weigh a ton at least."

"Oh, all right," Mac gave in, a bit grudgingly.

"One other thing," Mr. Fraser continued. "I'd be happier if we had an attached bow oar for steering as well as a stern oar."

"You go on about that oar, James," Mac snapped. "But I tell you that we don't need a bow oar! I've been on lots of rafts, you know!"

"If you're sure —" Mr. Fraser did not sound convinced.

"Yes, I'm sure!" Mac picked up a hammer and began pounding off the first rail log.

The noise did not make Jeremy wince and he realized his headache was gone. Maybe he'd swear by Dr. Wilson's Pink Pills for Pale People too.

Mr. Fraser watched for a minute, then turned back to the tent where he was baking bread and packing. Ben finally arrived to jeers of, "Here comes the sloth!" and everyone spent the day working.

Of course the raft was not finished by the time they left for church. Mac grumped that it was only because they had wasted time taking off the railing, but Jeremy doubted it. He doubted they'd take off tomorrow either.

When they reached the Police camp about a quarter of a mile down the beach, they squeezed into an already full tent. Jeremy hadn't seen so many people in one place since they'd left Lake Bennett.

Last Sunday had been Easter, so Dr. Grant took that as the theme for his service. He began by inviting everyone to pray for the sixty-three people killed in the avalanche on the Chilkoot Pass on Palm Sunday, the week before Easter. As Jeremy bowed his head, he remembered his fear of an avalanche on the White Pass — that seemed so very long ago.

After the service, the men and Jeremy shook hands with Dr. Grant. Mr. Fraser said, "We hadn't heard anything about the avalanche. It's very sad."

"Indeed." Reverend Grant shook his head. "But it didn't stop this mad rush for gold."

"Do you think Smith's gang started it?" Jeremy asked.

"No, it was an act of nature. There'd been a big snowfall a few days before, then it warmed up. Perfect avalanche conditions. There's seventy feet of snow now at the summit."

"There was about fifty when we went through," Bob said. "The customs house was nearly buried then."

As they trudged back up the beach in the twilight, Jeremy said, "Smith's gang could have caused it."

Rimmer retorted, "Why would they do that? They've got a whole town full of greenhorns to fleece. Why would they bother to climb that hill? It's steeper and higher even than the White Pass. Besides, they'd have to go up to Dyea and that's where the marshal is."

Jeremy could see Rimmer's logic made sense. But still . . .

14

Monday April 18th
Completed raft which took a week longer than I expected, got ready to start down river. Loaded all on except dogs & camp. 12' X 29' raft not able to carry as much as we supposed. Decided to leave the mare as she is not likely to live. Wrote home.

Tuesday morning they got away about eight o'clock. There were so many bags, boxes, crates, sleds and dogs on the raft that each person had to stay in his place. Mr. Fraser kept lookout in the bow, Ben had the left oar and Rimmer the right, Mac steered from the stern, and Bob and Jeremy sat on crates with the dogs. As the raft swished into the mainstream, Jeremy looked back at Sue, splay-legged on the shore, her ears at half-mast, watching them.

Jeremy's sadness deepened as the image of Sue grew smaller. She'd been the topic of heated words last night: Rimmer and Mac wanted to shoot her; Ben, Mr. Fraser and Jeremy wanted to let her live. There was some grass and the weather was improving; perhaps she had a chance. Little chance, the others argued: the grass was not nourishing, she was weak and there were wolves. At the last moment, Bob lined up in the let-her-live camp and the majority decided. Did she know she was being left? Jeremy quickly pushed the next thought out of his mind: if the men could leave the horse which had trudged on so valiantly, would they leave him next?

The water roiled by inches below the top of the raft. He pulled his feet up onto another crate because occasional waves splashed between the logs. "We're awfully low in the water, aren't we?" he whispered to Bob.

"I'd say we're drawing eighteen to twenty inches. Good thing we took the rail off."

Most of the conversation was Mr. Fraser's. "Rock to starboard! Now to port! Steer to the right, Mac! Not that much! Sandbar ahead!"

They stuck with a shudder. "Oops," said Mac. The dogs leapt to their feet and barked in alarm, but they were tied on short leads to the sleds. Bob, Ben and Mr. Fraser jumped onto the sandbar and Jeremy took Ben's oar. Between back-paddling and pushing, they turned the raft sideways to the bar. The men shoved it into the current before leaping on. When they were again under way, the dogs settled down.

The river was shallow and fast — six or seven miles an hour, according to Mr. Fraser — and full of dead trees and chunks of ice as well as rocks and sandbars. But the sun glinted off the white mountain backdrop, and off the river's surface as it wound between treed, rocky shores. Everyone was giddy with the delight of carrying on to the goldfields in this swift and easy fashion. "Ho to Klondike!" Ben yelled and began to sing, "Way up upon the Yukon River," to the tune of *Swanee River*.

"Keep it down, Ben!" Mac yelled. "I can't hear James!"

Bob dug lunch out of the food box: bean and bacon sandwiches on sourdough bread. They washed them down with water dipped from the river. With a full stomach and the sun beating down, Jeremy dozed off, in spite of the chill wind and his cramped position between crates.

A jolt awakened him. The dogs leaped up, barking and howling.

The current had pushed them onto a wide gravel bar which they could now see clearly. It had been disguised by six inches of water.

"If I had a bow oar, I could have avoided this!" Mr. Fraser's tone was clipped and his cheeks splotched with red. Mac's cheeks grew red too, but he pinched his lips together and said nothing.

Bob said hastily, "What's done's done. We took a calculated chance, starting this early when the water's still low. Figure out how we're going to get off." They contemplated the current rilling and riffling over the bar while they felt it bury the raft ever more firmly into the gravel.

"We can try pushing," Rimmer suggested in a dubious tone. About six feet of the raft had ground into the bar.

"We can't unload unless we put up with everything wet," Ben observed.

"Oh do shut up!" Mac yelled at the dogs. "Lie down! Lie down!" All thirteen looked at him and howled even more frantically.

"We can try pushing and back-paddling," Mr. Fraser stated in a tone that meant he'd made a decision.

"Won't work," Mac muttered, but he took up the stern oar again.

"Rimmer, Bob and I will push, you others use the oars," Mr. Fraser directed.

Ben and Jeremy took an oar each and braced it against the gravel. Mac sculled. The others leapt overboard, splashed around to get some footing and pushed against the bow logs. All that happened was that the gravel shifted and the current pushed the raft ahead another foot.

Mr. Fraser straightened up. "That's not going to work." They studied the situation again.

"If another boat came by," Jeremy offered, "It could pull us off with ropes."

"If wishes were horses, beggars would ride," snapped Rimmer.

Bob had been scuffing the gravel with his toe. "This stuff moves easily. We can dig a channel and let the current take us through."

"Pretty dratted wide bar, must be thirty feet," Rimmer complained in a surly tone, but all of them resignedly acquiesced.

They unpacked the shovels and picks and started digging. Jeremy's waterproof bags came only to mid-calf; little waves of icy water splashed into his moccasins. As they dug around the front, the raft tilted downward. That made the dogs start howling and fighting again. The current worked against them by rolling gravel back into their channel. Then Bob dug too close to Rimmer; the gravel he was standing on shifted and he was wet to his thighs. For every forward inch they gained, they had to dig five shovelfuls. Then they had to dig down the back ridge of the bar to free the middle of the raft. After two hours, the raft had progressed another foot and everyone was soaked.

They dug until six when they took a dinner break to eat cold beans, bread and dehydrated apple slices. They were all tired, but the chill breeze was too cold against their wet legs and sweaty bodies so they dug some more. The dogs had periods of restlessness; they used their energy howling or snapping and snarling at each other.

The crew dug and dug and dug. Jeremy thought it wouldn't be so bad if they were digging up gold, but they were just digging up rocks. Mr. Fraser probably was right about a bow oar. He thought that they could wait until more snow melted and the waters rose, but that might take a month. He kept digging.

They dug through the long twilight until they were exhausted. They'd progressed about six feet. Twenty-four more to go.

Back on the raft, each located dry pants and socks and their sleeping bags. Then they tried to get comfortable on the hard crates. No one could stretch out. The dogs took up a lot of room and were in foul tempers; when Ben accidentally leaned on Captain, he lunged and snapped.

They dozed or rested uncomfortably until four, then watched the dawn fade out the stars. Each reversed the order of the night before: put away sleeping bags, dry pants and socks, pulled on clammy wet ones, ate more beans and bread, and then began to dig.

Finally, at four in the afternoon, the raft was free. Rimmer was the last to scramble on board as the current so easily — so mockingly — swept them away. Nobody said anything. Nobody even cared to look around as they journeyed downriver. Jeremy ached in every muscle he owned.

Then there was another now familiar jolt and shudder and the dogs again leapt up, howling. Rimmer and Mac simultaneously let loose a string of epithets that included names for private body parts and strange activities in conjunction with names for mothers and the Lord. Mr. Fraser closed his eyes and slumped his shoulders. Jeremy felt tears of frustration gathering. Ben and Bob just stood at their oars, white-faced.

They worked without talking, driving their sore bodies to dig, push, or paddle. This was a smaller, deeper sandbar so it only took them two hours to become unmired. Jeremy felt nauseated with exhaustion and Ben was white and shaking. They steered to the riverbank and staggered off the raft. When Rimmer freed the dogs, they tore along the beach yelping and howling, then rolled on their backs to scratch.

Somehow — only because the tasks had become automatic — they managed to pitch a tent, locate wood, assemble the stove and start a fire. Heat, food and hot coffee helped and all were stretched out in sleeping bags before twilight ended.

In the morning, Mr. Fraser said, "We should rig a bow oar before we go on."

"Oh, you and your bow oar, James!" Mac snapped. "You've got it on the brain! I've rafted on Lake Superior, Lake Erie, Lake Ontario and the Welland Canal and I've never needed a bow oar!"

"Those are deeper waters. Obstacles are buried." Mr. Fraser's tone was quiet — menacingly so, Jeremy thought — and he had his hands fisted on his hips.

Bob said, "A bow oar and its rigging will add weight, James. We can't afford it. We're drawing a lot of water as it is." Rimmer nodded.

Jeremy thought of saying, Mr. Fraser's right, but he didn't.

Ben darted glances at the men while he washed and packed the cooking gear.

There was a long silence while Mr. Fraser and Mac stared at each other. Mr. Fraser looked at Bob and Rimmer. Jeremy stood up and moved toward a packed crate he had planned to cart to the raft, but he couldn't leave the tent.

Mr. Fraser sighed and sucked in his lips. He shook his head, slowly. "You're wrong, Mac. This river isn't the Welland Canal. But you're right, Bob. We can't afford more weight." He considered some more, then pursed his lips wryly, as if having some inner conversation. He sighed again. "I don't know how much attention God can pay to one little raft in the Klondike, but we're in His hands."

Jeremy's shoulders relaxed as Mac said, jovially, "You'll see, James. The river's getting higher everyday. There'll be enough water to cover the bars. We'll be fine." He added as a sop, having won the fight, Jeremy realized, "Though don't think I don't appreciate your caution and attention to details."

Mr. Fraser's cheek muscles tightened and he shook his head, but he rolled up his sleeping bag.

The dogs watched them load the tent and gear on the raft, growing increasingly snappish. When it was their turn to climb on they cringed and howled and dug their feet into the gravelly riverbank. Rimmer and Mac pulled, pushed and finally whipped them on board.

Mac pushed off with the back oar and the raft was grabbed by the current and flung downriver. Jeremy perched again on a crate, Rimmer, Mac and Ben manned the oars, Bob tried to calm the dogs and Mr. Fraser looked out, chanting his litany, "Rock to starboard, sandbar to port!"

The current was stronger than on the previous two days; the river had narrowed slightly and more ice was melting on Lake Leberge. Also there were more rocks in this channel and the fully submerged ones were hardest to see.

"Rock dead ahead!" Mr. Fraser yelled. "Get to starboard, Mac!"

Mac leaned on the oar with all his weight, but the raft was too heavy to turn quickly. It struck with a crunch and a shudder. The dogs jumped up and milled about, yelping. The crates and boxes creaked against their ties as they tried to comply with gravity pulling them toward the raft's left back corner. Jeremy and Bob hung on to a rope. Water slapped over the stern logs.

"Could have avoided this one with a bow oar," Mr. Fraser announced in a clipped tone. "You should have turned her faster, Mac!"

"I couldn't! You take over steering if you think you can do it better!"

"You know what I think!" Mr. Fraser snapped.

Ben said, "If we shift the gear to the high side, we should be able to work her loose." The men studied the mountain of equipment, sleds and dogs, and the raft's lack of free deck space.

"We have to pile it up even higher," Rimmer offered. "But it might work."

They unroped gear and piled it in the forward right section. Dogs seemed to be everywhere, snapping at everything that moved, tangling themselves between the men's legs.

At one point Ben mused, "I'd thought that once we got on a raft, travelling would be like a Sunday cruise, but it's as much work as climbing the White Pass." Mac banged down a crate and gave him a black look.

When they had all the goods rearranged, Jeremy worked to persuade the dogs to climb up on the precarious pile and stand still. The dogs kept trying to leap down.

But the stratagem worked; the river lifted the rear of the raft and shot them off the rock. Now the raft was unbalanced the other way and the men worked to hurl crates into the centre again. The current pushed them along relentlessly. "Take us to shore, Mac, so we can reload properly!" Rimmer shouted.

"Watch that boulder!" Mr. Fraser yelled.

Before Mac could swing the stern oar over, the raft rammed another rock. Rimmer's oar rotated and knocked him overboard. The dogs were thrown off too, most still attached to sleds or each other. Jeremy dug his fingers around a lashing and hung on as he watched the unbound crates, sleds, shovels and bags of flour disappear downstream.

"There's Rimmer!" he yelled. A head bobbed up and arms began flailing toward them.

Mr. Fraser lay half-off the raft on his stomach, Bob and Ben holding his legs. He fished around in the water, trying to cut through the dogs' traces so they might swim to shore.

Rimmer had hold of a rock; he'd saved himself from being swept away. "Fling me a line," he yelled, "I'll try to get it to shore!"

Mac knotted one end of a rope to a log, then attached the end of another that Jeremy handed him and flung it downstream. Rimmer reached out and grabbed. He tied it around his waist and started toward shore, fifty feet away.

Mr. Fraser cut Captain free; the dog burst to the surface, choking and gulping. But he couldn't reach the four others tied to the same sled and had to watch them drown. Captain struck out for shore following Rimmer's trajectory. Leo was also swimming, dragging his loaded sled behind him. Jeremy watched him get closer and closer to the bank; when the sled ground into gravel in a shallow eddy, Leo turned around and climbed on top, where he shook himself. Tom and Frank dragged a load of flour ashore. Rimmer made it too. They watched him stagger out, scramble up the bank and walk back up until he was opposite them. He fastened the rope around a large rock. It made a shorter route to shore than Rimmer and the dogs had had to take against the current.

Mr. Fraser stood up. "We've lost everything," he stated, surveying the empty raft.

"We'll find some gear downriver," Mac said.

"I'll go to shore and Rimmer and I can start looking," Bob offered. He grabbed the rope and swung himself in. "Oh My God, it's freezing!" He hooked his left arm over the rope and pulled himself forward with his right hand, but the current pushed his feet in front of him so that he was lying crosswise to the rope. He had to keep it away from his neck so the river wouldn't use it to strangle him. His progress was no faster than Rimmer's or the dogs'.

Five more dogs had now made it to shore, Sam trailing an empty sled.

"We've lost everything," Mr. Fraser repeated. "We can't go forward and we can't go back! And all because we had no bow oar!"

"You should have insisted!" Mac flared. "You should have designed the raft to have one!"

"You're the expert raftsman!"

"Now boys, don't get out of control," Ben interjected. "What's done's done. No need for verbal fisticuffs."

Mr. Fraser crossed his arms and glared at everyone. Mac banged his fist into his other palm and turned his back. Ben raised his brows and rolled his eyes at Jeremy, who realized he was holding his breath.

As they were debating — less acrimoniously — the best way to use the rope to get to shore, a boat containing two men appeared.

"Watch out for the rope!" Mac yelled. Ben pointed at it. "Steer for the other side!"

Through hard back-paddling, the boaters managed to slow enough to drift broadside against the raft's stern. A man with a bushy black beard observed the situation. "Had a spot of trouble, did you?"

"Just a spot," Ben admitted. "The rest of our party's on shore. We're about to go over by rope-trolley."

The brown hatted man said, "Climb in and we'll ferry you over. Might as well stay dry."

"Kind of you," Mr. Fraser said. "If we hang on to the line we can help by pulling — and free the channel for others."

He undid the rope and the three climbed into the boat. Ben sat in the bow hauling in the rope. "Skookum craft you got here," Mac admired. "You come from Lake Bennett?"

"No," Blackbeard replied. "Ice isn't out there yet, according to the Police. We built this a few miles back. Saw you go by day before yesterday. Thought you'd be farther on."

"Hit a sandbar." Mr. Fraser did not elaborate. As the keel grated on the gravel of the riverbank, he added, "Thanks for the lift."

"We'll keep an eye out for your gear and tell them at the next Police camp."

"Thanks," Ben echoed, the last to splash ashore. "It should be Hootalinqua."

As an afterthought, Blackbeard asked, "Have you matches?"

"Yes, thanks." Mr. Fraser pulled out a waterproof case from his pocket and held it up. "Keep this on me at all times!"

The crew watched as the strangers rowed into midstream and the current grabbed their boat again. The raft clung solidly to its rock at a forty-degree angle. No one said, We should have built a boat, but Jeremy wondered if the others were thinking that too.

15

—

Thursday 21st April 1898

We had fire but no tent, no dishes & not enough blankets & put in a very dismal & uncomfortable night. Mac & I tried sleeping in one sleeping bag but it was not successful.

Friday 22nd April 98

Rose early. Could not sleep as things looked very blue. Very little money, 4 dogs lost, harness, tools, everything. However, borrowed same boat that took us off & tried to get raft off & get some stuff out of river. Did not accomplish much so Rimmer & I started down river to look up stuff. 3 miles down we found his dunnage bag at "Dad's" camp, still on the sleds, stranded on a gravel bar in mid stream. Went to Police Station at Hootalinqua (8 miles from camp) where stayed all night & were kindly treated by everybody.

Sat. 23rd April 1898

Borrowed some rope & axes. About 11 a.m. started up each bank of river accompanied by Constable Fyffe. 3 men had secured a sled load & an empty sled & were drying the goods. One of them went on a raft with Rimmer & we secured the bacon &c, putting it higher on a bar for safety after which we went on to camp where we found Capt. Newcomb & Mr. Brown. Another boat containing 3 men was wrecked today & lost most of their stuff some of which we secured for them & they put us across river to go to camp.

Sunday 24th April 1898

Snowed through night & this morning. Let up about noon so we all went down river to get the bacon ashore. On way down Rimmer found that part of his clothes, blankets &c which had been spread to dry had been stolen so he followed down & got a policeman & caught 2 men with the stuff.

Wed - 27th April 1898

Took boat & spent all forenoon trying to get raft off & secure some stuff but without success. Even lost a pick which we had on a pole trying for things. Afternoon we got things together for a move.

The ten days since the accident were the most frustrating of Jeremy's life. They plowed up and down the steep, gravelly, wet river banks looking for gear or else made fruitless attempts to free the raft. As they did, the decision to build a boat just grew.

"Like Topsy," Ben said, when they finally acknowledged the decision.

"What's a topsy?" asked Jeremy. It was Sunday evening and they were sitting on reclaimed crates outside their one tent, sipping after-dinner tea and watching the sun's lengthening colours play over the river.

"You haven't read enough books, boy," Mac retorted.

Ben took pity. "She's a negro girl in *Uncle Tom's Cabin* who says she didn't come from anywhere, she 'just grew.'"

"It's a book about slavery," Rimmer said. "You should read it, it influenced the Civil War."

"The American Civil War," Mr. Fraser elaborated. "How far did you study in school?"

Jeremy realized he must have been looking as blank as he felt. "Um — I finished grade four."

"Have you read a book since?" Mr. Fraser persisted.

"Well — no." He wriggled. In the old days, before his contract, he could have said he'd read *Mr. Midshipman Easy,* but he hadn't. Catherine had read it to them. "I've had to live," he defended. "I've read the papers though." That was no lie. He read the headlines. Well, some headlines.

"Whether Jer's read a book is not going to help us build a boat," Bob stated.

Jeremy thought if they'd taken the extra time at first, like Captain Newcomb and Mr. Brown, they wouldn't be having to build a boat on top of having built a raft. Like black-bearded Mr. Allen and his friend, Skinner; they'd taken the extra time. Jeremy'd bet, if Mac would ever say so, he'd acknowledge that rafts that worked on the Welland Canal — wherever that was — wouldn't work as well as boats on the Yukon River. Jeremy would further bet that Mac would even agree to a bow oar now, but that topic had been avoided since the accident.

Mac said, with grating enthusiasm, "We really need two boats so we're not overloaded again."

Rimmer snapped, "We can only build one at a time."

"In case you haven't noticed," Bob's tone dripped with unusual sarcasm, "We have less stuff to pack now."

Rimmer continued, "We got enough logs out for one boat today, thanks to Allen's and Skinner's help."

"Let's take the logs out of the raft and float them down here." Jeremy stated. "They'd come off the rock log by log. We won't have to cut any more trees and we can saw those logs into planks."

Bob, Mac and Rimmer frowned at him. "I never want to see that raft again," Bob enunciated through clenched teeth.

"Trees grow here, the raft is eight miles back," Mac barked.

Rimmer pronounced, "The raft wood's wet as well as green. Harder to saw."

"Oh — well," Jeremy mumbled. Obviously his plan was wrong.

Mr. Fraser's black mood had waned slightly with every retrieved bit of gear, though he'd spent evenings writing figures on scraps of paper as well as writing in his journal. From his mutterings, Jeremy learned that the men did not have much more money than he had. Without their gear, they could neither go forward nor go home, as Mr. Fraser kept saying. So Jeremy had felt most rewarded by Mr. Fraser's pat on the back when he'd found the fifty-pound crate of bacon. Granted, the bacon was wet, but they'd spread it out in the sun and, last Sunday when it snowed, had hung it near the chimney.

The Police camp consisted of a long barracks-like log cabin and some outbuildings nestled on a low bench where the Hootalinqua River — which some people called the Teslin — was beginning to flow into the Yukon. The water in the Hootalinqua was muddier; it made a definite stripe where it flowed into the bluer, clearer Yukon — or Lewes, as some people called it. Behind the benchland and across the Yukon, treed hills sloped steeply upward. There were not as many policemen here as at Tagish Post, but there were more people in general and more arriving every day. Captain Newcomb and Mr. Brown had left Babe, their ox, at pasture here with some horses when they'd gone on in their boat.

Last week, Constable Fyffe had told Mr. Fraser that the photographer, Hegg, had spent an entire day taking pictures at Hootalinqua. Jeremy hadn't realized until now that his photo of the White Pass was probably gone forever. Even though they'd found some of his gear, they'd not found the tin of tea and, even if they had, the river would probably have washed away the image. He kicked at the rocks; *damn*, already it was so hard to remember earlier parts of the journey.

They decided to build a boat like Allen's and Skinner's; a dory was the simplest, Mac stated. Jeremy caught a flash of skepticism on Mr. Fraser's face, but he said nothing. Mac was still the only one of the crew who'd had much to do with boats.

Monday morning they finished constructing the saw-pit. Bob and Rimmer laid two logs atop six-foot posts and braced them. It took all of them to roll the twenty-foot log up the slanting braces. Ben and Mr. Fraser went off to the other on-going task of drying food and gear while Bob returned to cook's duty.

Jeremy watched Mac on the ground and Rimmer on the log take hold of the handles of the two-man saw they'd borrowed from the Police. Rimmer pushed and Mac pulled then Mac pushed and Rimmer pulled. Within minutes, Mac was covered in sawdust. He spat constantly and kept his eyes closed as much as he could. Rimmer, the one who could see, guided the saw so the boards would be even. It looked like a miserable job. Jeremy was glad that Mr. Fraser wasn't there to hear the men's language.

When they finished the first cut, nearly an hour later, Rimmer kicked the board to the ground and jumped down. "Take this end piece for making oars, Jer!" he ordered, then, to Mac, "you climb up and I'll take the bottom."

Mac wiped his eyes and mouth and flexed his shoulders. "I won't argue."

Jeremy said, "I could go look for the raft oars. That'd save some work."

"You won't find them," Rimmer stated. "They'll be matchsticks in that river. Anyway, they were too long for boat oars."

"What's the matter, boy?" Mac teased. "You don't want to do any work? We'll put you to whipsawing, this is real man's work!"

Jeremy lifted one end of the board and dragged it to the logs they'd formed into a crude worktable. Then he lapsed back into contemplation of the rhythmic whip-sawing and the warm sun on his back, enjoying the smell of fresh resin and sawdust.

Mr. Fraser returned. "Don't stand there gawking. Make yourself useful." He took out a pencil and drew an oar shape on the wood. He drew another oar upside down beside it. He handed Jeremy a handsaw. "Cut those out."

Jeremy sawed. Between the sun and the activity he soon grew too warm and stopped to remove his jacket and cap. He sawed some more. The sawteeth had suffered from being used on green wood and immersed in the river. This wood was green too, of course, but it was no longer frozen and its pitch gummed up the saw and jerked it to a halt. Every few minutes Jeremy had to rub the blade with a cloth soaked in lantern fluid. By the time Mac and Rimmer had another plank down, Jeremy had cut out the rough oars.

Jeremy sat down on a piece of scrap lumber and flexed his shoulders. Surely it was lunchtime?

Mr. Fraser materialized and Jeremy scrambled to his feet. "Good," he pronounced, examining the oars. "Now you remove the bark and smooth the wood with this." He clasped one oar between his knees and pulled down on the handles of a drawknife. "Watch you don't cut too deep."

The drawknife wanted to cut deeply and Jeremy took a while to find the right pressure. Once he'd chipped off the bark, the knife produced long curls of wood and the oar grew smoother and rounder. He stroked its surface with pleasure. And he could straddle a log while he worked.

Rimmer and Mac finished another plank just as Bob yelled, "Lunch!" Jeremy carefully put down his oar and knife and the three started to the tent. While they were eating, Mac said, "James, too bad your friend Perry didn't put in a sawmill here instead of at Cariboo Crossing."

"Or that we'd stayed there to build a boat," Ben added. Jeremy wondered if they'd be just as far along if they'd done that.

While Jeremy made oars, Ben and Mr. Fraser measured and

sawed the rough boards Mac and Rimmer produced. They had decided that the boat should be thirty feet long and eight feet wide.

On the occasions that all saws were quiet at the same time, Jeremy could hear the scrapes, creaks and clatters of the ice breaking up. Great chunks floated by them or crunched to a halt on the sandbars where they rested until the river's current found a way to push them on. Trees and branches drifted by as well, some getting caught on each other and wedged together on the banks. There were more obstacles in the river now, Jeremy thought, than when they'd been rafting.

Mr. Allen thought so too, apparently. He appeared shortly and, after watching a while, offered to help, "since Skinner and I aren't going on until the river's safer."

The men were grateful for another hand. Jeremy caught Mr. Fraser and Ben exchange a look, and he wondered if they were thinking that Mac would not be their only expert now.

The week passed and the lumber took a boat-like shape upside down on the worktable. Sawdust and shavings grew around it and the dogs tore back and forth, unaware that soon they would have to get back on the river. Mr. Fraser walked down to buy more nails from the supplies at the Police camp. He stomped back muttering, "A dollar a pound! Highway robbery! You can buy twenty pounds for a dollar in Vancouver!" and thereafter made sure that each nail used was really required.

Jeremy was so proud of his oars that he was pleased to make a second pair. He enjoyed working the drawknife down the handles and over the blades, smoothing and rounding them. In fact, he realized, it was the only task since leaving Vancouver that he really had enjoyed.

A few hundred people spent that week at Hootalinqua waiting for the worst of the ice to go out. Most, like Mr. Fraser's crew, were busy with their own affairs but, at one time or another, they paraded up and down the now-worn trail to exchange greetings and just to see how everyone else was managing.

One of these groups contained Mr. and Mrs. Black, Sven and Ole, Jeremy discovered, when he returned from a latrine visit. He stopped by the tent, his heart beating hard. Here was his worst fear — well, his second-worst fear, Soapy Smith was his absolute worst — that the Robinson party would catch up with them and ask where they were going. It was probably happening right now and it was all his fault.

Mr. Black was saying, ". . . trying to buy a boat so we don't have to build one again." He looked hopefully at theirs.

"A lot of work," Mac said. "Don't suppose many people would want to sell. We sure wouldn't."

"No Sirree," Bob agreed. "What happened to your other boat?"

"Leaked," Sven offered. "Not enough caulking."

"Then ice rammed us," Mrs. Black elaborated. "We made it to shore, but just. Mr. Robinson broke his leg. He's laid up for six weeks."

"Too bad." Jeremy followed Mr. Fraser's gaze toward the river and the ice floes crashing past. "I suppose he won't be going on then," Mr. Fraser continued.

"Oh, they'll show up later," Mr. Black said. "Far as I know." Ole strolled over to the fire where Ben was heating caulking pitch.

Sven said, "A while back your boy told us you weren't going to Dawson."

There it was, baldly stated. Jeremy closed his eyes and bit his lip.

"Oh, that kid don't know nothing," Rimmer declared with a laugh.

"He's a great one for lies." Mac added. "Did he tell you he had a father with a mine?" He laughed. "Yeah, sure. You can't trust a thing he says." Jeremy snorted. Mac didn't have to lay it on that thick.

"Well, where are you going?" Sven persisted.

"Fort Selkirk's the next stop, but not until we get this boat finished," Mr. Fraser enunciated tightly. He turned and picked up the drawknife Jeremy had been using to make the seats.

"And after that?"

"After that, we're following the river," Bob stated.

Sven's eyes had narrowed. "Makes me almost think they know something they don't want to share," he sneered to Mr. Black.

"And if we did, we'd keep quiet about it, wouldn't we?" barked Mr. Fraser.

"No offence meant, Mr. Fraser," Mrs. Black soothed.

"Indeed no," Mr. Black echoed. "We got our own plans too," he said to Sven, as well as the rest of them. Then he raised his voice so Ole could hear, "And those include getting us a boat!" He turned back to the main crew as Ole rejoined them. "Too bad we can't talk you into selling this, but if you're sure . . . ?"

"We're sure," Bob replied, then, as if he couldn't resist adding, "You just might have to build one, like everybody else!"

"We'll see about that," Mr. Black laughed.

"Now, Mr. Black," Mrs. Black admonished. "Don't you go challenging the future. Tra-la," she added as the group walked away.

Jeremy came around the corner of the tent at the same time as Ben, carrying the pot of steaming pitch, crossed back. "What did that big Swede want from you?" Bob asked him.

Ben put down the pitch. "To know where we're going."

"What did you say?"

"It was none of his business."

"You didn't have to lay it on so thick about me, Mac," Jeremy said in an injured tone.

Mac laughed. "Don't sulk, kid. You got us into this one. Just hope we got out of it."

"But you lied when you said you can't trust a thing I say," Jeremy persisted, with increasing outrage. "I haven't told a lie since Lake Bennett!"

"Ahh, leave it be, Jer." Mac turned back to his hammer. "I just stretched the truth a little."

Jeremy studied his back, frowning. Wasn't stretching the truth a lie? In fact, hadn't they all lied, Mr. Fraser included, by not telling the whole truth? Where was the line between lying and telling only what one wanted to tell?

Later, when the lingering twilight had faded to a burnished steel blue, Rimmer rolled up his sleeping gear and announced, "It's a nice night. Think I'll bed down by the boat. Get some fresh air."

"You mean," Bob said, "The boat could tempt certain men who don't want to build their own? If that's what you're thinking, that's what I've been thinking, so I'll join you."

Mr. Fraser nodded approvingly. "To emulate Our Father Which Art in Heaven and avoid leading people into temptation would be a kind thing to do. If the rocks get hard," he added, "feel free to wake the rest of us for a shift."

16

Tuesday 10th May
Cold & showery with high wind. Ben & I caulked the boat & started to pitch it. Rimmer packing meat &c. Mounted Police en route for Dawson & Major Walsh arrived from LeBarge.

The boat was a definite improvement over the raft, they all agreed. They were less crowded than in the raft because of fewer dogs and the gear they'd never retrieved. Bob, with some bitterness, called the extra room a mixed blessing. The boat was more responsive to Mac's steering and now Mr. Fraser could fend them off any rocks with his bow oar. Of course, the river had risen from all the melting snow; rocks, such as the one on which they'd capsized three weeks ago, were no longer a danger.

They named the boat *Rosie O'Grady* because Ben had been singing or humming the song for days. He couldn't get the tune out of his head, he said apologetically, and tried singing other songs. But minutes later he'd burst into "— I love sweet Rosie O'Grady and Rosie O'Grady loves me!"

Whenever Jeremy heard the song, he had an image of the girl in the red dress. He hadn't seen her since the summit; maybe she was still at Lake Bennett, camped with her father. But maybe, he'd thought in the past few weeks, she'd show up here. What would he say to her? Is your name Rosie O'Grady? If your name isn't Rosie O'Grady, it should be! Would you like to walk by the river? No! He couldn't say that, that was too bold!

The song had driven the crew to the limit of their endurance as they'd dipped the caulking in hot pitch and tamped it in the cracks, nailed in the seats, or packed up the gear. Then Jeremy and Bob found the song in their heads and Bob said in disgust, "It's as contagious as smallpox."

Jeremy had mixed feelings about the boat's name; when he'd inadvertently burst into song, his voice had cracked and boomed uncontrollably. All the men had laughed. Jeremy hadn't spoken again for what felt like hours; when he finally had to, his voice squeaked before cracking. The men laughed again. Bob looked over with an amused smile. "Your voice is changing. Don't worry, it's happened to all of us."

Nice of Bob, Jeremy supposed, but too hard to believe. He wondered about taking a vow of silence.

Bob's and Rimmer's night beside the boat had been uneventful, if uncomfortable, and no one had seen members of the Robinson crew since. However, a couple of days later Mr. Allen told them, just before he and Skinner pushed off, some Indians camped on the other side of the Police barracks had reported a canoe missing. Mr. Fraser's crew looked at each other significantly. Then they forgot about the Robinsons, the Blacks and the two Swedes in the relief of getting back on the river.

Actually, everyone was relieved but Jeremy. He was worried. The arrival of Major Walsh's party at Hootalinqua on Tuesday had reminded Jeremy that the men had promised only that he could go with them as far as the Pelly River. So he sat in *Rosie O'Grady* with nothing to do but worry. He thought of asking the men — no, asking Ben — if they were going to leave him there, like Sue, the horse, but what would he do if Ben said yes? He comforted himself that Mr. Fraser had not mentioned it to Major Walsh, and the Yukon Commissioner hadn't seemed to remember. But then, the Major's attention had been focussed on getting to Dawson and the state of the ice in the river. All this was little comfort now they were on the last leg down to Fort Selkirk — which was situated at the mouth of the Pelly River.

And they were travelling on a Sunday, to boot. Jeremy had opted to stay put, as they usually did on Sundays, so he could have one more day to worry, but the barricade of ice that they'd harboured *Rosie O'Grady* behind last night had melted. The boat was in such danger from passing floes that even Mr. Fraser could see that the only thing to do was carry on.

Jeremy buzzed with dread and helplessness. His mouth was dry, no matter how much water he scooped out of the river, and his heart hammered. He barely noticed the rocky canyon walls, sloping treed riverbanks or the dazzling mountains that swirled by, even though Mr. Fraser frequently commented, "Very fine scenery indeed."

They drifted along on the current until Mr. Fraser shouted, "Look out ahead!" They were coming upon floes of ice three feet high that had jammed together. Everyone back-paddled to slow the *Rosie* down and they bumped undamaged into the edge of the first flow where the current held them.

Bob looked behind them. "If any more ice comes before this breaks up we could be crushed."

"Break up, break up," Ben urged.

With a crashing and crunching, the floes re-organized themselves. Some started again down river, leaving gaps that widened. The *Rosie* swept along with them.

"Try to stay behind the worst of it," Mr. Fraser ordered, but it was useless. The best they could do was fend off the nearest ice and steer between the chunks, hoping that they would not jam together again. After a tense mile or two, the river widened and so did the gaps between the flows.

"Whew," Rimmer voiced for all of them. "That was more excitement than I needed."

Jeremy returned to his worrying.

Mid-afternoon they sighted small low islands and the mouth of the Pelly River disgorging brown water from the east. Within a mile they saw the buildings of Fort Selkirk on the Yukon's west bank. Boats were pulled up onto the river's edge below it and dogs and people milled about. When their dogs spotted this, they struggled and howled to get out. Four forgot that they were tied on short lines and nearly strangled themselves before Rimmer got them sorted out. Even at that, when Mac had steered into a clear space, he had to unload them first. "Dogs are more nuisance than they're worth now the snow's gone," he muttered.

Up the bank and set back twenty feet, a two-storey log house and a smaller building sat surrounded by a fence and fronted by a flagpole, from which the Union Jack fluttered. Five other log buildings straggled along the shoreline to the south.

Ben whistled. "Almost a city!"

"Hardly," Jeremy retorted.

"I meant these are more people and buildings than we've seen since Lake Bennett," Ben defended and Jeremy realized he must have sounded crankier than he'd meant to — maybe as cranky as he felt.

He didn't know why he felt so cranky as he watched the men pack camp gear up the bank. Before he'd met them, he'd been planning to go to Dawson, hadn't he? He hadn't been counting on them then, had he? He could manage by himself, he'd done so for half a year in Vancouver, hadn't he? He'd just get on with it, go find his fortune in Dawson. He didn't need them, did he?

"Don't stand around wool-gathering!" Mr. Fraser called. "Get busy!"

Jeremy started sorting out his own gear, intending to pile it separately, but soon stopped. Since the rafting accident, all their reclaimed gear had become hopelessly mixed up. He wasn't even sure that he had enough to go on by himself. Well, they'd just have to outfit him, wouldn't they? It wasn't his fault everything got dumped in the drink. He hadn't been steering. He hadn't decided to build a raft.

"Get busy, Jer! Pull your weight!" Bob this time.

"This is Fort Selkirk," Jeremy stated.

"Yes." Bob's tone was patronizing, as if Jeremy had said *the sky is blue.*

"This is the Pelly River. Isn't it?"

"Yep. You saw it, just back there."

He looked at Bob. Was it possible the men had forgotten? In confusion he reached for a crate. If he asked them outright, they might remember and say, *oh yes, thanks for reminding us.* He started up the bank. On the other hand, all these people would be leaving soon. He had to find a new crew before that.

He bet Mac remembered; he was the one who most hadn't wanted him along. Pretty soon Mac would remind the others. Jeremy put the crate down and looked around.

Oh, there was Mr. Fraser talking to Major Walsh! That fixed it! They'd be arranging his passage right now! Mr. Fraser never forgot anything, he'd just waited until here instead of Hootalinqua! They'd said the Pelly and they meant the Pelly!

Jeremy straightened his shoulders and stomped over. ". . . the Police left this morning, but I have to — Hello." Major Walsh started at Jeremy's sudden appearance.

"Sir, I am ready to go with you to Dawson whenever you are leaving," Jeremy announced in clipped tones.

Now Mr. Fraser was startled. "Wait a minute. What's this about?" His cheeks started to redden and his lips tightened. "At the very least you could have told us first you wanted to go to Dawson — oh." He deflated as he remembered. He turned back to the Major.

"Oh. Yes, I mentioned to you at Bennett the possibility of our young friend here —"

"Yes, I remember," the Major cut him off.

"— however, I think our crew had better have a talk about this before he tries to make his own arrangements with you." The Major nodded.

Jeremy had never seen Mr. Fraser so flustered, smiling at the Major and glaring at him. He was probably going to get a royal bawling out. Well, he wouldn't put up with it this time. He didn't need them. He could get on by himself.

Major Walsh was saying, "I'm leaving as soon as I get Yukon District business organized here. Maybe tomorrow, maybe Tuesday."

"I'm sure we'll have things straight by then." Mr. Fraser let his breath out in a heavy sigh.

"I will stay in touch with you," Jeremy said in a most Mr. Fraser fashion.

"Yes, do," the Major said. "Meeting your father, aren't you? He has a claim, as I recall."

"No, I made that up." Jeremy looked him in the eye.

The Major blinked. He digested, ruminated and apparently decided to leave it alone. After a noticeable pause, he stated, "I have to get on with business. You'll be around for a while, James?"

"Yes, James." Both smiled with their eyes and not with their mouths, as if that movement would have disturbed their moustaches. "We had a bit of bad luck in the river and need a few things before we carry on."

As the Major nodded and turned, Jeremy said quickly, not wanting to lose his advantage, "I'll be in touch too."

As if mesmerized, Mr. Fraser and Jeremy watched the District Commissioner walk away, then both broke the trance at the same time. As Jeremy started away, Mr. Fraser said, "Ahh —" and Jeremy said, walking, stumbling, "I'd better ahh-umm."

He slid down the bank. There was the boat. There were Bob,

Rimmer, Mac, other people, dogs. Leo and Captain, his favourite dogs now, caught sight of him and barked. He looked south. More boats were pulling in. More people, dogs. His knees trembled. He stumbled over the rocks along the riverside, while the dogs pranced beside him, expecting adventure, perhaps a head-pat. There wasn't much riverbank, but soon there was a bend and an overhanging bush. When he sank down behind it, tears took him over. Leo and Captain cocked their heads, then lay down beside him and waited.

When he'd finished crying, he felt tired but calmer. He continued to sit on the rocks and watch the sunlight play on the moving water and the face of the dark high cliff across the river, even though he was chilly in the shadow of the bank. Absent-mindedly, he rubbed the dogs' heads.

Boots clunked over the rocks. Leo and Captain leapt up, tails wagging. All five men brushed by the bush, looking solemn. Mr. Fraser cleared his throat. "If you really want to go to Dawson we understand, but you are welcome to continue with us."

"We've got sort of used to a six-man crew," Rimmer said.

"You're a good worker," Mac offered.

"Oh heck, we even like you!" Ben contributed.

"But you said —" Jeremy began.

"That was a long time ago," said Mr. Fraser. "People do change their minds." He looked gruff and uncomfortable. "If you hadn't brought it up, we wouldn't have."

"Some of us had completely forgotten," added Ben.

"You've stuck to your contract like a man," Bob observed. He considered, then corrected, "Like a gentleman."

"Do you really want to go to Dawson?" asked Mr. Fraser.

Jeremy shook his head. "No," he whispered. "No."

"Then you'll continue with us," Bob stated. "That's settled. Now, back to work."

"Will you tell me where you're going? Where *we're* going?"

"Yes, but not here," said Mr. Fraser. "There are too many people here."

"Soon?" he persisted.

"As soon as we get away from here," Mr. Fraser promised. At Jeremy's look of disappointment he lowered his voice and added, "I can say that, for now, we're going up the Pelly, but the least said, the better. There's a supply barge due as soon as the ice goes out. We'll leave right after that gets here."

Mac tugged on Jeremy's coat collar. "Come on now, there's a tent to pitch and chores to do. And hair to cut. Look how shaggy we've all got." He was smiling. So were Bob and Ben and even Rimmer.

As Jeremy stood up, he ducked his head and blinked. He was in danger of crying again, but, this time, for different reasons.

17

Clear & warm. Placed surplus supplies in warehouse & took load
with 2 canoes over to mouth of Pelly. About a dozen boats passed
& several stopped.

The next morning at breakfast, Mr Fraser stated, "I fear our
boat will be too heavy to track upriver. If we can't secure
another canoe, we should build a smaller boat."

The rest groaned. They were eating in front of the tents. Jeremy
looked down at *Rosie O'Grady* overturned on the bank. Mac countered, "Our boat's not too heavy, James. We're strong, we'll be able
to do it."

Mr. Fraser frowned. "The Pelly's in full spate. We'll have enough
trouble lining our light canoes."

For all these months, Jeremy hadn't realized the crew had been
hauling two canoes. They'd been in halves, stacked one piece in
another — a long box of canoe. All he'd known was that it had
been a heavy box, one he'd tried to avoid lifting.

Ben nodded agreement with Mr. Fraser. "We need to smoke
that extra crate of bacon Jeremy found. Salt alone won't be enough
protection as the weather warms up."

"More work," Bob muttered. "But you're right about the bacon. Its dunk in the river probably rinsed out a lot of salt."

Rimmer stood up and put his plate in the bucket of washwater. "We can build a smokehouse out of logs if we chink them well, but I'm against building a boat. Someone said yesterday there're lots of Indians passing by so maybe we can trade for a canoe."

"We can trade my tent," Jeremy offered.

"You need gumboots and Mac needs a sleeping bag," Ben pointed out. What else do we need?"

"Nails, shovels, picks," contributed Mr. Fraser.

"Prospecting gear," added Bob.

"I need gumboots too," Mac said, "and food. Flour and beans at least."

Ben, Mr. Fraser and Rimmer drew smokehouse detail. Mac, Bob and Jeremy, carrying his tent, headed up to the trading post. It was drizzling and a cool wind blew, but last night's frost had melted.

Mr. Fraser had informed them yesterday that the original Hudson's Bay buildings were burned in 1852 because the Indians viewed the company as a trading competitor. This made Harper's trading post and house the oldest buildings in Fort Selkirk. The store smelled of the rank animal skins piled on the counter. Some store, Jeremy thought. Where were all the goods?

The storekeeper, a small man with a weather-beaten face, introduced himself as Pitts and said, "A supply barge is rumoured to be coming downriver. Could arrive any day now — even today."

"Looks like you need it," Mac observed.

"Indeed. I got cleaned out in the fall. Unless you want furs or moosehide, you'll have to wait like the rest."

"I was hoping to trade this for some gumboots." Jeremy held out his tent.

"I think I have an old pair that might fit you." Mr. Pitts walked to the back of the store, rummaged in a cupboard and returned, carrying a pair. "Not much call for this size."

They were pretty old, Jeremy noted as he pulled them on, but they were better than moccasins and disintegrating bags.

"The tent's a wall tent, worth more than old boots," Bob remarked. "Will you give us credit against some other supplies?"

"Sure, there's always call for a tent."

"Do you have any prospector's gear in your cupboards?" Jeremy asked.

Mr. Pitts laughed, went over to the cupboard and returned with a box. "You've asked for the only two things I have. These came from the same source as the gumboots." From a fabulously rich miner, Jeremy hoped, examining a battered gold pan.

"Shovels and picks? You'll have to wait for the barge," Mr. Pitts answered Bob. "You'll need hip-waders too. If any come down, I'll throw them in for the tent. And a sleeping bag or blankets," he said to Mac. He grew suddenly curious. "What happened, you get swamped?"

"Yes," Bob said in a tone that discouraged more questions. "We want a canoe. If you hear of one, would you let us know? We're just down the bank a piece."

"Sure thing," Mr. Pitts assured them as they left.

Jeremy stored his box and moccasins in the tent, and threw the dirty, wet, frayed canvas bags into the bush. He joined Mac and Bob who were inspecting the progress of the smokehouse.

The framework was up already — six feet high and two feet square. Mr. Fraser and Ben sawed logs on makeshift sawhorses and Rimmer propped them against the frame. "No nails," Bob said, grabbing a log. "We'll have to lash the logs. How much rope do we have?" Mac went off to look. "Jeremy, dig up some stuff for chinking. Moss or grass or cut up your old bags."

Jeremy located scissors, hauled the bags off the brambles they'd landed on and cut them into long strips. Bob used a stick to poke them between the logs Rimmer lashed onto the frame. The dogs milled around or flopped down exactly where someone was about to walk.

When his bags were all poked in, Jeremy wandered up the hill escorted by Leo, Captain and Tom. On a garbage heap behind the store he found old sacks and strips of soggy felting and dragged them back. Then he pulled up grass and knocked lichen off the trees. It took a lot of stuff to chink even a small smokehouse, he thought.

By noon it was done. Bob and Ben carried over the slabs of bacon and Rimmer placed them on a rack five feet above ground and beneath the chimney hole. Mr. Fraser lit the pile of sawdust and kindling and told Jeremy to bring over the branches they'd cut off the logs. When the fire caught, he laid the branches on top and shut the log door. They watched smoke curl satisfactorily up from the roof hole before going back to their tents for lunch.

There wasn't much to do in the afternoon if they weren't going to build a boat, except to keep the fire fed. Jeremy knew they'd be here for at least five days; it took that long to smoke bacon. He slid into a sleepy, absent-minded state on his up-turned crate and watched the river. Every hour brought down more and more vessels. Some couldn't be called boats; contraptions was more accurate. He wondered how a few of them even floated. All stopped to report to the Mounties, then the majority cruised on to Dawson, their occupants waving and shouting as they passed by.

Rimmer walked down to talk to an Indian who'd pulled his canoe onto the bank. Jeremy watched their gestures. Rimmer returned muttering, "Highway robbery! He wants a hundred dollars for his canoe!"

Jeremy stumbled to his tent for a nap, leaving the men writing letters and tending the smokehouse fire.

When he emerged, he first thought no one was around, but then he saw his crew and all the dogs on the riverbank, staring intently across the river. Coming out of the Pelly were six canoes, each containing three or four Indians and some dogs. Jeremy arrived just as Mac said, "Maybe they'll trade, they don't need that many canoes, they can double up." They watched the fleet paddle across the Yukon, avoiding collisions with other boats, and draw up on the bank.

When their dogs heard the Indians' dogs, they charged them. The bank became a whirligig of fur and growls. The Indians banged at the mêlée with their paddles and Jeremy's crew yelled, "Tom! Captain! Frank! Stop it!" A woman dumped water on the dogs and another woman herded some of them into the river. Eventually they calmed to throaty growls. Mac muttered, "Damn dogs're more trouble than they're worth now there's no work for them."

"*Klahowya Tillicums,*" Rimmer said, placing his hand on a canoe, "*Nesika hyas ticky huyhuy okoke canim kopa nesika skookum* boat." He pointed to the *Rosie.*

The adults stared at him. A small girl covered her mouth and giggled. This tribe was taller and sharper-featured than the Indians Jeremy was used to in Vancouver and Victoria. All were dressed in skin parkas, leggings and moccasins and some of the men had scraggly moustaches. The adults talked among themselves while the children peeked out from behind their legs. Two men started over to the *Rosie;* Bob and Ben hurried along behind. The rest watched the Indians inspect the boat, look up the Pelly and say something, shaking their heads.

"Jeremy, go get a side of bacon," Mr. Fraser ordered, watching the four return, then said to Rimmer, "See if they'll trade for bacon."

"*Nesika huyhuy kopa cosho itlwillie?*" Rimmer asked.

The Indians again consulted among themselves as Jeremy left on his errand. When he returned with their last chunk of previously smoked bacon, the Indians' dogs hurled themselves at it. Jeremy stumbled backwards and nearly fell down. The Indians laughed and the woman hurled more water at the dogs. Bob rescued the bacon and held it out. Mr. Fraser pointed at the meat and then at the canoe. After another conference, one of the men took the bacon and kicked at the dogs, which hadn't once taken their eyes off the chunk. Other people removed belongings from the canoe.

"Thank you," Mr. Fraser said and nodded.

"*Mahsie,*" Rimmer corrected. "*Hiyu mahsie.*" A man nodded back and handed him the canoe's line.

"Stick Indians," Rimmer announced, as they made their way back to camp. "Probably haven't ever seen a civilized man before. Maybe they don't even know Chinook."

"Why are they called Stick?" Jeremy asked.

"Tinneh's their other name." Mr. Fraser was always happy to supply information. "The Coast Indians call them Stick because the trees here are like sticks compared to the coastal trees."

Bob and Mr. Fraser hauled the canoe up the bank beside the first canoe and the *Rosie* while Ben went to the smokehouse to check the fire. Jeremy felt a bit sorry that the Indians had rejected their boat; he gave her a pat, then looked to see if the others had noticed. "Where'd you learn to speak like that?" he asked Rimmer.

"Chinook?" Rimmer ran his fingers through his beard. "Picked it up freighting in Washington. Trade language, been used for years. Indians use it between different tribes too."

The crew took turns keeping the smokehouse fire stoked during the night. When it was Jeremy's turn at two o'clock, he needed no lantern. The sun had dipped behind the hills, but twilight lit the brief hours before its return. Dusk blended into dawn now and the streaked cliff across the river was as easy to see as the cobblestones he picked his way over. There was no such thing as night any more, and he tried to remember how dark it had been in February. He tried to remember snow, how he'd hated it, and could barely remember, even though the river still carried chunks of ice. If he'd not lost his photograph in the river, he'd have a way of remembering.

One day Jeremy had looked up river by his bush for saplings to turn into poles; in the few days since he'd cried, dead-looking branches had sprouted lush green leaves and flower buds. Between one day and the next, the field behind the buildings had changed from brown to green dotted with white and yellow flowers. Flocks of geese and ducks flew north, songbirds chirped and trilled and swooped over their reclaimed territories. Everyday the river moved up its bank, forcing them to relocate their tents on higher ground.

Two days later, a cry went up along the banks, "Supply barge!" Jeremy put down the drawknife and the poplar saplings and leapt up. Mr. Fraser also put down the pole he was tipping with metal so the rocky river bottom wouldn't wear it out. They hurried to the wharf where they were joined by the rest of their crew.

Steaming downriver was a small sternwheeler towing a scow. "How can a boat come downriver before it's gone upriver?" Jeremy asked.

"It wintered at White Horse Rapids," Mac replied.

"It won't have many supplies if it's coming from there," Jeremy added, feeling disappointed.

But the scow did indeed have unused supplies from the Police camps, and someone had scoured the trails for discarded items — gumboots, blankets, tents, stoves, even bicycles.

Mr. Fraser shook his head with grudging admiration. "There's a man who'll get rich without the hard work of mining."

Jeremy watched Mr. Pitts, the storekeeper, haggle with the barge owner and wondered if he'd have to pay again for Magnus' things he'd discarded.

Amid the pushing and shoving crowd, they eventually procured the items they needed, including hip waders in Jeremy's size. He also got a new pair of trousers when Ben pointed out how short his had become. Carrying their goods, they started back to their camp. Ben observed, "There's an awful lot of smoke over there."

"That's our smokehouse!" Rimmer started to run and the rest followed. Smoke roiled between every log and, as they watched, flames shot up from the roof.

"Get buckets!" Mr. Fraser ordered. Jeremy and Bob dashed uphill, threw their purchases on the ground and grabbed six pails. They ran to the river, scooped up water, ran to the smokehouse and poured it on the flames. The rest of the crew formed a bucket line and Jeremy and Bob joined in. They passed pails as fast as they could and soon the structure was only smouldering. Mr. Fraser pried open the hot, blackened door and pulled out the slabs of bacon. Parts still sizzled, more cooked than smoked. "That's what we get for hurrying," Mr. Fraser proclaimed in disgust. "Who put too much wood on?"

"I checked it just before the scow arrived." Mac clipped his words. "And no, I didn't put too much wood on!"

"Logs probably got too hot and the chinking dried out," Ben offered.

"The logs were green and full of sap," Bob pointed out. "That's what caught."

Rimmer added, "The bacon was nearly done anyway, James. It'll be fine as long as we cook it well."

"Mm," Mr. Fraser muttered, staring at the sorry-looking slabs, but he let the topic drop.

III

18

Wed 1st June 1898

Picked up Camp & started up Pelly. Left Selkirk about 9 a.m. & got to where we left stuff at mouth of Pelly about 11:30. Very rapid water here. While lunch was being prepared we took one load above ripple (100 yards) & after lunch loaded up and started upstream. Very hard work indeed, banks full & overflowed so we could neither track, pole or paddle. Dogs nearly drowned.

The ice let go of Lake Bennett on May 28, freeing ten thousand goldseekers. All week they'd been rushing into Selkirk where they were required to report; now, as Jeremy's crew steered around the small islands at the junction of the Pelly and the Yukon, the main flotilla bore down on them. Hundreds of home-made boats, canoes, and rafts packed the river. Their occupants hooted and hollered and cheered, and dogs barked and howled. One man yelled, "Hey, boys, you're going the wrong way!" Jeremy just waved his oar.

"If we'd stayed at Bennett till the ice went out, we'd be just as far along as we are now," Bob observed, over the din of their dogs.

"Because of that dad-ratted raft," Mr. Fraser snapped. "If things had gone according to plan, we'd be at least two weeks ahead of this mob."

Ten thousand people! It looked like so many more than when Jeremy had last seen them, strung out in tents between the icy shores of Lindeman and Bennett. How could there be enough gold for all these people? He could feel the crowd's excitement and for a moment longed to go in its direction. Then he thought, if his crew hadn't just made the mouth of the Pelly, the flotilla would have swamped them.

"What a crazy sight!" Ben exclaimed.

"Worse than Skagway," agreed Bob.

"Worse than the mob on the docks when we left Vancouver," added Mac.

"We knew from those over-booked steamers it would be wild," Mr. Fraser stated. "Who called this mass hysteria? At least we have a plan."

"Most of them'll turn at Dawson and go home when they discover the good claims are staked — that's what happened in previous gold rushes," Rimmer finished.

"What is our plan?" Jeremy asked. "You said you'd tell me when we were away from Selkirk."

"I'll tell you when we're camped," Mr. Fraser retorted. "Till then I need my breath to get upriver." Jeremy wrinkled his face in frustration.

The dark high cliff they'd seen from Fort Selkirk formed the Pelly's northwest bank. To the southeast, low treed hills rolled into blue-purple distance. The river was as wide as the cliff was tall, the waters high and swirling, but the major difference between the Pelly and the Yukon was the crew's direction of travel: downriver, the current had sometimes been their friend; upriver, it was always their enemy.

Within a few yards, Jeremy found out what hard work it was to move a canoe upriver. The Pelly was in full flood and spilled in ripples and eddies around hidden rocks. With all six paddling, the canoe managed to stay stationary against the current. With four paddling and two poling, the canoe gained a little headway.

Jeremy wished he'd made the poles longer than ten feet; in some places they wouldn't reach bottom, so he or Mac had to feel around for a rock to push against before the others could lift their paddles for their next stroke. But by the time they came in sight of the bay where Ben and Mr. Fraser had cached the other canoes two days ago, their technique had improved.

The river's edge lapped at the beached canoes. "Why didn't you put them higher up!" Mac exclaimed.

"They were well up the bank when we left," Ben shot back. "The bank was twenty feet high. Now it's about ten."

Jeremy leapt out to haul the canoe in, grateful for the thigh-high gumboots he'd got from the supply steamer.

While Bob made lunch, Jeremy and Ben helped Mr. Fraser load the first canoe and take it further upstream. There was a ledge just above high water; by clinging to hand holds and overhanging branches, they dragged the canoe forward with ropes one hundred yards. There the ledge sloped underwater so they tied the rope to an outcropping and inched back to the bay.

After lunch they lined the other canoes forward. The dogs followed along the ledge. As he untied the first canoe, Mr. Fraser noted, "The water's too deep to pole and we won't get anywhere paddling. The only way is to track and that means wading."

Jeremy looked at the racing water, murky with silt. Trees and branches overhung the bank and dead trees swept down by the river taunted them with tangled roots and branches.

The men checked the canoes' lines — a long bow line attached about four feet out to a short line tied to the canoe six feet behind the bow. "Why the short line?" Jeremy asked.

"The bridle? Keeps the canoe's nose pointed upstream," said Ben. "If it weren't for that line, the canoe could go sideways and ship water."

Mac chuckled as he climbed into the stern of the first canoe.

"Tough job, steering, but somebody has to do it."

Bob climbed into the second canoe and Rimmer picked up the paddle for the third. Ben took hold of the lines to Bob's canoe and Jeremy fell in line for the third. Mr. Fraser grabbed the rope to the first canoe. They inched forward slowly, testing the hidden ledge. It seemed wide enough. Water sloshed around their ankles.

The dogs followed to the end of the dry ledge where they whined and barked. "We can't help you," Rimmer stated. "Figure it out for yourselves."

"We could put them in the canoes," Jeremy suggested.

"They wouldn't stay without being tied," Rimmer replied. "Besides, there isn't room." Sudden splashes made Jeremy look back. The dogs were swimming after them.

Progress was slow because of the current and the rocky, slippery footing. Mr. Fraser stepped into a hole; Jeremy bumped into his canoe and over-balanced. Water sloshed over the tops of his gumboots and leaked down to his feet, shocking him with cold. Then he nudged into a large boulder and had to shuffle around it. Other times the crew detoured around logjams. As much as possible, Mac and Bob and Rimmer tried to keep the canoes pointing upstream with their paddles. At the end of the first hour, the crew had only progressed about half a mile.

"This is ridiculous!" Mr. Fraser shouted. "We'll pull in where we can wait till the water goes down!"

"Good idea," Rimmer agreed for all of them.

Jeremy was the only one who heard Mr. Fraser mutter, "Even if it means more lost time."

They took turns steering and tracking. Jeremy tracked with Mac and Bob while the others steered and rested; Jeremy steered while they tracked. But he was so wet from the river and sweat that he shivered in the cool breeze and offered to track again.

When they could walk along sandbars, tracking progressed smoothly, as it was supposed to, but as soon as the sandbar ended they'd be back to wading.

Everyone threw occasional glances back at the dogs, swimming when they had to, climbing onto sandbars or logs and shaking themselves, before being forced to swim again. The distance between the men and the dogs lengthened as the dogs grew tired, but still they followed. Jeremy felt very sorry for them.

The river broadened. Close by was a small island surrounded by riffles that signaled hidden rocks. Their side of the river was swampy, but it had a bank that looked walkable — once they passed yet another logjam. There was nothing for it but to head farther out. The water sloshed around the trackers' thighs as they towed the canoes broadside to the flow. "Look out!" Mac shouted. "We're shipping water! I'm drenched!"

"Not much we can do about it!" Mr. Fraser shouted back.

When they hit the eddy that had shoved the logs together, the river's drag on the canoe increased. Jeremy grabbed at some roots to steady himself. For a minute the canoe pointed upriver again so that the men's steering helped, then they tacked across the current on the other side of the jam. Now they had to fight the current's attempts to press them into it; whenever their footing was insecure, the current nearly won. With his paddle, Mac fended the canoe off logs and branches. "Get farther upstream!" he yelled. "Any one of these will puncture the moosehide canoe!"

Jeremy, Ben and Mr. Fraser tried to move farther away, but the current wouldn't let them. It was all they could do not to be impaled themselves.

Finally they gained the bank, lined the canoes a few yards to safety and stopped to rest. Jeremy's legs were frozen and he had no feeling in his feet. Mr. Fraser was looking at the logjam. Jeremy turned too. "The dogs'll have a hard time getting around that," Mr. Fraser muttered. "Can you see them?" he asked Jeremy.

"One, two, three — they're doing all right. There's Leo and Patch —"

"Five. Oh, there's another, six. And seven." As Mr. Fraser counted again, Jeremy watched the heads bobbing in the river. The dogs were really struggling now. The steerers had climbed out of the canoe and turned to look as well. "Not much fun for anyone," Mac grumped.

"I don't see Captain and Tom," Mr. Fraser announced.

"I'm going back for the dogs. Leave one canoe here. The rest of you keep going."

"I'll come with you," Jeremy said.

"You help us," Mac said. "We can take the three canoes on."

"No, I'll go with Mr. Fraser."

"We'll be back shortly. It won't take long." Mr. Fraser had already started wading. Jeremy stumbled after him.

The current, as if delighted that they'd changed direction, rushed them along and now they had trouble staying upright in the torrent.

"Go around the logjam," Mr. Fraser ordered. "If we try to go over it, it might unlock and kill us."

Jeremy had been planning to climb over the logs, but now he slogged sideways, with the current, and sideways again.

They found Tom and Captain entangled in the next logjam downriver. Tom had his paws around a log and his nose above water. Captain was wedged under a log, his head at an awkward angle. Mr. Fraser dug out Tom, and Jeremy, Captain; the dogs had no energy even to wag their tails.

As they started back upriver, Jeremy said, "They're nearly drowned!" Mr. Fraser agreed. He carried Tom, a half-dead weight. Captain was slightly better off; he swam feebly with Jeremy pulling the loose skin on his neck. Jeremy wondered how much longer the dogs would have lived, but he didn't have the breath to wonder aloud.

Finally they were around the logjam for the third time, and discovered that none of the men had gone on. "Where'd you find them?" Mac asked.

"Next driftwood down." Panting, Mr. Fraser set Tom on the

ground. The dog's eyes were half-closed and, other than shivering, he made no move. Mr. Fraser pulled off his wet jacket and started rubbing Tom. Jeremy did the same with Captain.

"It's no good," Mr. Fraser announced. "They need a fire or they'll die from exposure." He looked upriver. "A camping spot can't be far —"

Mac cut him short. "Put them on the canoe, then, James."

Jeremy looked at the canoe. It was as full as it could be without sinking. Its rim rested only a few inches above water.

"No. We'll walk them up, it's faster. I'll build a fire and come back." He picked up Tom again.

Jeremy tried to pick up Captain but he was too heavy. Fortunately, the dog seemed able to carry on.

"He can manage, Jer. You steer and I'll track," Mac said.

"No," said Mr. Fraser. "These dogs need attention now. You watch that none of the others get stuck in this driftwood. I'll be back soon."

Jeremy followed him upriver, Captain staggering beside him. They ran out of bank and had to wade again around a point. Jeremy's foot hit a rock and he fell down. Mr. Fraser was soaked too, his arms full of wet dog.

Another half mile on Jeremy saw a plateau three feet above high water. In the grassy meadow were some abandoned buildings. There was also a tent.

As they staggered up the bank, two men and a woman appeared. Mr. Fraser set Tom down and looked around for a source of firewood. Captain collapsed beside Tom. The strangers hurried over.

"Have you any kindling?" Mr. Fraser asked. "These dogs need to get warm immediately."

The three said something to each other in a strange language. The woman pointed. One man hurried back to their camp and returned with an axe. The other man brought a pile of brush that they'd already collected for their own use. "Fire," he stated.

"Have you been here long?" Mr. Fraser asked, as the brush caught and he fed it other pieces.

The woman smiled and said, "Today." Wow, I thought we set up camp fast, Jeremy thought, until she held up two fingers. Oh, Jeremy corrected himself, two days.

Mr. Fraser yarded Tom and Captain closer to the fire. Jeremy, shivering too, practically stood in it. "You keep the fire going," Mr. Fraser instructed. "I'm going back for the canoe."

"I'll come," Jeremy retorted.

"No." Mr. Fraser walked away. As Jeremy watched and shivered, he realized he didn't have an ounce of energy left. He sank to the ground and fed another log to the fire. Pulling off his gumboots, he dumped out the river then peeled off his socks and stuck them on sticks over the fire. He shoved his blue feet as close to the flames as he could bear.

The foreign men arrived back from the bush with more armsful of wood. "Thanks," said Jeremy.

"Bad," the shorter man said, jerking his head to the river.

"Yeah," agreed Jeremy. "Very bad. Where are you from?"

"Norge. Oslo," he added, when he saw Jeremy's blank look. "Norway," the tall redhead clarified before they crossed back to their own tent.

Norway sounded like a country he'd heard of, but he couldn't remember where it had been on the map that had hung over the blackboard during geography. Maybe he should plan to read some books when he was rich. He stroked each dog's head. Captain opened his eyes, but Tom didn't. Jeremy put more wood on the fire and swivelled around to dry his back.

Were these people going to the same place his crew was? Would his crew again not tell him where they were going because these strangers were here? He was consumed with curiosity — and had been for months. He also realized, as his shivering lessened, that he was starved.

Leo and Patch staggered around the point and shook themselves. Jeremy called them. Both gave a half-hearted wave of their tails and stumbled up to the fire. Three more followed shortly.

He was nearly dry when Rimmer, Bob and Ben arrived with two canoes. Jeremy was surprised to see Mr. Fraser with them. The last two dogs dragged behind. The men hauled the canoes up the bank then staggered to the fire. Everyone was wet. They all held their hands out to the warmth.

"Where's Mac?" Jeremy asked.

"Canoe swamped. He's reloading."

"I'm going back for him now," Mr. Fraser stated. He was soaked and looked terribly worn out.

"I'll come with you," said Rimmer. "You three get camp set up and dinner going. We'll be back soon."

"Ha ha," Bob intoned, without mirth.

"Once more unto the breach, dear friend, once more." Mr. Fraser clapped Rimmer on the shoulder.

"I thought it was the Pelly," Rimmer muttered. "This is no time for Shakespeare."

It was eleven-thirty when they returned with Mac, the canoe full of wet goods. The three slumped by the fire. Jeremy, revived by food, brought them cups of tea and plates of beans, bacon and bread. Mac glowered at everyone and refused to say a word.

Why's Mac so cross? Jeremy wondered. It's no harder on him than anyone else. Anyway, Mr. Fraser made the most trips. He rescued the dogs. Would Mac have done that? Why had Mr. Fraser teamed up with Mac in the first place? Mr. Fraser was so fussy about details and Mac never did what he said he was going to do in the time he said he'd do it. Oh well, Jeremy answered himself, they're friends.

19

———

Thursday 2nd June 1898
Fine & warm. Waters falling rapidly (about an inch an hour). Lay in camp all day being very stiff, sore & tired. An outfit of 5 men (Gillies) and 2 boats arrived & lay over.

The next morning everyone staggered out of bed late, groaning about their sore bodies. The dogs lifted their heads briefly but did not get up. Jeremy watched Mr. Fraser check Tom and Captain and pronounce that they would recover.

"We should have left the dogs at Selkirk," Rimmer observed. "They're more trouble than they're worth when they can't work. They're just mouths to feed."

"How dare you say that!" Jeremy stroked heads. A few tails wagged. "They're part of our crew! They've worked from the beginning!"

"They're just pets now. You don't take *pets* on a hard trek, kid!" snorted Rimmer. "Everyone has to keep working!"

Bob got breakfast very slowly and after eating, while they were sitting on crates in the sun drinking tea, Jeremy said, "Since we're not going on today, this is the perfect time to tell me where we are going and why."

"Oh, I don't know," retorted Bob. "We should build up more suspense for you."

"You want to spoil a surprise?" Ben gave him a pained look.

Even Rimmer shook his head. "Young people shouldn't know everything their elders do."

"Oh you — !" Jeremy spluttered. He was pretty sure they were joking, but what if they weren't?

The men laughed. Bob nudged him with his elbow. "Sure, we'll tell you, kid. Anything to stay still. The only muscle that doesn't hurt is my tongue."

"We're going up the Macmillan River," Mr. Fraser stated, pulling out a map. "See, it comes into the Pelly here." Jeremy saw. "And branches here." Mr. Fraser traced its length with his finger.

"But why?" Jeremy asked. "Why aren't you going on to Bonanza and Eldorado like the others?"

"Exactly that reason," said Bob. "That area was pretty well all staked before news of the strike got out. If you weren't in the Yukon in '96, forget it."

"Why the Macmillan? Why not this river?" Jeremy pointed to the Stewart.

"Two reasons," said Mr. Fraser, still holding the map so Jeremy could see. "One, gold has been found on the Stewart and surface gold always washes down from somewhere. The headwaters of the Stewart and Macmillan are fairly close together. As you can see, this whole area's unmapped. Could be that the motherlode of the same gold that's on the Stewart or the Klondike is in this area."

"And the second reason," Mac elaborated, "Is McHenry's find. In the '80s a man named McHenry came out of this area with forty pounds of gold."

"Wow," said Jeremy.

Mac nodded in agreement. "I met him by coincidence in '87. The name McHenry was notorious on the Welland Canal so I asked him if he was the McHenry who was also known as Townsend, and he said he was McHenry but not Townsend, as he was accused of being, and after the trial he'd come out to the Fraser River gold rush, then to the Cariboo and the Omineca and the Dease, kept working his way north until he'd found this lode." Mac's voice sparkled with enthusiasm. "He said he was getting too old to come back in here and he told me how to find the pass, since we were both from the Welland area."

"1887! Why haven't you looked for it before this?" Jeremy asked.

"Time flies."

"What if someone else has found it?"

Mac poured himself more tea. "Haven't heard that anyone has."

Jeremy pondered. "How do you tell the pass?"

"That's my secret till we get to the head of the Macmillan."

Jeremy glanced at the other men. They nodded and raised their eyebrows as if in resigned acceptance.

"Fair enough," Rimmer said and Jeremy wondered if they'd asked this question before and met with the same answer. Was this why Mr. Fraser put up with Mac's sloppiness?

Jeremy took another tack. "What was this McHenry so famous for?"

Mac laughed. "Murder. He was tried twice in the '50s and acquitted both times. No one could prove he was the Townsend who was a member of a notorious gang that killed three men, including a policeman. But everybody believed he was."

"But you said he said he wasn't," Jeremy reminded him.

"I'd say the same if I'd been acquitted," Ben stated. "It's a famous case. I studied it in law school. There's no statute of limitations for murder so, if he admitted he was Townsend, he could be tried a third time."

"He'd be pretty doddery now if he's still alive," Rimmer mused.

"In his seventies, I guess," Mac said. "He looked well-worn a decade ago. Said he was too rheumaticky to come back up here."

"He was nearly thirty at the time of the trials," Ben added.

"Do you remember hearing about the case when you were boy, James?" Bob asked.

"Yes. Even over in Alexandria it was big news. Such grisly, premeditated murders. We boys played at being the Townsend gang whenever we could get away from chores." He smiled, remembering. "Bang, bang, you're dead, then we poled across the creek, pretending it was Lake Ontario and we were escaping to Buffalo."

All the men smiled. If asked, Jeremy would have said that of course Mr. Fraser had been a boy once, but he was having trouble with the mental image.

"So we're going looking for the McHenry mine —"

"And we won't be the only ones," Bob interrupted Jeremy. "Not with gold fever at the pitch it is. That's why we didn't tell you. We didn't want to start another stampede."

"I would have kept it a secret." Jeremy bristled with injured pride.

"We didn't know that then." Bob smiled. "We do now."

Jeremy was mollified.

"Imagine," he said, "Murderer's gold! Forty pounds. How much is that?"

Mac moved his hands to indicate a space about six inches by three inches by one inch. "I told you gold is heavy."

"How much would that gold be worth?" Jeremy asked.

"In today's prices, over seven thousand dollars."

"Wow! Maybe that's why McHenry didn't go back! He was rich enough."

"Could be," Ben agreed, "since the average clerk or labourer makes about six hundred dollars a year, but I'm inclined to bet he didn't go back because of his age, human nature being as greedy as it is."

"If I got seven thousand dollars, I'd be satisfied," Jeremy objected. "That's enough to buy a house on Georgia Street and a bicycle and a really good camera!"

"By the time we locate pay dirt," Rimmer said, "We'll have earned it. Every bone I own aches."

"*If* we find it," cautioned Mr. Fraser.

Jeremy tightened his lips. Mr. Fraser could be such a wet blanket.

Jeremy was the only one who didn't ache, so he drew the job of collecting deadfalls for firewood. Since the sun was hot they rigged up the stove and oven on rocks outside the tent. Mr. Fraser picked up the mixing bowl to make bread, saying that kneading the dough might help his shoulders. Bob decided to make a pie out of evaporated potatoes, carrots and bacon as a respite from the ever-present beans. Ben took the fishing rod to the river.

When Jeremy had bucked, split and piled enough wood for the cooks, he wandered up the meadow to explore the abandoned buildings. Leo looked as if he'd like to follow, but then thought that more sleep was a better idea.

As Jeremy crossed the plateau, the constant roar of the river receded to background noise. Now he could hear birds trilling complicated patterns and the wind blowing through the ankle-high grass. The air was filled with the scent of grass and silver-leafed shrubs hung with yellow flowers. More flowers, pink and white, bobbed among the grasses.

Only two walls of the building remained. The back portion of the sod roof had collapsed. Peering in the door, Jeremy could dimly make out a cookstove, its pipe knocked askew by the fallen roof. A bed frame or long table made of logs protruded from one wall.

He entered and waited for his eyes to adjust to the gloom. Who had lived here? Miners? Had they found gold? Why had they abandoned the camp? Mice or rats had taken over, judging by the droppings on the dirt floor. He picked up a horseshoe-shaped magnet and put it in his pocket.

Outside, he sat down in the sun. Small birds swirled and dipped

over the river. Above them, eagles coasted on updrafts. Dark
spruce, spotted with clumps of lime-green poplars, rolled to the
horizon. He had a sense that, with one step, he could clear the
river and stride on over the land. He could hop the mountains
when he got there. He lay back on one elbow, pulled up a blade of
grass, chewed the sweet new growth and smiled at the part of him
that strode over the river.

They'd find McHenry's mine — a cave of shining gold — bars,
coins, jewellery — and they'd be rich. Pounds and pounds of gold.
The dogs could haul it out. Anyway, they'd be going down river,
though they might have to build another boat. They'd cover the
heap of gold with a tarp to keep it from sliding into the river. The
months of slog would be worth it when they got that gold. All the
work, all the cold plodding on, all the hauling, dragging, loading
and unloading, and all the wet feet. Never do that again when they
got the gold. Fancy McHenry telling Mac where it was just because
they were from the same place. That Welland Canal. Like if
Cowlick Sunday from the Orphanage showed up here and told
him where his gold was just because of the Orphanage.

Like if the pretty girl in the red dress was lying on the grass with
him and if he could really talk to her —

His body seemed to be expanding, he could feel his blood rushing, his skin tingling everywhere —

He rolled onto his stomach and looked across the river — striding, striding —

There were new tents going up at the edge of the clearing.
Jeremy hadn't noticed anyone arrive but now saw two boats pulled
up the bank. His crew seemed to be talking to a number of men.
The Norwegians wandered over. Jeremy stood up, brushed himself off and started across the meadow.

He could hear the newcomers' accent before he could decipher
their words: it sounded just like Soapy Smith's accent. He paused
for a second, holding his breath . . . ? No, that couldn't be. His crew

would have told him. But his crew hadn't met Smith. No, these men just sounded like him. Still, the accents were enough to fill Jeremy with the fear he'd felt in Skagway.

"Yes Suh, that rivah is mighty full," a big man with a broad-brimmed hat was saying. "Gillies is mah name and the rest of mah pahty is Royston, Brownlee, Baker and Woolidge." He rattled off the names so quickly Jeremy couldn't fit them to their owners. "We're from Atlanta, Georgia." Pronouncing it *Jawgia*.

Mr. Fraser introduced their crew and said they were from Vancouver. "Except for me," said Rimmer. "I'm from Colorado."

"How was your trip up the river?" asked Mac.

Gillies shook his head. "Hellish. We spent last night about half a mile from the mouth and only got this *fah* today. We decided to lie *ovah* a bit."

"The water seems to be going down about an inch an hour," Mr. Fraser stated. "I marked the high line at midnight and it's down more than a foot."

"Well, that's something. Say, bet you fellas haven't heard they're building a railroad." Gillies paused and grinned as if aware of the effect this news would have.

"Railroad?" Rimmer echoed. "Where?"

"Thought you probably couldn't have heard. Yep. Skagway to White Horse. Met some fellas yesterday just come down from the Rapids. Ten million dollars put up for financing."

"We'll have a cup of tea by the fire," Bob ordered. "You can dry off and tell us about it."

"Now that's a nice idea, isn't it, boys?" The *boys* nodded, and started toward the fire. Bob cocked his head, including the Norwegians. They understand more English than they speak, Jeremy thought, noticing the same intense interest on their faces as he was feeling.

"Tell us what you've heard," Mr. Fraser prompted Gillies and his men, when they all had cups of tea.

"Construction's probably started by now. Our informant had left Skagway in April and said that they were unloading rails then."

"What route are they going to follow?" Mac asked.

"White Pass. Going to be the White Pass and Yukon Railway."

"How will they ever build a railway through there?" Jeremy wondered.

Mr. Fraser frowned at him. "The Canadian Pacific got through the Fraser Canyon. This'll be no worse. There are some good engineers nowadays."

"If there's gold to be got out, someone'll figure how to do it," Royston or Woolidge offered.

"You mean like — ," Jeremy couldn't help letting his awe show, "if we'd waited to come, say, next year, we could ride on a train? You mean we wouldn't have had to walk? To make so many trips? We wouldn't have had to carry our stuff? Just put it on a train?"

The men looked at him and laughed, but their laughter was kindly. He'd said what they were thinking — that all the hardships they'd suffered in getting to the White Horse Rapids were soon to be unnecessary.

"Remember this, young lad," Brownlee or Baker shook his finger sternly, "You're a pioneer, being one who came up before the train. We're all pioneers."

That idea pleased Jeremy. "Yeah, just sissies'll take the train," he joked.

"Have you any other news from outside?" Bob asked. "That's one of the hardest things about being here, not knowing what's going on in the world."

"Or knowing how your family is," added Mr. Fraser.

"Let's see," Gillies pondered.

Royston said, "Of course you know we're at war."

"No!" exploded Bob.

"Who with?" asked Mac.

"Spain."

"Oh, you mean the United States is at war, not Canada," Jeremy clarified, looking at Rimmer.

"Yes," Gillies said. "*Remember the Maine.* Men are leaving the goldfields to sign up and free Cuba. Even Skagway has a recruiting office, apparently."

"Did the person you talked to say anything about Soapy Smith?" Jeremy asked.

"Smith?" The newsbearers searched their minds. "No, can't say that he did."

"Be nice if he signed up and went to war," Jeremy said.

"When we came through Skagway in March we got out as fast as we could," Baker or Brownlee continued. "I've never seen so many disreputable ruffians in one place. Enough to put the fear of God in any red-blooded American."

"I lost money," one of the Norwegian men offered. "A man take my — took my —" he parted his hands as if opening a billfold.

"Wallet?" Ben supplied.

"Wallet." The man nodded. "Hundred dollars and boat ticket. Police do nothing. Bad city."

"Did some men say they'd find the thief and run off in different directions?" Jeremy asked.

"Ya."

"Then they didn't find anyone?"

"Ya." The Norwegian nodded hard.

"That's Smith's gang's scam — one of them." Jeremy shivered. Soapy reached all the way up here; he was all through the gold rush, all these people . . .

Shortly, with thanks for the tea, Gillies' crew departed to set up camp and the Norwegians left also. Fraser's crew continued to sit by the stove.

"Do you think they're looking for McHenry's gold too?" Jeremy whispered.

"No," Mac replied. "Gillies said they were going up the Pelly past the Macmillan and I think the Norwegians are going that way too."

"With time getting on," Mr. Fraser said, "and with all our delays, we're not going to have much good weather to search. If we team up with some others we can cover more territory. Many hands make less work."

"Who?" Mac asked, frowning.

"I don't know. Depends on who comes by."

"We'd have to share," Mac pointed out.

"It'll take us the rest of June to get upriver. That only leaves July, August and part of September to prospect. More men makes it more likely we succeed. With just the six of us, we might find nothing. A share of nothing is nothing."

Ben said thoughtfully, "That makes sense. It depends on who comes along. If we like them."

Bob and Rimmer slowly nodded, but Mac continued to frown. For once, Jeremy agreed with Mac.

20

——

Saturday 4th June 1898
Day fine & clear. 3 men & 1 boat arrived in morning (Anamosa) & lay over. 3 more men arrived at noon & lay over but the Norwegians left for up river. In forenoon Ben, Rimmer & I brought up small canoe & load. Then Ben & I went down to mouth of River in small canoe to arrange with man, left there in charge of cache by Rogers' Group, to take charge of & feed our dogs. Bob walked dogs down bank. Made arrangements ($10.00 per mo) then went over to Selkirk for more dog feed. Left there at 4 p.m. & reached camp at 9 very tired. Many boats passing.

Sunday 5th June 1898
Showery. Gillies' & Rogers' Outfits started up River this morning & last comers (Wilson's Outfit) went to Selkirk. Anamosa Gang building a boat.

Jeremy's throat constricted as he watched Bob and the dogs disappear downriver. Captain and Leo had their tails up and waving as if going on an adventure. Tom had his up too. Well, Jeremy thought, all were that up-curled-tail sort of dog. That's what they do. Oh well, he thought, and retreated to the abandoned building, where he sat in the sun-warmed grass. He did not have the strid-ing-over-mountain-feeling of the other day. He had a sinking-into-ground-feeling, *sulking,* Matron would have said — *Oh, he's just sulking* — and he let himself indulge as he pulled up tender new grasses and chewed them. What would it have been like if Hank had been able to come? If Collie and Prince hadn't died? Or Blackie the horse? If they — men and animals — were all together, as they'd been in the beginning? But — would that have meant Soapy and his gang too? Jeremy bounced up, went to the bush and collected kindling.

While the crew waited for the water level to fall, Mr. Fraser con-vinced three crews to join up with them. Fuller, Miller and Larson came from Anamosa, Iowa and Wilson's party from Cle Elm, Washington. Two of Rogers' party came from California and two from Oregon. They'd all heard rumours of McHenry's lode, but when they found out that Mac had talked to McHenry and knew exactly where to go, they were impressed enough to throw in their lots. The ten new men were a blur of strangers to Jeremy. He felt shy and resentful that his familiar crew could not go on alone.

Mac had recovered his sociability and found out what work the newcomers did, while everyone sized each other up, just slightly less obviously than the dogs would have done. The Iowans — all in their twenties and all with blond hair — were sons of grain farmers. Wilson and Fraser had mixed farms near Cle Elm and Gassman was the town blacksmith. Wilson had a very long upper lip and Gassman looked too thin and wiry to be a strong black-smith. Rogers and Osborne both had greying hair and beards. Recently, they'd been in real estate in Oakland, but, they assured Mac, they'd met while prospecting in Nevada. Lane had a dry-goods business in Portland but "times were hard." Townsend, his brother-in-law, was "in banking."

The Cle Elm Fraser was also James. When he discovered the problem he laughed and said, "You can call me Jas." However, there were three more James as well as the two James Frasers: James Miller from Anamosa, James Rogers and James Lane. These James would have to be addressed by their surnames. Jeremy snickered. If the James had all been named in an orphanage their matron had unfortunately skipped over the Matthews, Marks, and Lukes.

There were two Johns in the new group, but they could be called Wilson and Larson. Frank Fuller, Charles Osborne and Bill Townsend had the relief of no duplications. Jeremy drifted in and out of the convoluted conversation; he'd never remember all the names. As it turned out, he didn't have to worry about Gassman's first name; his Cle Elm crew just called him Gas.

Gillies' and Rogers' groups decided that the river had fallen enough to start out on Sunday, but the rest stayed put another day.

Between showers on Sunday afternoon, Jeremy walked back up to the abandoned cabin, wondering if he would have that feeling of striding over the river and mountains again. He'd hoarded the feeling and examined it both nights before he fell asleep; it was as if a door in his mind had opened, a door he hadn't even known was there. He tried not to remember the feelings he'd had when he thought about the pretty girl; he refused to think about her.

Towering cumulus clouds churned across the sky, casting moving shadows on the ground which was too damp to sit on. But there was a drier log. As he looked around, he was aware of a sage-like smell from pale green bushes drying in the sun. Cloud shadows darkened the river to a roaring menace, then as suddenly rolled on to leave the waters sparkling and apparently benign.

Ben crossed the meadow from the woods where he'd been cutting firewood. He leaned on the axe and joined in Jeremy's survey. "Some view," Ben said, then, "What do you think of our new partners?"

Jeremy looked up at him. "I dunno. What do you think?"

"They seem upstanding enough. Good workers. Rogers' boat's nifty. Good thing, I doubt our canoes will last too long."

"But they'll be ahead of us," Jeremy objected. "They'll get there before we do." By *there* he meant the gold. "They could find it and not share it."

Ben laughed. "You trusting soul! They'll need our help as much as we need theirs."

"Do we really need their help?" His voice sounded whiny, even to himself. Ben looked at him, still amused. Jeremy felt himself blushing. "We've come all this way by ourselves . . ."

Ben cut him off. "It's taken us much longer than we allowed for. We were supposed to be there by now. We don't have much choice if we want to do any prospecting."

Prospecting. That meant actually looking for gold, not just the tedium of travelling to it. *Prospecting* was what this journey was supposed to be about. Had he really believed they'd ever do any? His heart speeded up in anticipation.

"Anyway, give me a hand to get the firewood out before you pick some dandelion greens."

"Dandelions?" Jeremy cleared his throat.

"The new leaves. Bob says his mother always cooked them this time of year." Ben raised his eyebrows and rolled his eyes. "He says they're good for us."

As they walked to the pile of wood, Jeremy bet that Bob had told Ben to pick the dandelions, not told Ben to tell him to do it. Oh well . . .

They chucked wood onto the tarp and gathered the corners together. Jeremy watched Ben drag the load down the meadow to the cook-site. As Ben's brown hat and blue-checked shirt receded, Jeremy realized that never once had these men beaten him. Never, in all these months. Not when he'd lied about his "father." Not when he'd got mad at Rimmer for saying the dogs were just pets. Any one of the crew had had a reason to beat him, and they never had.

He picked the dandelion greens and washed them in the river.

When Bob served them, limp from boiling, Jeremy thought he might as well have picked grass, but he was so hungry he probably would have eaten grass too. Mr. Fraser commented that the greens were just like spinach and added a piquancy to the beans and bacon.

Next morning they dismantled camp and started upriver. Mac and Mr. Fraser had the Indians' canoe, Rimmer and Bob the larger of the collapsible canoes, and Ben and Jeremy the smaller. The Anamosa crew had assembled a prefabricated boat the day before and now had two vessels. Wilson, Jas and Gassman had one. According to Mr. Fraser's high water mark, the river level had fallen over six feet and was still dropping. But the current hadn't changed direction, as Jeremy fancifully wished, and the going was nearly as hard. They had to line the boats up the shore and this meant frequent wading which inevitably meant getting wet. Jeremy was very glad of his hip-waders. When they camped that night, just past a steep cliff and a rocky island, they were all wet and tired and only six miles farther from where they'd been that morning.

There was more of the same the next day. Mac held onto a bush too long while Mr. Fraser, with Jeremy's help, was turning the canoe's bow upstream with the line. The canoe almost swamped, Mr. Fraser almost swore, Mac almost got out and walked home. The men had to haul the canoe ashore, unload her and bail her out before they could go on. Jeremy went back to his and Ben's canoe. However, even with that mishap, they estimated the day's progress to be seven miles.

While they were eating supper, Jeremy spied a canoe coming downriver. Mr. Fraser hailed the paddlers and asked them if they were going to Selkirk to please bring their mail up when they returned. "Five months without a word from anybody," Bob commented when the canoeists had agreed and disappeared. Jeremy didn't care about mail; he'd never received a letter in his life.

The days melded into the same repetitious pattern of hard

work that moving their gear over snow had been. They were wet all the time, and because of that, as cold as in winter.

When Jeremy complained of the wind, Bob snapped, "Be glad for it. When it stops the bugs'll start. What do you want, hot with bugs or cold?"

"Warm. No bugs," Jeremy retorted.

They spent evenings mending the moosehide canoes or making new poles or paddles and often did not get to bed until midnight, and once not until four. When they did lie down, their muscles screamed and it was hard to get to sleep, in spite of their fatigue.

All were grateful when Sunday came and they could rest. The crews travelled separately, exchanging the occasional word but not sharing after-supper cups of tea. Jeremy was glad that there had been little change in the patterns of his crew.

On Thursday — Mr. Fraser said it was Thursday — they overtook Rogers' crew which had started out a day earlier than they had. Ben winked at Jeremy and he grinned; in spite of their general misery, they were puffed with pride.

According to Mr. Fraser, studying the map, they'd come about fifty miles from the mouth of the Pelly. According to his authorities, Dawson and Ogilvie of the *Geological Survey of Canada,* who, Jeremy had been told many times by now, had surveyed the Yukon a decade ago, it was twenty-four more miles to the mouth of the Macmillan River.

"And how far up that, I'd like to know?" Rimmer commented. He was bathing his broken blisters in bichloride solution.

"As you know, Rimmer," Mr. Fraser replied dryly, "We don't know. It hasn't been explored yet. Dawson met some miners who'd been up it a bit, but they didn't find any prospects so they came back down."

"What about McHenry?" Jeremy asked. "Didn't he explore it?"

"No," said Mac. "He came up from Dease Lake, from the east." Jeremy hesitated before asking his next question. He wanted it to go away so he wouldn't have to ask it, but instead it grew more pressing. "How do you know the Macmillan is the right river then, if he came from the east? Maybe it's this river or that river." He pointed to the Pelly and the Stewart on Mr. Fraser's map.

"Because he described it, boy! Because it can't be those rivers! This is the only river it can be!" Mac stomped off in disgust.

Jeremy, feeling foolish and chastized, looked at Mr. Fraser. "Those are good questions," he replied, "But everything we've studied proves Mac's right. The Macmillan is the only river leading into McHenry's prospects. If you look here on Mr. Oglivie's map you'll see it's not too far from the source of the Peel River." Jeremy looked. "Now the Peel flows north into the Arctic Ocean and the Macmillan flows west. That means there has to be a divide in this area. You must have studied the Great Divide in geography?"

Jeremy blinked.

Mr. Fraser sighed. "Anyway, that's why we think McHenry's find, if it exists at all, would be in this area." He folded his map, and Jeremy had to be satisfied.

Later, a large canoe with five or six men hove into sight coming downstream. Ben ran to the shore and waved. They back-paddled to a stop. "How much farther to Dawson?" the bowman yelled.

"Fifty miles to Fort Selkirk, couple more days to Dawson," Ben yelled back. Jeremy and the others had gathered. "Where you coming from?" Bob asked, for all of them.

"Edmonton! We left last August! They promised a road or at least a trail! It's a hellish scam! There's nothing but mountains and bog! One of our men died of scurvy and two drowned in the big canyon upriver just two weeks ago. We lost all our animals. Are we too late? Is all the gold gone?" The six men were skeletally thin and the one in the stern had pasty blotches on his face.

"It's pretty staked around Dawson and thousands more went downriver when the ice went out," Bob answered.

Rimmer asked, "Is this canyon that claimed your friends before the mouth of the Macmillan or after?"

"We don't know the Macmillan. It's taken us two weeks from there but we had to look for their bodies. Never seen such country, it's the backyard of hell! Amazing we're not all dead!"

Mr. Fraser said, "There are police at Fort Selkirk. You can report the deaths to them. Do you want to stop for some tea?"

"No, we've taken so long, we'll just carry on to the gold. A thousand men, you say?"

"Thousands!" Bob yelled.

The strangers pushed off, paddling furiously as if to speed the current up.

"Ten months," Jeremy breathed. "Nearly a year."

"Makes our trip seem puny." Mac, as usual, was restored to good humour.

"They looked awful," Jeremy continued. "Half-dead. Did you smell them?"

"A graphic illustration of the importance of looking after your body in the bush," Bob lectured.

"Maybe they couldn't," Jeremy defended.

"There is always time to wash," retorted Bob. "That's an example of gold lust replacing common sense."

"Commerce," stated Mr. Fraser, when they were again seated. "Look at the competition between Vancouver and Victoria and Seattle and San Francisco to sell outfits to would-be miners —"

"Like us," Ben interjected.

Mr. Fraser nodded. "It's the making of Edmonton. Lure people by advertising that it's a good route to Klondike and get their business." He looked at them as if he weren't really seeing them and continued, "You know, this Klondike business reminds me a lot of Winnipeg in 1882, when the Railway got through to there. Boom town. You wouldn't believe the construction and new businesses! I moved there, that's where I met Walsh, he was running a coal company —"

"What were you doing?" Jeremy asked.

"Oh, selling real estate, importing dry goods . . ." Mr. Fraser waved his hand dismissively. "My point is, the boom didn't last. The CPR got built really fast across the prairies. By next spring, Winnipeg was just a flood of mud and bankruptcies. One of the fastest booms and busts in history. I went back to Port Arthur. Winnipeg's where I got married though," he added with a wistful smile. "There was such hope then."

"There won't be a bust for Klondike," Mac stated. "There's too much gold here. This is really it."

"Your famous CPR is not gold in the ground, James, it's a business," Rimmer said. "Klondike won't be bust, already it's not a bust."

"All gold rushes peter out eventually," Ben said.

"Of course, when you've got the gold out." Rimmer clucked impatiently. "That won't be in our time, though. All the assays of the finds show there's lots of gold, more gold than anywhere else in the world. You mark my words, we'll be mining Klondike for years and years."

Jeremy grinned. Gold was just up the river. Mr. Fraser was an old man and 1882 was history, before he was born. Rimmer was right, gold wasn't the same as a railway. Winnipeg — that was east? in the middle of the country? — wasn't the same as Klondike. He almost felt like going on again right this minute. Striding upriver toward the motherload — the men had used that word — the way he'd felt he could cross mountains last week. Until he looked at the laden canoes on the bank and his body remembered how hard it was, foot after foot after foot after foot.

21

___

Thursday 23rd June 1898

As our skin canoes are leaking & we'd have to lay over a couple of days to put canvas bottoms on them, Mr. Wilson (Cle Elm Crowd) agreed to help us build a batteau like theirs & as they have whip-saw & all tools we gladly accepted whereupon all hands turned in to help us. Anamosa Crowd helping & Rogers & Osborne while the rest of their party are going to remodel their own boat which is a hard one to haul up stream. This p.m. one of the Johnson brothers & 4 other men came along in canoes & passed on. Did not bring our mail.

So this was the Macmillan River! Finally! "Yay!" Jeremy shouted when Mr. Fraser declared it so, having studied the map. And Mac actually agreed with him, unlike yesterday and the day before when the men had squabbled over which was the right fork.

"We're here," Jeremy added, and grinned at Bob and Ben and Rimmer. Ben grinned back, but no one else said yay. "When do we look for the gold?"

He glanced at the loose gravel on the banks of the river and told himself sternly that he hadn't really expected to see lumps of gold lying there. Not really. The river, though not as wide as the Pelly, looked remarkably similar to all the other rivers he'd seen.

"We have to set up camp first of course." Bob stated.

Later, when Jeremy heard Bob propose to Mr. Fuller and Mr. Gassman that they go up a creek a bit and look for colours he leapt up from the chopping block and shouted, "Me too!"

Bob glanced at everyone else engaged in some task or other. "If you want. Get your pan and shovel."

"And your hip waders," added Frank Fuller.

Innumerable times since February Jeremy had unpacked and repacked the gold pan he'd acquired with Magnus' gear. It had been lost, unused, when the raft capsized. He'd replaced it at Fort Selkirk with a rusty, battered pan traded in by an exiting miner — a fabulously wealthy miner, Jeremy hoped. Now, after carting the peculiar flat-bottomed, slope-sided pan all these miles, he was actually going to get to use it!

He snapped the suspenders of his hip-waders over his shoulders, located a shovel and the pan, then searched his dunnage bag for a leather poke, just in case.

When Jeremy rejoined the men, they were similarly attired. Bob and Gassman carried hatchets for hacking through the underbrush.

They waded up a rocky creek which spilled into the Macmillan from the north. Cottonwoods and willows in full lime-green leaf dangled overhead, casting patterns of sun and shade on the water and creek-banks. It was not too hot and not too cool and, best of all, as Gassman noted, the breeze kept most of the newly hatched mosquitoes away. Underfoot the rocks were slippery. Water swirled around Jeremy's calves and sometimes his thighs. All concentrated on their footing and so hardly talked.

A few miles on the creek curved sharply. A little bay had formed beneath a steepish bank. "This looks possible," Bob announced.

Jeremy watched the men shovel gravel into their gold pans, dip water into them and swirl them around. It didn't look hard; he did the same. Water splashed into his eyes and rocks and sand fell out. He refilled his pan and swirled gently. Nothing happened.

Gassman, who was closest, said, "You never panned before, huh? Watch." He refilled his pan, added water, then picked out the largest rocks. "Tip your pan back and forth and side to side at the same time." He held his pan at a slight angle and rotated it in a circular, rocking motion, spewing out gravel, sand, dirt and sticks. Jeremy imitated the motion. He recalled Mr. Hammond in Saanich teaching him to milk a cow. *No, no, stroke the teat and bend it and pull it all at the same time! No, no, not that hard!* Panning had a technique too.

"Gold is heaviest," Gassman instructed. "So you let the water take out all the junk. Keep adding water and shaking till you're down to a bit of black sand, then I'll show you what to look for."

Jeremy added water to his gravel and swirled around and around, back and forth, trying to keep the pan tilted not too high and not too low. Water carrying dirt, sticks and rocks drained back to the creek. He added more water. Smaller rocks and some sand swished out. What if he was washing out the gold as well? Finally he was down to a small heap of sand caught in the angle of his pan. "What do I do now?"

Gassman took Jeremy's pan, swirled the sand about, looked at it intently and added water. He tilted and shook and drained — more gently, Jeremy noted. He stroked his fingers through it. "Nah, you don't have nothin," he declared. "Neither do I. How's your luck, boys?" he shouted at the others.

Fuller shook his head, rinsed out his pan and stored it. "A few flakes," said Bob, "But nothing worth anything."

"Can I see your flakes?" Jeremy asked, before Bob could dump them.

Bob rolled his eyes but walked over, holding out his pan. "This is gold," he sifted the sand, picked a minuscule grain and held it out on his finger, "But there's not enough to worry about."

Jeremy held his breath and looked. A dark flat flake the size of an insignificant splinter dried on the end of Bob's fingers. "That's gold?" he said, letting out his breath.

"Yep." Bob flicked it off. "Not enough to think about. We'll carry on."

"But —" Jeremy looked down at the creek, at the rocks and sand, "If there's gold here —"

Fuller joined in impatiently. "It's not enough, boy. You got to have colours. Enough at least for a ten cent pan. That's flakes. A little flake like that, it's half a half a half a cent, if anything."

"Oh," said Jeremy. But it was gold, they had found gold, he thought, as they slogged farther on.

The creek meandered in a series of curves but the spruce and poplar, scrub willows and roses were so thick that it was faster to wade than to cut across land. Eventually the creek banks grew steeper. The men scanned them. Bob ran his hand over a darker band of dirt. "This could be old creekbed." He chipped some dirt and rocks into his pan and began washing. Jeremy did the same. Fuller and Gassman scooped gravel from the creek.

Jeremy picked out the biggest rocks, then swirled and washed. Eventually he was down to black sand and a few small glitters. "I've got gold!"

"Let me see," said Gassman, stilling his own pan. "He has four or five colours," he announced to the others.

"What do I do now?" Jeremy asked, thinking, *gold, I've found gold.*

"Same thing again. Only get your dirt from another place."

"What do I do with the gold?"

Gassman laughed. "Nothing. That's poor pay. It'd take forty thousand of those little flakes to make an ounce. If you get over twenty colours in a pan then you're ticking with steam. Anything less, forget it." He turned back to his own pan.

But Jeremy hauled out his poke and carefully wiped the five flakes into it. He pushed them down the leather sides, drew the drawstring and returned the poke to his pocket.

"This is better," Bob announced, studying the bottom of his pan. "I've got about fifteen colours, some of it coarse."

"Are you going to save them?" asked Jeremy.

"No."

"Let me then," Jeremy said quickly, before Bob could empty his pan.

With an exasperated look, Bob stood up, handed Jeremy the pan and turned to study the dark streak in the bank. Jeremy put the colours into his poke. He couldn't feel them through the leather.

Bob waded fifty yards upstream and picked at the bottom of the streak until he had loosened enough to wash. Jeremy sloshed halfway up to him, scooped dirt out of the bank with his shovel and crouched over his pan. Again some colours — nineteen — and, was that a little nugget? He put the gold into his poke and refilled his pan.

Before he added water, he looked around. Bob had moved farther upstream; Fuller and Gassman were occupied with the gravel in the creek. Where he was, the bank and trees shaded him but sunshine danced on the creek which rippled in a constant monotone. Nearby, some ravens croaked and grumbled. In spite of the mosquitoes that whined everywhere and landed undeterred by his frequent applications of oil of citronella, Jeremy realized that he was entirely happy. He'd come to Yukon to find gold and here he was, finding gold. It was hard to believe that he was finding it and not still just thinking about it. Jeremy smiled and began washing his new pan of dirt. He hummed a little tune while he swirled the contents of his pan. He added words to his tune: *gold, gold, gold, I've found gold, gold gold.*

They carried on upstream for another hour, then Bob said, "Isn't much here. We better get back and see how the boat-building's going."

"But I've found two pans with over twenty colours, that makes this worth panning, you said," Jeremy protested.

"Nah, we'll do better farther up the Macmillan," said Gassman, fastening his shovel to a loop on his backpack.

"We're looking for a bigger lode," Fuller added kindly. "There's too much work to make anything of these few colours." He started downstream.

Reluctantly, Jeremy looked at the bank. He hadn't worked that hard for his gold. If he kept on, he could fill his poke. Surely a pokeful of gold would be worth a lot? But then, what would a bigger load of gold look like? Would it just be lying around so he could shovel it into his knapsack?

He splashed downstream after the men, but he vowed that, until they reached the load, he'd pan every chance he got, just to be sure.

From a distance, the camp area seemed furiously active. There were stacks of lumber by the saw-pit and two benches on which to build the boats. Two more canoes were pulled up on the river-bank, and another tent. "We've got company," Jeremy said.

"Looks like it," Gassman agreed.

Bob glanced at Jeremy and cautioned, "Don't say a word about where we're going."

Jeremy clicked his tongue in disgust. "I won't."

"Don't get your knickers in a knot. I was reminding all of us," Bob added, but Jeremy hmmphed in disbelief.

They found the James Frasers sorting through the pile of angled branches they'd collected to support the boat's ribs. "Company?" asked Bob with a raised eyebrow.

"Grants, from New York," said Mr. Fraser. "Brothers, I gather. Don't seem to know where they're going or why."

"We were out in the bush when they got here," Jas Fraser added.

"Asked so many questions I thought they were lawyers. Oh, here they come."

The five turned to watch the newcomers cross the bench. Jeremy was puzzled: why wasn't Mr. Fraser welcoming these men as he had everyone else they'd met?

The Grants were tall, thin and dark-haired. Both walked with the same gait, shoulders moving before legs as if they had to punch room for their bodies to step into. Jeremy remembered the twins at the Orphanage, Home Boys, they hadn't stayed long, the rest just called each *Twin*. These Grants could be twins.

"More members of your party, Frasers," the one on the left said in a jocular tone. "Hello. Bob Grant, from New York, this is my brother, Bill." Both stuck out their hands but when Jeremy shook them in turn, they twitched to get away. "We've seen you before, haven't we?" he said to Gassman, who slowly nodded.

"Looks like you been prospecting." The Grant on the right, Bill, stuck his hands in his pockets and rocked back on his heels.

"A little exploring," Fuller answered.

"Any luck?" Bob Grant winked at Jeremy.

"Nah." He shook his head.

"No colours at all?"

"Not enough to carry on," said Jeremy.

Bill asked, "Where were you washing?"

Gassman answered. "Up that creek a mile or so. The boy's right, there's nothing there."

"Guess we won't go there, right, Bob?"

"Right, Bill."

What do these men mean? Jeremy wondered. Sounds like they're talking three things at once.

The Frasers went back to their branch sorting. Fuller and Bob removed their packs, which reminded Jeremy of his. He took it off, then unsnapped the suspenders to his hip-waders. He wiped sweat off his forehead and slapped at the mosquitoes.

"Big crew you have here." Bob Grant addressed Fuller, Gassman and Bob. "Going on up the Pelly?" There was a long silence.

"Could be," Fuller finally said. Bill looked at Jeremy.

Bob laughed. "We're looking around. Not sure where we're going. How about you?"

"Same here," a Grant replied, swatting mosquitoes. "There's gold all over this Klondike." Bill took a step toward Jeremy and smiled. Jeremy peeled down his hip-waders and stepped out of them. That was cooler. Mosquitoes zoomed to his legs and the sweaty rubber.

Mr. Fraser stood up and Jas did too, more reluctantly.

"*Did* you find any gold, boys?" Mr. Fraser's eyes drilled Bob and Jeremy, included Fuller and Gassman.

"Nah, nothing worth anything," Bob said. A look was going back and forth between them that Jeremy thought was important. He felt even more puzzled.

"The boy did the best of us," Gassman laughed. "Working that streak in the bank."

"Show them what you got, Jer," Fuller commanded.

"No!" How could he have thought Mr. Fraser and Bob and now even Fuller and Gassman were his friends? They'd laughed at him for collecting those flakes. Now he was supposed to show strangers his poke? "No!" he repeated.

"Come on," Mr. Fraser urged. "I'd like to see what you've got." Jeremy glared at him. Through his glaring, he slowly registered that Mr. Fraser seemed to be pleading. What was going on?

Bob — or Bill — Grant laughed. "We're not going to take it from you, boy. Just want a looksee."

Jeremy registered silence. No sawing. Only the interminable river and the constant mosquito whine. Ben and Charlie Osborne, Mac and Rimmer arrived. What was going on?

Don't tell them where we're going. Oh, a decoy. But his gold? It was his gold. Jeremy was totally torn. He'd marked the creek in his mind as a place to come back to and he still didn't think the men were right to discard it. Now, if he showed his poke with its flakes and two nuggets, these Grants would clean that bank out. On the other hand, he wanted to mine that creek. Maybe he should encourage the Grants and go with them, switch crews. But why was Mr. Fraser asking him for something?

With a sigh of resignation, Jeremy slowly pulled out his poke. The Grants drew closer. "There isn't much here. You can't even feel it." He loosened the drawstring. "You can't really even see it."

Bob or Bill made a grab. "Let me check."

"Take it easy," Mr. Fraser said. "It's the boy's."

Bill or Bob took the poke, hefted it, and looked inside. "You're right, not many colours," he dismissed, though he looked at his brother as he handed it back. "Good for you, kid, keep it up and you might get rich someday."

Face burning, Jeremy shoved his poke into his pocket. He wasn't five years old. He picked up his waders and pack and stormed off to the tent in his stocking feet. They were probably all watching him go, probably laughing at him for saving those little flakes. The nape of his neck itched and burned from their gaze but nothing would make him look back.

He flopped down on his sleeping bag and crossed his arms over his chest. The sun beat through the canvas; it was so hot he could hardly breathe. Mosquitoes whined and bit in spite of the mosquito netting. But he didn't want to go outside; he wanted to be alone. There were too many people here now, it had been better before. It had been the same at the Orphanage, there was hardly any time to be alone. Living alone in Vancouver was sometimes lonely, but it was better than never being alone. It made sense to be lonely when he was alone, but it didn't make sense to be lonely with people; that's what he would be, if he went outside. "Crap," he whispered. "Damn." What if he walked outside and shouted that, wouldn't Mr. Fraser be furious? He smiled and whispered again, whispered every single bad word he knew. Then he slapped four mosquitoes on his neck and looked at the bloody smears on his hand.

Mr. Fraser pulled back the tent flap and peered in. He untied the netting, entered and carefully tied it behind him. "It's an oven in here! Aren't you boiling?" He looked hot and tired and uncomfortable as he sat down on his cot. He didn't wait for Jeremy to answer, just continued, in a low voice, "Thank you for doing that, Son. I wouldn't have put you on the spot if I hadn't thought it was for the best."

Jeremy said nothing. He couldn't think of anything to say and even if he could have, he wouldn't have said anything.

Mr. Fraser took off his hat and wiped his forehead. He blinked and his moustache twitched. He swiped at a mosquito. So did Jeremy. Mr. Fraser lowered his voice even more. "I can't explain now. I will later. I just wanted to say thank you." He stood up and put on his hat. Jeremy met his eyes and held them, then nodded slightly, once, before turning his head away. Mr. Fraser left the tent and re-tied the netting.

Jeremy still didn't have a clue what was going on, but the *thank you* had been nice — not that it made up for forcing him to show his gold. Making him look like a stupid kid. He sat up and slapped more mosquitoes. Well, he'd show them, he'd pan every chance he got — in fact, there might even be gold here. He'd split wood for the cook stove, then he'd —

Bob came in, followed by Ben. "Sorry about that, Jer," Ben said. "Those Grants arrived just after you left. They're really bad news. Gassman said their crew —"

"They might hear you," Jeremy said flatly.

"Nah, they're packing up," Bob said. "They can't wait to get up the creek, thanks to you." Jeremy's lip curled into a sneer.

Ben continued, "They arrived after the Cle Elm bunch was scattered — Gassman says they've run into them three times and wherever they are, bad things happen. None of them warned us so we were pleasant, but the Grants wanted to know far too much and were making noises about joining us. We had a tough morning. I was mainly out of it, sawing, but I saw them poking and prodding into everything, why, they even opened a crate! We were all working so it was hard to keep our eyes on them. Not that they offered to work. You were a godsend when you came along. And to actually have some gold!" Ben grinned.

"Yeah, I should have given you every flake I found," interjected Bob. "Made that creek look like a real lode!"

"They practically wet their pants over your poke!" Ben added. "You saved our bacon, Jer. They'll go up that creek and not follow us, thanks to you."

Jeremy looked at them smiling at him. Again, he didn't know what to say. Saving their bacon was nice, but the creek — He heard his tune, *I've found gold, gold, gold,* in his head. "It's hot in here. I was just —" his voice cracked and he coughed " —going to split some wood for supper."

"It sure is hot," Bob echoed, sounding relieved. He patted Jeremy on the shoulder. Jeremy stood stiffly still. "Anyway . . ." He patted again.

"Back to the instruments of torture," Ben joshed, pulling aside the netting. With a last lame pat, Bob left too. Jeremy followed them out. Compared to the heat in the tent, the river bank was cool.

22

Sat. 9th July
Off early & struck forks of river about mile beyond last camp &
took dinner. Went 3 to 4 miles when Mac induced all to camp
about 3 p.m.

Jeremy was the only one not irritated with Mac's insistence on quitting early; he'd have hours more to pan especially now when they had finally reached the north fork of the Macmillan. Every day, when he was not needed for other chores, he found a likely looking back eddy or creek mouth and tried his luck. The pickings were slim, as the men they'd met today had said, but Jeremy was content with whatever flakes he found. Slowly they were amalgamating into a small bulge that he could feel through the leather of his poke.

As he panned, he mused about Mr. Fraser's bad temper. Ever since those men had forgotten to bring their mail upriver, over two weeks ago now, Mr. Fraser acted as if he was mad at everyone. Like today. Mac couldn't help it if he had a toothache. His cheek was really swollen and he was swigging Perry Davis' Painkiller like water. So what right did Mr. Fraser have to get mad?

When he wasn't outright mad, he just didn't talk. Or he ordered everybody to do what he wanted — like how he'd limited them to firing only one shot on Dominion Day. Only one shot for the biggest holiday of the year, next to Christmas! "We don't want to run low on ammunition," he'd said. Mac had protested, "The Americans will think we're stingy and unpatriotic." Looking back now, Jeremy agreed that the Americans probably had. They'd said nothing at the time, but on their holiday three days later, they'd fired twenty-one shots.

Jeremy was the only one to spend his spare time prospecting. The others were waiting until they got to McHenry's Pass, as he had come to think of it. Even if he weren't finding the occasional small nugget and dust, he would still be panning, he thought. It was exciting, searching for likely gravel, washing it, seeing what was left. He'd learned that the best gravel lodged on the inside bends of the creeks or on the downstream side of ridges in the creekbed. He'd figured out that he had to look up on the banks also in case the creek had eroded its bed. When there was no creek near their camp, he panned the bays and eddies of the North Macmillan.

The continuous gurgling and splash of water was soothing — as long he wasn't tracking a loaded boat upstream. The sun warmed his back through his shirt as he squatted, washing dirt in the customary mesmerizing motion. Around him were trees and brush and rocks and mountains that stretched for hundreds of miles in all directions and, even a quarter of a mile from camp, he felt as if he were the only person in the world.

It was a funny feeling, he thought, because it made him feel as if nothing he could ever do would matter yet at the same time he felt that everything he did — his footsteps, his discarded heaps of dirt, his scars on the bank — was monumentally important.

If the men paid any attention, it was just to tease him. Gassman had started calling him *Prospector*, which Fuller and Miller had shortened to *Pros.* When anyone asked how his panning was going, he always answered, "fine," even when he'd found nothing. It wasn't a lie, Jeremy realized, because even nothing was fine with him. There was always the next pan of dirt.

Sometimes, like now, when he found over twenty colours to a pan, he continued in the same spot, digging deeper and wider. He'd given up any hope that he could convince his crew to stay put and work these areas; all they wanted was to get to McHenry's gold. Of course, he did too, but still . . .

He stood up and tried to dab the sweat off his forehead without dislodging his mosquito netting. For a week now everyone's latest attire had included a large square of netting worn over the head and anchored by a hat. He was hot beneath it, and the ends scratched his chest where he'd tucked them into his shirt. Jeremy still laughed when he saw the others; Ben had said, "We look like characters out of a Jules Verne novel."

"Or a beekeepers' convention," Rimmer had added.

Jeremy wasn't convinced the discomfort of the netting was worth it. For every mosquito or blackfly it discouraged, four were undeterred. Once something got under the net, he might as well not be wearing it. And nothing discouraged no-see-ums.

Behind him were rustlings and crunchings as if someone was approaching through the bush. He turned, wondering who else would be here.

The animal looked equally startled to see him. A big dark brown bear, it reared up on its hind feet as if to get a better look.

"Get away!" Jeremy flung his loaded, dripping gold pan. "Get out of here!"

The pan hit the bear in the chest then clattered through the bushes. The bear growled and lowered itself to all fours. Jeremy scooped up some rocks and flung them, yelling. For an instant, the bear looked as if it would charge, but with a shake of its head, it turned and loped off the way it had come.

Jeremy yelled a few more times then found himself trembling and gasping for breath. He sat down on the low bank then immediately stood up and turned around. What if the bear returned and he had his back to it? He leaned his shaky arms and knees against the bank and took deep breaths. He'd never been this scared. At least not since Skagway, at least, not since the raft overturned.

He'd also lost his goldpan. The goldpan with gravel in it. What if it had contained an enormous nugget? He should find it, but the bear might be coming back. If we'd kept the dogs with us, he thought, they'd have barked. He hesitated, listening for the bear, but could hear only the creek. He could borrow someone's gold pan. Then he scolded himself, vaulted up the low bank and pushed aside the thick bushes. No bear. He searched the bushes and ground. No bear. The pan couldn't be very far away, as the bear had been so close. Close enough to smell, he remembered now, rank like a fish-eating pig. There was his pan, caught between some branches. He wiggled it out. No bear. The goldpan was empty, of course. He couldn't distinguish the gravel he'd dug from the gravel on the ground.

Rose bushes grew over his head. Wind rattling cottonwood and aspen leaves obscured the sound of the creek, even though he knew he was so close. It had to be behind him — or had he turned around? He concentrated on sounds, a bird, bees in the roses, mosquitoes, a bear? the wind — It dropped momentarily and he picked up the gurgle of the creek to his right. Its sound was so constant he'd stopped hearing it.

Jeremy pushed through the undergrowth, no bear, and down the bank. He came out ten feet upstream from his pick and shovel. He frowned; he'd swear he hadn't taken more than a few steps. How easy to get lost, no one would ever find you. All those people going up and down the rivers, but a hundred yards away from the banks and there's no one. Just bears, wolves and cougars. A wave of fear rolled over him again and he longed for the safety of the city. Or the dogs. He really missed the dogs.

Now he had a dilemma: he'd found two pans with twenty colours and wanted to keep panning but the bear might come back. Or another bear might show up. He looked around — nothing. Were the bushes rustling again or was that just the wind? He shovelled gravel into his pan, trying to keep one eye on the bank.

He could ask Mr. Fraser to teach him how to shoot, then he could shoot bears. But no one would lend him a gun, he was pretty sure. The sun was hot on his back and the creek water cold on his boots as he swished his pan around, standing up. Before he bent over to scoop in more water, he looked up the banks on either side. He could have hit the bear with his shovel or pick, if he'd been able to get to them. They were leaning against the bank. He sloshed over to them, dragged his shovel to the creek edge, then leaned it against his side with his arm around it. Panning was even more awkward, especially bending to scoop water. In the end, he propped the shovel against a rock within reach.

Jeremy collected the few flakes on the end of his wet finger and rubbed them into his poke. He loaded up his pan again and stirred the contents with his finger, hoping, as he always did, to pick out an enormous nugget. Then water and sloshing back and forth, around and around. Ten or fifteen minutes later, he sorted through the black sand caught in the angle of the pan's side and bottom and again wiped the few, minute flakes into his poke.

Hunger made him realize it was probably dinnertime. He glanced at the sun but it was high overhead as usual so he packed up and waded down the creek toward camp, looking and listening for the bear.

When he arrived, he spotted Mac sitting on a rock, holding his palm over his jaw. "How's your tooth?" Jeremy asked.

"Same," Mac muttered over the heel of his hand.

Jeremy's tongue was investigating his own teeth. He didn't

think he'd ever had a toothache. "You look more swollen to me," he offered, then he caught Mac's scowl and said, "Oh, sorry."

Rimmer arrived and held out a pill and a cup of water to Mac. "We're nearly ready. Take this morphine."

"Ready for what?" Jeremy asked, as Mac took the pill and cup.

"I'm going to pull his tooth. He can't go on like this."

"Oh, are you a dentist?" Jeremy had never been to a dentist.

"Of course I'm not a dentist!" Rimmer barked. "A dentist would have proper dental tools! Don't ask dumb questions!"

Jeremy figured that maybe Rimmer didn't want to pull Mac's tooth. Perhaps he should get some food and go back to his colours. Though there was the bear.

In front of the tent, Mr. Fraser tended a fire under a steaming pot. "Hello," Jeremy greeted, "Are you cooking? What's for dinner?"

"I'm boiling pliers." Jeremy started to smile at the idea of boiled pliers for dinner, but Mr. Fraser frowned severely. "Sterilizing them. To pull Mac's dad-blamed tooth out of his jaw so we can get on with what we're supposed to be doing."

"Oh." Jeremy contemplated the last part of Mr. Fraser's sentence. Mac's toothache had not improved Mr. Fraser's temper. "Is there anything you want me to do?"

"No." Jeremy hefted his shovel and pick and started off. "Wait!" Jeremy turned. "Bob and Ben have gone hunting. You have to help me hold Mac still." Jeremy nodded and put down his implements.

Mr. Fraser removed the pot of pliers from the fire. Rimmer led Mac, who was reeling as if drunk and fumbling with his shirt buttons, to a blanket half-spread over a log. Rimmer helped him get his shirt off, then lie down with his head on the log. Mr. Fraser placed a folded blanket under Mac's head. "Comfy?" he asked.

"Mmm," Mac slurred, his eyes closed. "Just get the damn thing out."

"Which tooth is it?" asked Rimmer.

Mac took a long time to answer. "Third upper from the back. Upper." He seemed to collapse from the effort of speaking.

Rimmer looked at the still-steaming pot and pliers. "Those are too hot to handle. Dump the water out."

"No. I'm keeping the water for a hot compress." Mr. Fraser fished out the pliers with two forks. Clouds had been gathering for some time and the evening was cooling down. Shortly Rimmer could hold the pliers.

They were large pliers to fit in a mouth, Jeremy thought. They looked well used. "Whose pliers are they?"

"One of the Cle Elm's," replied Mr. Fraser.

Gassman's, Jeremy guessed. He was a blacksmith.

Rimmer looked from the pliers to Mac, sprawled with his eyes closed, to Mr. Fraser and Jeremy and back to Mac. "James, you kneel by his right side and Jer, you take his left. Hold him down or else give him your arm to grip. Just keep him still at all costs. I don't know how much pressure I can use and if the tooth's really rotten it might break in his jaw. That'd be a real mess."

They positioned themselves with Rimmer on the log to Mac's right. Jeremy realized that, if he'd kept on panning the creek, he could have missed this chore.

"Open," Rimmer instructed and Jeremy grabbed Mac's arm.

"Rimmer's just looking right now," Mr. Fraser pointed out. Jeremy relaxed.

Rimmer straightened up. Mac closed his mouth and swallowed.

"I see the tooth. Now I'll try to get the pliers on it and test it, Ready?" Mr. Fraser and Jeremy both nodded. "How you doing, Mac?" Rimmer asked.

Mac groaned. "Get it out before the morphine wears off." He opened his mouth again.

All Jeremy could see was Rimmer's hand, the plier handles and the back of his head. Mac's arm felt tense and knotted. The procedure seemed to be taking a long time. A raven chirred from a branch and a mosquito buzzed near Jeremy's ear. Suddenly Rimmer's arm muscles contracted and Mac's back arched. His feet kicked as if trying to run away. He grabbed Jeremy's and Mr. Fraser's arms and emitted an awful gurgling sound.

Rimmer sat back. Clasped in the pliers was Mac's bloody tooth. Jeremy was assailed by such an over-powering stench of rotting flesh that he turned his head and held his breath. Mac let go of Jeremy's arm and struggled to sit up. Blood and pus poured from his mouth and the air filled with even stronger stench. Jeremy fought against gagging.

"That's good, let it drain," said Mr. Fraser. He dipped a cloth in the hot water, rang it out, folded it and handed it to Mac. "Hold this on your cheek. Jeremy, get me a cup of that sterilized water and I'll mix up the mouth wash."

Jeremy dashed off as fast as he could, escaping the smell before he threw up. When he returned, Mr. Fraser opened the package of antiseptic and shook crystals into the cup. He swirled the mixture around. Mac had tears on his cheeks and blood on his chin and chest. Blood stained the ground beside the blanket.

"I think I got it all," Rimmer said, contemplating the tooth he still held in the pliers.

"Looks like it," Mr. Fraser agreed. He handed the mouth wash to Mac who rinsed and spat slightly lighter blood. Jeremy backed up; he didn't like blood and gore and pus, he realized.

"Stoke up the fire and heat this water for compresses," Mr. Fraser ordered and Jeremy escaped again.

When he next saw Mac, he was cleaned up, re-shirted and dozing on his cot, holding a compress to his swollen cheek. After supper, Rimmer gave him another morphine pill and he seemed knocked out for the night.

When Jeremy finally crawled into his sleeping bag, he realized he'd told no one about his bear encounter.

23

Sat. 16th July 1898

Rained through night till 8 a.m. All very tired so decided to rest & do some moose hunting. Repairing clothes etc. Showers through day. Wilson & Charlie out p.m. Fraser & Fuller got 12 trout, fair size. After supper Wilson, Mac, John & Charlie went out hunting.

Sunday 17th July

They came in about 3 a.m. to get boat & help to bring in a moose Wilson had shot. Got her (a young cow) to camp about 5 a.m. was very fine & dressed about 600 lbs. Day very warm

Friday 12th August

Fine & warm & hazy. River crooked narrow & climbing rapidly so that the riffles were steep, swift & close together. Water shallow so boat had to be lifted over. All hands worked hard & were about played out when we struck the forks about 6 p.m. & head of navigation on this stream. Think we are 260 miles up Macmillan & 335 miles from Selkirk.

Jeremy was elated when Mac announced, "We've brought the boats far enough. Now's the time to start prospecting."

The river had narrowed during the past week and they'd been hauling the boats uphill as well. The water had become colder, swifter and shallower and the rocky riversides made tracking slow and disagreeable. Ahead of them, the Macmillan narrowed even more and appeared to enter a canyon.

"Now you have to tell us how we're to recognize your pass when we find it," Mr. Fraser ordered Mac.

"There's a knob on the mountain to the right of it." Mac pulled out a pencil and sketched a picture on a flat rock. "There are two mountains to the left that go up like this, and the knob to right. McHenry swore you couldn't miss the knob."

"Oh great!" Gassman exploded. "Never believe anyone who swears you can't miss something!"

Mac frowned. "It was practically his deathbed statement!"

"Did he give any distances or direction?" Bob asked.

"He came southwest to meet the river so that makes it northeast, and he said about a day's tramp."

"Did he tramp fast or slow? That could be a difference of fifteen or twenty miles," Bob calculated.

"Did he say where he hit the river?" asked Osborne.

"I assumed the headwaters. He mentioned a slough. He could see the river when he came out of the pass."

If it really was this river, Jeremy thought.

"Best we break into parties, go out for a few days and then rendezvous back here," Mr. Fraser stated.

Osborne nodded. "That'll give a better idea of the country."

"Good idea," said Mac, and so it was decided.

After putting together enough food and gear, Rogers' and Anamosa's crews started up a creek that came in from the north. Wilson's crew continued upriver in their small boat, accompanied by Mac and Rimmer, who planned to branch off further up. Protesting only mildly, Ben agreed to remain in the main camp to guard their gear and to smoke the rest of the moose meat. He had law-school thoughts he could think to keep him busy, the others pointed out.

Ben ferried Mr. Fraser, Bob and Jeremy across the river and, after good-byes, they slipped into their packs and headed north-east. Each pack weighed about fifty pounds, not including picks, shovels and gold pans.

Bob took the lead, whacking the underbrush with his machete, then came Mr. Fraser, compass in hand for easy reference. Jeremy was last. Within steps, his shovel caught on a branch and the handle banged his thigh. He tried to remember how high the shovel protruded and to duck lower under the next branch. As they moved inland from the river, the cottonwoods and marshy grass gave way to thin, dark spruce interspersed with clumps of aspen. Bare mountaintops towered in the distance, steeper here than on the Pelly. Prickly rosebushes were the main undergrowth, but the flowers had finished now and the hips were reddening. The trees grew a manageable distance apart and, with Bob clearing trail, the only thing Jeremy had to worry about was overhanging branches.

Within a mile his pack straps dug into his shoulderblades. He tried to ease them with his thumbs; then he had no free hand to steady his gold pan as it clanked against the shovel and his thigh. Still, this hike was not as bad as the White Pass, he consoled himself, could never be as bad as the White Pass, though there were mosquitoes and heat. And he was in much better shape he congratulated himself, noting his bicep bulge through his shirt.

"There's a gully at the bottom of that benchland," Mr. Fraser announced. "It'll be easier walking and we can see what the prospects are."

"Looks like it heads southeast," Bob observed.

Mr. Fraser snorted. "Between you and me and the gatepost, if two spires on one side and knob on the other is the only description Mac has of this mythical Pass, we don't have a hope in a chicken coop of ever finding it! We might as well see what prospects are generally." Bob smiled ruefully, as if agreeing. "This is unmapped country even if it has been explored, which I don't think it has," Mr. Fraser continued.

"It's possible McHenry lied," Bob added, "Thinking he might come back himself."

Mr. Fraser nodded. "It's extremely possible."

Jeremy contemplated their cynicism. It hadn't occurred to him that Mac didn't know exactly how to find McHenry's gold. But then, Mac had been definite about rafting and look what happened. Still, Jeremy fought disappointment. McHenry's forty pounds of gold was much more than the flakes he'd found. He said slowly, "It's possible we will find the Pass." Bob and Mr. Fraser nodded but their eyebrows were dubiously raised. "It's possible we'll find the load of gold," he persisted.

"It's always possible," Bob reassured.

"We have only a month or six weeks till the snow flies," Mr. Fraser observed.

"It's possible that we'll find the Pass," Jeremy repeated, trying to keep his tone reasonable.

"Possible, but I'll put my money on improbable, knowing Mac." Mr. Fraser's eyebrows had formed straight lines over narrowed eyes.

"So we might as well carry on," said Jeremy, still reasonable. "Isn't a gully at the bottom of benchland a good sign of prospects?"

Both men smiled. "It is. And — we might as well carry on." Bob turned toward the gully.

They slid down a sandbank and walked along the rocky gulch. Jeremy kept his eyes open for signs of gold, but there was no water here to pan. Although they followed the shade cast by the cliff, heatwaves shimmered off the rocks. The cliff blocked the breeze they'd previously enjoyed and their sweat attracted even more mosquitoes. Some got in under Jeremy's net headgear. Between swipes at them, he sipped from his water bottle.

After a few hours, during which the gully veered from southeast back to east, they came to a little creek. Jeremy removed his pack, hat and mosquito netting then pulled his shirt over his head and flung it into the icy water. He sighed with bliss as he wiped his face and neck and pulled his shirt back on. Mr. Fraser and Bob wet their neckerchiefs and retied them after they'd mopped their faces. Each drank as much as he could hold and then refilled his water bottle. Trees grew on the banks of the creek a few yards away and they sat in the shade and ate bread and moosemeat. Then they panned a few shovelfuls of gravel.

"Nothing here," said Mr. Fraser. "Just galena."

Jeremy looked up from his pan. "What's that?"

"This." Mr. Fraser shoved a bluish rock at him. It glittered in the sun. "Lead ore."

"Lead's good, all those lead pencils."

"They aren't lead," said Bob, "they're graphite."

Jeremy turned back to his pan. "Why're they called lead then?"

"Who knows?" Mr. Fraser threw the galena into the trees. "Time to move on."

Jeremy examined what remained in the angle of his pan: some black sand and four tiny flakes. "I've got some gold!"

"I keep telling you, *Prospector*," Bob scoffed, "a few flakes that small are nothing! It'll take longer than your lifetime to make a living from these pickings! Come on, we're looking for the bigger lode!" He picked up his pack and followed Mr. Fraser up the creek.

Jeremy scowled as he pulled out his poke and rubbed the four flakes inside, but he hastily packed up and followed too.

It was cooler walking up the creek, but the mosquitoes liked the water. Jeremy had bites on his bites. Every half mile they washed some pans, but even he found nothing. After some time ascending the creek, they noticed that the boulders, around which the creek sought its path, were getting bigger. The thin, short trees grew farther apart and tiny flowers sprinkled the clearings between them.

"Might as well put our pans away," said Mr. Fraser. "We're near-ly at the tree line."

"We can leave our packs here, have a looksee and pick them up on the way back," Bob stated.

Jeremy shucked his off and rubbed his sore shoulders. Perhaps he shouldn't have wet his shirt; that made the packstraps rub more. Walking up what had turned into a rocky mountain creek was hard enough without a pack. "But what if we see McHenry's Pass and we want to go on?"

Bob snorted. "There's a law against anything being that easy!"

Mr. Fraser said, "We have to rendezvous with the others so we'll have to backtrack." Then he added, "Don't get your hopes too high, Son."

Son. Jeremy felt his face flush. That was the second time Mr. Fraser called him *Son.* It was a bit embarrassing, but he liked it. He smiled at Mr. Fraser's back.

As Jeremy followed the men, he wondered why they'd come to Klondike — to this unmapped area — if they didn't really believe in McHenry's mine. Why not go somewhere they knew had gold?

They stopped a few paces above the treeline. The mountain peak loomed half a mile above them, but its slope looked easy to climb. Jeremy glanced back, the way Mr. Fraser was facing. Miles and miles of trees fused into a green blur, which became a bluish blur and then a jagged purple blur on the horizon. Bob said, "Might as well go to the top and see what we can see."

"I'm bushed, I'll wait for you here." Mr. Fraser sat down. "Take this to get some bearings." He handed Bob the compass.

Jeremy started up the rock and shale. It'd be grand to be the first to see McHenry's Pass. The sun reflected off the rocks and he could feel their heat through his boots. A constant breeze dried his sweat. At least there were no mosquitoes up here.

Behind him, Bob said, "There's an animal trail, see it? Moun-tain goat or sheep probably. It'll be the easiest way."

Jeremy followed the faint trail up to a small, level area just below the highest peak — "the mountain's shoulder," Bob said, when he arrived. From there, they could see in all directions. Mountains, mountains and more mountains, some cradling small lakes or creeks, some splaying up from plateaus, some snow-topped or wearing low clouds. Jeremy felt overwhelmed as he slowly rotated.

"It's like there's no other people in the whole world," he whispered.

Bob clapped his shoulder. "Makes a man feel insignificant." Jeremy nodded. "And grateful," added Bob, a minute later.

Grateful, Jeremy mulled, contemplating the expanse. Grateful for Bob and Mr. Fraser, grateful he wasn't alone, he decided, in this wilderness. Eventually he said, "I don't see two peaks with a round knob to the right, though, do you?"

"No. That creek over there," Bob was looking northwest, "is undoubtedly the head of the river the others went up. So," he turned east again, "looks like our creek carries on around this mountain. We should keep up it tomorrow."

They picked their way down the goat trail. Mr. Fraser asked, "See any sign of the Peel River?"

"No, but there's another range of mountains northeast we can reach if we follow the creek."

They returned to their packs and decided to camp there. Jeremy gathered wood, Bob made a fire and Mr. Fraser laid one tarpaulin on the ground and rigged the other over it with ropes. After eating beans with moosemeat and toasted bread washed down with cups of tea, they stretched out in their sleeping bags. Jeremy fell asleep in seconds.

The others were still snoring when he awoke. It was hard to know what time it was when the sun was always up — he'd thought that every morning this summer — but he felt awake so he pulled on his boots and jacket, crawled out of the makeshift tent, peed, then started a fire with wood he'd piled last night. As he filled the teapot at the creek, he sniffed moisture in the air and noted the heavy dew. It was cold so it must be early. He threw some bigger pieces of wood on the kindling and propped up the blackened pot.

Mr. Fraser emerged and went off behind a tree. "Cloudy," he observed, when he returned. "Smells like it might storm." Mr. Fraser was always commenting on the weather. Jeremy'd bet he even wrote it down in his journal.

Mr. Fraser got out the frying pan, bacon and pancake mix he'd made at the main camp. He hacked slices off the bacon, put them in the pan and placed it on the fire. He dumped mix into his gold pan and added water from the creek. As the bacon sizzled, Jeremy swallowed saliva.

Bob crawled out, ran his hands through his hair and beard, went off and presently returned. "Mmm," he nodded.

The water in the pot was boiling so Jeremy threw in tea leaves and moved it to a stone to steep. Mr. Fraser turned the bacon, shoved it to one side and poured in some batter. Bob stood and blinked. He and Ben were the slowest to wake up, but Bob never stayed in bed until he had.

Soon, all three were eating from their gold pans. Jeremy felt like a real miner. He'd been carrying a plate and bowl to his pack when Mr. Fraser had passed him. "That's extra weight. Take a fork, spoon and mug. You can eat out of your gold pan."

As he ate, he thought that it was grand how many uses there were for a gold pan — eating, mixing batter, baking, washing, shaving — if any of them bothered with that — and of course, prospecting.

They were packing up when a gigantic boom rolled overhead. Jeremy dropped the frying pan he was scrubbing with sand, then ducked as lightning flashed. Immediately large raindrops splattered. He dashed to the tarp Bob had just started to unrope and joined the others under it. Thunder and lightning repeated simultaneously. "Right overhead," Mr. Fraser yelled. Sheets of rain fell around them, split only by rumbles, booms and yellow flashes. In the seconds between strikes, their surroundings were darker than they'd been in months.

Jeremy's heart battered his ribs. "Are we safe here?"

"No," said Bob.

"Then let's go!"

"There isn't any safe place!" Mr. Fraser yelled. At the next boom and flash, Jeremy ducked. Mr. Fraser continued, "Under trees isn't safe because lightning hits the highest point. In the open isn't safe because you're the highest point!"

Bob said, "I knew someone who was killed just by sitting on a root. A strike came down the tree and up the root. The chap didn't even know he was sitting on a root." Bob paused for the next volley. "Rest of us weren't hit. Took a while to figure out how he'd got it. A shallow root. Real shame." He shook his head.

Jeremy felt the ground for roots. He hugged his knees and bent over them, trying to make himself as small as possible.

"Roots here are very shallow," Mr. Fraser commented, "Since they're all on top of the permafrost."

"Tom McAllister," Bob went on, remembering. "We were out hunting when a storm came up. Poor old Tom. His hand fused to his gun barrel, we couldn't get it off."

Jeremy said, *Shut up, Bob,* in his head, then winced and shuddered at an especially loud crack. How could they not be as scared as he was? Too scared to talk. Should he lie down so he was low? Then he'd be covering more earth — more roots.

Mr. Fraser poked at the pool forming in the tarp above them. Water poured off and trickled in. Bob kicked some dirt in its way to make a dam. "Good thing it's raining," he observed. "In case a strike starts a fire."

"I remember McAllister," Mr. Fraser said. "Had the smartest pair of matched chestnut mares in Port Arthur. Rightly proud of them. Poor Tom, what a way to go. I was in Winnipeg at the time."

There was another boom and rumble. Jeremy squeezed his eyes shut and burrowed into his knees. A cold wind blew rain under the tarp.

"Ah," said Bob. "That was a bit of a lag before the flash. It's moving on."

"You can always tell when there's going to be a storm," Mr. Fraser said. "There's a metallic smell to the air and it's too still."

"All the birds and animals know," Bob added.

I didn't, Jeremy thought, daring to open his eyes. A bright flash closed them again.

"Definitely a lag," Bob said in a satisfied tone.

Thunder rumbled and banged.

"But you can't tell which way the storm's going yet," Mr. Fraser added. "We don't want to tramp back into it."

As quickly as it had begun, the seconds between flashes and sounds lengthened and they watched the storm move southward. Slowly Jeremy recovered, but with each rattle of thunder his heart battered. We could have been killed, he thought as he resumed packing, we really could have been killed.

24

Friday 19 August 1898

Froze hard last night & boots, sox &c frozen, put them on wet, got breakfast & started up to head of valley. Found pass into next, followed this & up to head of that where another pass let us through into another gorge down which we tramped striking east branch of main river about noon & about 2 miles above where we expect to meet Mac. Went down there & not finding him had lunch & put our packs up a tree & started for camp to meet him. Walked 4 hours (10 miles?) to camp & found him there, feet too sore to travel. He allowed them to get sore and raw through care-lessness. Ben cooked & baked & I got wood & washed sox. Saw large brown bear on way in 30 yds from us. He appeared to be going to attack us but we whistled & astonished him so he let us pass.

Sat. 20th August 1898

Ben & I intended starting out this morning but we slept cold last night & our boots & clothes need so much mending took until noon to get partially prepared. Then rest of prospectors came in so we did not go out. Wilson crew came in yesterday just ahead of us & Rogers was in camp. Day fine, cold at night, frost.

No gold. While Jeremy washed the black sand a few bends upriver from the main camp, he wondered exactly what the men meant when they said *no gold*. Whenever that was pronounced in his presence, he scraped flakes into his poke, which now contained a definite bulge. Obviously, *no gold* meant *not enough gold* if a pan had to hold over twenty flakes before it was worth the trouble, and there was the time Bob had scoffed at even twenty flakes. How much gold would they consider worth the trouble?

No one had seen a sign of McHenry's Pass. As the various groups returned to camp shaking their heads, one man after the other said to Mac, "Are you sure you've got the description right? Sure he didn't tell you anything more? Sure we're in the general area?" Mac's responses grew more and more explosive and he limp-stomped away, looking surly.

It wasn't much of a description, Jeremy realized, reflecting on all the mountains and passes he'd viewed while out with Mr. Fraser and Bob. It'd be great to find McHenry's load, but they weren't going anywhere right now and he didn't have anything to mend, so he might as well pan.

When Bob tried the other bank yesterday, Jeremy didn't believe he hadn't found some colours. He bet Bob hadn't looked very hard. The pans Jeremy washed yesterday contained flakes and today's pans also. Not many, maybe three, maybe fifteen, and they were small flakes, but still gold was gold, wasn't it? He picked six flakes out now and added them to his poke.

He'd like to find as much gold as the money he'd have made if he'd stayed in Skagway selling newspapers. One hundred papers a day at thirty cents — thirty dollars — less his cost, three dollars, and the fifteen dollars Soapy would have taken — he should find twelve dollars worth of gold a day. He didn't think he was doing that. Eight flakes in this pan. He shovelled in more gravel and water.

Then there was the number of days he'd have sold papers if he'd stayed in Skagway. Say half of February and five more months — somewhere around 165 times 12 — wow, nearly two thousand dollars!

He doubted he had that much, that'd be more than enough to live on for years, the way he lived. But did he want to live on the streets anymore? At first it had been better than the Hammonds', but now a tent was better than the street. Even a tent covered in snow.

Today's weather was the mosquitoes' favourite: cloudy, humid and still. Sweat tickled down his face and off the tip of his nose. He rubbed his forehead with his arm, then had to pry the stuck netting loose from his nose and cheeks. Before refilling his pan, he scooped water and splashed it over his head. Clouds of mosquitoes swarmed away, only to return as the water dripped off. When he stopped to listen, there were no sounds but the river's gurgle and the mosquitoes' whirrs.

Oh, twenty flakes! Should he tell the others? Nah, they'd just say they were too small. What had Bob said — he wouldn't live long enough to get rich at this rate?

Jeremy stood up and looked at the sand bar he was panning. He scraped the loose gravel away with his shovel and looked again. The black sand he'd been working extended in a streak along the bank at the back edge of the bar. Loose gravel and lighter sand hid most of it. He prodded the depth of the black sand. A few inches until he hit clay, but the streak must be ten feet long.

He set to work at the downstream end and shortly examined his pan. Three little nuggets among the coarse grains and dust. These were the biggest bits of gold he'd found, different from the previous flakes. He put them in his poke and washed another pan. Would the men think this gold was no gold?

Jeremy worked up the paystreak, finding dust and coarse grains. After picking out the bigger bits, he tilted his pan and stared at the remaining sand, rusty with gold dust. He stirred it with his finger but couldn't isolate the fine grains. There must be a way to separate it, he thought, as he regretfully let it all wash out.

A few more pans and his poke was nearly full. It was so heavy that when he put it in his pocket, it dragged down that side of his pants. He took it out and put it in his pack.

Back at camp, he found Bob sitting on the chopping block surrounded by scraps of the mooseskin canoe and a pot of warm glue, resoling his boots. Jeremy rolled up a log and sat down beside him. The putrid smell of glue mingled with the warm yeasty smell of bread baking in the cook stove. Jeremy hoped the bread was nearly done; he was, as usual, hungry.

"I was thinking —" he began.

Bob frowned. "We've told you that's dangerous."

Jeremy smacked his tongue in mock irritation, as he'd learned to do when teased. "Not all gold's nuggets or flakes. What do miners do when it's really fine?"

"You mean like dust?"

"Yeah, and mixed with sand."

"Mercury," said Bob. "Gold amalgamates with mercury. Then you squeeze it in a wet canvas or chamois to get out the excess and then you heat it. The mercury evaporates and you're left with gold."

Jeremy considered. "Too bad we don't have any."

Bob looked at him sharply. "Why? Have you found gold dust?"

"Oh — I just meant — what if McHenry's load is in dust, then we should have mercury."

Bob put down one boot and picked up the other. "Didn't you get a complete prospector's outfit in Fort Selkirk?"

"I don't know. What do you mean?"

"All prospectors carry mercury. If your outfit's complete, you should have a bottle marked *Hg* or *Quicksilver*."

"Oh, I hadn't noticed!" Jeremy started up.

Bob looked at him. "One thing about mercury though —"

"What?" Jeremy was itching to get to his packs.

"Oh," he waggled his boot dismissively, "If it's for McHenry's lode you don't need to know until we find it. And that might be never." His eyebrow arched.

"Oh come on, Bob, I'm just trying to learn something!"

Bob gave him a knowing look and quirked a corner of his lips. Jeremy blushed; Bob knew he had a reason to use mercury now. But Bob didn't pursue it. He placed his boot on the leather and took out a pencil to trace the pattern.

"You have to stay upwind when heating mercury so you don't breathe the fumes. They're deadly. Another thing," Bob added, "you can use a magnet to separate magnetite, which is a lot of the black sand. Do that before you fool around with mercury." He drew around the sole's outline.

"Thanks." Jeremy started toward his tent, then stopped and came back. "What do you heat mercury in?"

Bob looked up and raised his other eyebrow. "In the field you use your shovel. Just be sure to stay upwind. *Prospector.*"

Jeremy found a bottle marked *Hg* in the box he'd acquired at Fort Selkirk. There was also a magnet, but the magnet he'd found in the abandoned camp looked stronger. He put them in his pockets then searched for some canvas and an empty container. In the kitchen gear, he found a nearly empty tea tin, poured the tea into a new tin and took the container back to his tent, where he emptied his poke. He tried to do it slowly and quietly, but the gold made such loud rattles he thought anyone around would hear. It covered the bottom of the tin. He ran his finger through it before he replaced the lid and put the tin in his prospector's box.

Passing the stove table, he cut off half the cooling bread and ate it as he returned to his paystreak.

Once he'd washed a pan down to a line of black sand and gold dust, he held the magnet over it. Little black grains leapt up like fleas and clung. He tried scraping them off, but they just moved farther along the magnet. Thinking he could rub them off with the cloth, he put the magnet on the ground while he reached for the cloth. When he turned back, the magnet had attracted so many more grains its outline was fuzzy. Jeremy sighed in exasperation as he wiped the magnet clean. By wrapping the magnet in the cloth and passing it over the pan, he separated the rest of the magnetite. When he removed the cloth from the magnet's field, the grains fell to the ground. Then he set the magnet down while he got out the mercury — bad idea! The magnet was again covered with black fuzz.

There wasn't much matter remaining in the angle of his pan so he decided to wash more sand before using the mercury. This time he placed the magnet underneath his pan where it clung to the bottom. Instantly, a pile of black grains collected. Jeremy moved the magnet and the grains moved too. He pulled the magnet away, set it carefully on the cloth and brushed out the magnetite. That was easier, he thought.

Now he uncorked the glass bottle and poured a few drops of mercury into the pan. He tipped it back and forth and watched the silver balls dart around. Quicksilver was a good name. When he added another drop of mercury, all the little balls rolled into one clump. He picked it out — it felt smooth and slippery and his fingers wanted to play with it — and placed it on the cloth. He rinsed his pan and filled it again.

Jeremy continued in this way until the mercury bottle was empty and he had an amalgam of about four inches in diameter on the cloth. Had Bob said to squeeze it through a wet cloth? He hoped so; everything was wet. He put the magnet in his pocket and twisted the ends of the cloth around the amalgam. He grunted with effort as he twisted and squeezed and pressed. Reluctantly, mercury oozed out and dropped into the gold pan. Jeremy squeezed until his hands trembled and he was panting; the ball felt much smaller. When he undid the cloth, the amalgam was darkened by what it contained — gold, he hoped, but only half-believed.

He'd panned half the paystreak before he couldn't retrieve any more mercury by squeezing. Six lumps of amalgam about two inches big tried to meld together in his shovel bowl. As he dumped each load of firewood on the bar, he admired them, excited to find out how much gold they contained. If you had enough mercury, he thought, you could just pour it on the black sand and you wouldn't have to pan.

He lit kindling close to the creek edge and blew on it impatiently. Once the big wood had caught, he held his shovel with the lumpy blob over it. The air was so still that the smoke rose straight up then layered itself between currents. It would be hard to stay downwind.

"Day not warm enough, you got to build a fire?" Jeremy jerked around. Frank Fuller had limped across the bar without Jeremy hearing him. "Good God! Have you found enough gold to need quicksilver?"

"I'm just practising." Jeremy hunched his shoulders and turned back, but he couldn't hide what he was doing.

"Pretty big practice lump, *Pros.*" Frank was tall and thin. His bony face contained a vertical furrow down each cheek, as if hair migrated from his early balding scalp to his curly reddish beard. Frank stared at the streak of black sand then at the fire and back to the sand, looking from the disturbed area which Jeremy had worked to the untouched part. "Why haven't you told anybody?" Frank asked finally. "We're supposed to all be partners."

Jeremy kept his eyes on the amalgam which had begun to shrink. "No one thinks the puny flakes I've found are worth anything."

"From what you're cooking, these aren't just puny flakes."

"I just started. I would have told." I hope I would have told, Jeremy thought.

He struggled to hold the shovel steady and throw more wood on the fire. The amalgam was visibly shrinking. He moved around the fire as the plume of smoke did. So did Frank, who was continuing to look at him uncomfortably. Suddenly he yelled, "Watch your shovel!"

The handle had charred; it could burst into flame any minute. Jeremy plunged the shovel into the river where it sizzled and steamed. The amalgam rolled off the shovel and buried itself in the gravel. "Oh no, oh no!" Jeremy muttered, scrabbling to retrieve it. It was so hot he dropped it on the bank.

When he could pick it up, he turned it this way and that. It was heavy for its size, about two inches in diameter. A good day's work, he thought, as he put it in the poke. Not until then did he notice that Frank had disappeared.

Back at camp, he saw Frank talking to Bob and joined them. "You really have found something this time, Frank says." Bob's tone was neutral.

"It's just fine dust," Jeremy replied, "But I've run out of mercury. Have you any?"

"Don't I need to keep it in case McHenry's lode is dust?" Bob shot back.

Jeremy winced. "Okay. I didn't know how much gold there was." He pulled out his poke and showed the nugget he'd made. "That's from half the streak. It's worth doing the rest then, isn't it?"

Bob turned the nugget over and passed it to Frank. "I'd say so, even though you don't have all the mercury out. How deep did you dig?"

"He's working the surface." Frank passed the nugget back to Jeremy. "We should see what's under it."

Bob put his half-repaired boots down and they went off to get shovels and picks. Jeremy scrounged through the kitchen tent, emerging with cold meat and bread. When the men returned, Bob handed him a bottle of quicksilver.

"I nearly burned my shovel handle," Jeremy volunteered, as he led they way back to the sandbar.

"They're free for the taking." Frank jerked his head toward the scrub aspen and poplar.

"The rest want to move on as soon as the other crews get back," Jeremy said. "If there's a load here, maybe we should stay put."

"We'll see," Bob said and Frank elaborated, "Don't mount your horse before you've caught it."

Through the rest of the afternoon and evening, Jeremy panned the surface and Bob and Frank dug exploratory holes, fortunately for Jeremy, behind him. By the time Jeremy had re-built the fire and evaporated Bob's mercury, the bar was dotted with holes that collapsed as water found them, and Bob and Frank declared the area a bust. Jeremy however, had another large-sized lump of gold.

25

Tuesday 23rd

Having considered it expedient to have Ben return to camp to hurry
Mac forward, he left about 5 a.m. We rose later & explored two
passes to right which were easy & 5 miles brought us over to Peel.
Concluded neither was pass Mac described or desired.

Wed. 24th August 1898

We rose early & started for main camp about 7 a.m., taking everything with us which made heavy packs for us. Arrived about 4 p.m.
Found Mac &c had not started. Washed my clothes. Day showery.
(Have walked over 200 miles myself searching pass useless
prospecting). Saw large moose on way in.

Monday 29th

Fine & clear in morning. Wilson, Larson, Lane, Mac & I started up
east branch again hunting pass. Camped about 10 miles up at
first pass to east. Rained in night.

Tuesday 30th August 1898

Dull in a.m. Took lunch with us & went east through pass about
one hour's walk & struck large lake about 5 miles long & 1 to 2
miles wide lying n.& s. Returned to camp, had dinner & packed

up & went to head of valley. Wilson, Mac & I went to summit of first pass while others getting supper. Mac says not The Pass (knew it was not). Raining lightly all p.m. so were very wet.

The men had a funny way of prospecting, Jeremy had thought in the last week. He'd especially thought it when they passed a creek or sandbar that called out to him to be panned. The men didn't want to stop to explore prospects; they wanted to get to the head of the Macmillan where they planned to tramp some more, looking for Mac's pass. Mr. Fraser said it might be possible to cross over to the Peel River. One day Jeremy had even wondered if, should they find McHenry's gold, would the men stop to dig it? Or would they just keep looking for another spot, somewhere gold was, say, just hanging from trees? Then he scolded himself for questioning his crew: what did he know about prospecting?

The next morning, Mac hobbled around, complaining again that his feet were too sore to take him anywhere. Mr Fraser said, "Right, then we'll prepare to leave on Monday," and he collected the ingredients for a number of loaves of bread.

Bob winked at Jeremy. "A spot of prospecting?" Jeremy grinned.

Rimmer joined them, carrying his shovel and pan, as they set out along the river. The crew had climbed considerably in the past week and now the mountaintops did not loom above them as they had when Jeremy and Bob had climbed to the top on their first foray into the bush with Mr. Fraser. The river, now a stream, gurgled and splashed around large boulders. Occasional yellowed aspen leaves spiralled down onto its gravelly banks and bars. The air was thin and, out of the sun, cool. After a while Jeremy yelled in surprise, "Hey! There are no mosquitoes or blackflies!"

Bob chuckled. "We're either too high up or it's too late in the season!"

"Heaven," said Rimmer, "or the closest thing to it, is the absence of pesky bugs."

They stopped to wash samples of the bars, but even Jeremy had no luck. After some hours, the stream became a series of small waterfalls and they had to clamber up beside them. They came to a meadow on a shoulder of the mountain and could see down the other side. Their stream continued to the left; another one ran down the mountain to the right. "See two peaks and a knob anywhere?" Bob asked. From his tone, Jeremy thought he could be asking if anyone saw an elephant, but he looked anyway.

"If this is Mac's Pass, we couldn't see the landmarks from here, we'd be too close," Rimmer said.

"This new stream runs the opposite way," Jeremy pointed out. "Aren't we looking for that?" He spied a low-growing blueberry bush nearby and picked a handful.

Bob and Rimmer did the same.

"Could be the headwaters of the Peel or its tributary," Bob mumbled through berries.

"That would mean we've tramped over all the land that's not mapped!" The idea made Jeremy breathless.

"Not all of it," Rimmer snapped. Still, he looked out at the rolling plateaus and peaks as if he were the first man to see them. He took a reading from the compass and added, "We might as well carry on."

Jeremy picked more blueberries and looked around wistfully. "What if this is Mac's pass and the gold is right here?"

"It isn't," Bob stated, following after Rimmer.

How can he be so sure? Jeremy wondered.

For some miles they scrambled down beside the new stream which grew wider and noisier as it progressed. Jeremy could see three passes in the distance, but made out no peaks or knobs — but then, the air was hazy.

"This could be the Peel, it's veering northwest," Rimmer ventured.

"Then that Pass could have been the right one." Jeremy looked back, but his view was obscured by the trees. His pack had become very heavy and he was starved. "When are we going to eat?"

"Are you ever not hungry?" Bob asked.

"Not very often," Jeremy answered.

They came to a gravel bar and plopped down their packs. Jeremy gathered wood while Rimmer started a fire and Bob put beans in one pan and water in another. Jeremy was so hungry he was happy to have his beans lukewarm. They had sourdough bread too and, shortly, mugs of tea. Then Jeremy lay back and watched the sun make patterns on the trees. The creek rattled by and occasional ravens croaked. Bob and Rimmer dozed.

Remembering what they were there for, Jeremy got up and panned the gravel. Three nuggets about a quarter inch in diameter nestled in the crease of his pan. "Hey! Look at these!"

Bob and Rimmer jerked awake and examined them. "That's the best you've done so far," Bob commented.

"Not bad," Rimmer said, yawning, as he picked up his shovel and pan.

All of them went to work and found small nuggets or coarse gold in each pan. "Is *this* enough gold for you?" Jeremy finally asked.

Rimmer said, "It's pretty good, pretty good."

"For surface panning." Bob added. "If we had a hydraulicker we could really go to town." He looked around. "The way the bank goes up there and levels off," he pointed, "That could be the old streambed. Hydraulicking would be the most efficient."

"What's a hydraulicker?" Jeremy asked.

"Hydraulics is using machines that are run by water. A hydraulicker'll dig," explained Bob.

"We're hell and gone from anywhere," Rimmer scoffed. "No way could we get machinery in here!"

"Maybe not now," Bob agreed, talking loudly over the noise of the creek, "but someday this country will be opened up. Remember what that fellow said, they're getting the railway in." Jeremy carried on panning.

"That machinery they're using in the States now," Bob leaned on his shovel, "blasts through banks like this in no time. They're getting gold out of smaller surface deposits than this with the new machines. There's enough wood here, enough water . . ."

Jeremy looked up. "We should stake a claim. Get out what we can this way and come back with machines." He refilled his pan and began washing again.

Bob and Rimmer still contemplated the topography.

Jeremy had another thought. "Maybe *this* is McHenry's load!"

"If so," Rimmer said, "that old man gave Mac senseless directions." A pause and he added, "Might be worth staking."

Bob stirred finally and started up the four-foot bank. "I'm going to test the bench."

Each pan yielded Jeremy a few nuggets or coarse gold, which he tamped into his poke, then placed it beside him on the gravel, not bothering to tighten its drawstring in his hurry to wash another pan. I bet this is where McHenry found his forty pounds of gold and nobody's been here since him, Jeremy thought. Or maybe not, maybe it was somewhere close by and we can have an extra forty pounds too.

Bob washed the gravel from the bench. "Some flakes," he announced, rinsing out his pan.

Jeremy looked up. "You didn't save them!"

"There weren't that many. I'm testing just to get a sense of what's here." Bob climbed up the bank and Jeremy watched him begin digging in another place.

He should have saved them. Even if it's just testing, what's the point of not saving them? Jeremy's joints and muscles were stiff from crouching and so he washed straight-legged for a while. Rimmer had worked to the other end of the bar. Jeremy wondered how he was doing. After a few more pans and a few more nuggets, he strolled down to find out.

"Pretty good," Rimmer replied when Jeremy asked him. "More flakes down here than nuggets." Jeremy returned to his spot.

Eventually Bob rinsed out his pan and scooped up water for tea. He rebuilt the fire and when the tea was made, he called them both over. Jeremy was glad to stretch and then sit down. "This is the best site yet, isn't it?" He grinned.

"It's not bad. Might have possibilities," Bob agreed.

"I got this much." Jeremy hefted his poke. It was nearly half full.

"There's nuggets all through this bar," Rimmer offered, with a little more enthusiasm than his usual "pretty good." "But they're thickest right in here."

Bob said, "I propose that we prospect our way back up the creek. From the lay of the land, I'll bet my bottom dollar there are more placers roundabout. These nuggets got washed out from somewhere."

Jeremy sipped his tea. "I'd like to keep working this bar. We know there's gold here and we don't know for sure it's anywhere else."

"You're a real bird-in-the-hand boy, aren't you?" Rimmer laughed.

Jeremy frowned. "What's that?"

"A saying — a bird in the hand's worth two in the bush."

"Yeah, I guess so then."

Bob pulled out his watch. "It's nearly seven and we have enough food for two more meals. We can stay the night and start back tomorrow, panning as we go; that way we see what there is and then see what the others say."

Rimmer nodded and Jeremy asked, "Shouldn't we stake this before we go?"

"Nah." Rimmer threw the dregs of tea away. "There's no one here but us. We can do it when we come back."

After wolfing down beans and bread, Jeremy spent the evening washing gravel and filling his poke. Sometimes he caught himself humming or whistling. Gradually he became aware he was squinting to try to see better. He thought storm clouds were gathering and looked up; the sun had dropped beyond the mountains, creating a purple dusk. How long had it been since the sun had last set — May? He stood up and stretched.

"The sun's set," he yelled at Rimmer, a darker shadow down the bar.

"Yep!" Rimmer yelled back. "Not much summer left now!"

Jeremy returned to his task, trying to ignore an itchiness, a dislocation, an irritation, provoked by the loss of the sun. Even the return of the evening star did not make up for the loss. Only when he could no longer force his back and legs and arms through their motions, did he give up and roll into his sleeping bag, determined to be panning again at first light.

He awoke before the others and, ignoring his screaming muscles, rekindled the fire and put water on to heat. The sun was overhead and he could forget that tonight it would set even earlier. He'd washed about a dozen pans of gravel before Rimmer and Bob emerged from their cocoons. "Still the same luck," he said, when they came over to inquire. He was having to put these nuggets loose into his pockets.

"We'll eat and pack up and start back," said Bob. "If we check prospects along the way, we should get in by evening."

"I'll stay here until you get back." Jeremy washed the gravel as fast as he could.

"You'll have no food," Rimmer pointed out.

Jeremy picked out two small nuggets. "I can last till tomorrow, you'll be back by then."

"Might take us longer. Who knows who's gone off somewhere else. Now come and eat." Bob crunched back to the fire.

Reluctantly Jeremy finished off his pan and did not load up another. He vowed he'd come back and stay here for the rest of the summer, no matter what the others said. As they pulled on their packs and began to retrace yesterday's path, Jeremy gave a long look at the gravel bar and its surroundings, memorizing its exact position.

When they got back to camp late in the evening, they found

only Mac, Ben, Wilson of the Cle Elm crew, and Mr. Fraser there.

"We found gold! Lots of gold!" Jeremy yelled, taking off his pack and collapsing onto a crate. "We found the pass too, maybe, and the Peel River!"

"Wonderful! Terrific!" Mac rubbed his hands in satisfaction.

"Wow," said Wilson, "so soon!"

"You mean our own Bonanza?" Ben grinned. "If it happened once, it can happen again!"

Mr. Fraser looked to Bob and Rimmer for corroboration.

"It's not bad," Bob said. "The kid's loaded with nuggets from the stream. We tested some of the benchland too and got good flakes. Of course it wouldn't be financially feasible without machinery —"

Rimmer had sat down too. "It's definitely worth taking a look at, whether it's the right pass or not."

"Did you see the markers?" Mac asked.

"No, but it was hazy. The stream flows north-northwest. Have you any supper left? I'm sure Jer's starving." Rimmer winked at him.

"Where are the others?" Bob asked.

"Out prospecting. They won't be back for a couple of days," Mr. Fraser said.

"Show us your nuggets, Jer," Ben directed. Jeremy pulled out his poke and opened it.

"You got all those there?" Ben's incredulity was satisfying.

Wilson held his hand out. Jeremy passed his poke and watched Wilson heft it. "Impressive." He handed it back.

"Yeah. And I've got more in my pockets too. I was picking three or four out of each pan. I want to get back right away!"

"Right away is right!" Mac chortled. "We'll go tomorrow! I didn't think we'd find the pass so easily!"

Wilson ladled out three plates of moosemeat stew, saying, "Somebody will have to stay here to tell the others."

"Nah," said Mac, "we'll pack our stuff and leave a note. They can follow when they get in. We won't need this camp anymore."

"We did blaze a trail," Bob offered, his mouth full. "The site's only about fifteen miles away."

Mac ran on, "Since we found the pass so easily, maybe we don't need the others —"

Mr. Fraser frowned. "Have you forgotten we made a deal?"

"No, no," Mac said hastily, "I was just thinking out loud. Of course we wouldn't cut them out." Mr. Fraser's frown continued another moment, then he turned to pour some tea.

Jeremy was so tired he nodded off on the crate, then jerked uncomfortably awake as his plate dropped to the ground. "Go to bed," Mr Fraser ordered. "You can pack up in the morning."

Jeremy collected his poke and his pack and dragged to the tent. Before he spread his sleeping bag, he emptied his poke and his pockets into the tea tin. It was about a quarter full and satisfactorily heavy. Would he have to share his gold with the others? Was that part of the deal?

In the morning they realized they could not leave the camp unmanned; the boats and the others' tents and gear would be unprotected. While they drew straws to see who would remain, Jeremy held his breath and prayed, *not me, please not me.* Ben held the short straw and tried to hide his disappointment.

"You can reassign the job and join us as soon as the rest come in," Mac consoled, clapping his shoulder.

The other six packed their gear and enough food for a week and started off, following Bob's blazes. When they got to the pass where the two streams began, Mac said, "This isn't the right pass."

"Maybe not, but they did find gold," Mr. Fraser stated.

"It's not the right pass," Mac reiterated. "You gave me your word you'd all look for the right pass."

"I didn't, did I?" Jeremy asked, trying to remember. Mac ignored him and scrutinized the men.

"How do you know it's not the right pass?" Wilson asked. Mac glowered.

"At least come and see what we found," Bob said in a calm tone.

Grudgingly, Mac started off, muttering, "Shoulda known you wouldn't've found it so fast."

When they reached the gravel bar and bench, Mac said, "Just a few nuggets to a pan here. When we find the right pass, we'll find much more gold."

"It's enough for me," Jeremy announced, feeling angry and nervous.

"Look," said Mr. Fraser, "There are sixteen of us when the rest get back. We can divide up. If you think this ground is worth working," he looked at Bob and Rimmer, and not at Jeremy. "Some can work.it and some can look for the *right* pass." That was the closest to a sneer Jeremy had ever heard from Mr. Fraser. He added to Mac, "Will that keep you happy?"

"If that's the best we can do —" Mac frowned. "Though it's a waste to prospect here when we know what's waiting."

"A bird in the hand's worth two in the bush," popped out of Jeremy's mouth before he realized he'd even thought it.

Mac turned on him. "Oh shut up!"

26

Wed. 31st

Froze hard last night. At breakfast noticed 2 caribou on top of mountain about mile from camp. Wilson went & killed both while rest of us went up Valley to west. Mac condemned this also & we returned to camp. Wilson brought down smaller caribou & we had liver & heart for dinner, then took packs & the caribou & returned to main camp. Raining & we are all wet. Another 50 miles walked through brush & with packs. Over 250 miles I have walked now pass hunting!

Wed. 7th Sept. 1898

Fine warm day. Miller, Townsend, Mac & I started 9 a.m. with a week's grub up creek at camp for another hunt for The Pass. We made about 4 miles & camped. Wet & cold

Sunday 11th Sept 1898

Day warm. Walked hard all day & reached camp about dark. Tired & wet &c. I have walked 380 to 395 miles Pass hunting! At camp found they had killed a moose.

During the last month, Jeremy was the only constant prospector on the gravel bar he'd named McHenry's Load. Others came and went, depending on who was excused from hunting Mac's pass or who was not needed in the main camp. As the hope of finding the pass grew fainter, Mac became more stubborn and insistent, according to the others. Jeremy panned on, ruminating that the men might prefer to explore than dig for gold, otherwise why had they not stood up to Mac? Some were grumpier and more sarcastic than others; Gassman called Mac deluded, and every time Mr. Fraser dropped by, he sarcastically announced how many miles he'd walked looking for the "invisible" pass.

Since the sun had first set a month ago, night had increased by noticeable chunks so that now there were hours of darkness. Losing work time made Jeremy anxiously wash pan after pan of gravel from dawn until dusk then fall into his bed, grudgingly grateful that he was forced to stop for a few hours.

He'd filled one tea tin and now worked against time to fill the second, but he had an ongoing worry. Was he supposed to share his gold? When the others prospected, they kept what they found. This had contented him until he realized that maybe they were to divide it all when they were done. He knew he wouldn't be here without them and also knew he couldn't have found as much gold as he had without the others bringing him meat or fish and bread. He knew that hunting, fishing and baking took time away from prospecting, so should he pay them in nuggets for his food? It was obvious they would never find a pass that Mac would approve; all the time tramping about away from the gold was their choice, yet would he still be expected to share? If he knew he had to share, would he work so hard?

One morning the trees and gravel bar were covered in a dusting of snow and fingers of ice lined the creek banks. Bob pointed to it and said, "We have to go. We don't have long before freeze-up."

"You mean today?" Jeremy couldn't hide his consternation.

"Today, now, this morning," Rimmer stated. "Don't even think about panning," he added, as Jeremy looked at the area he'd been working yesterday.

"But we haven't been here very long," Jeremy whined. He knew he whined but he thought of all the gold — all his gold — still among the gravel.

"You can register your claim at Fort Selkirk and come back next year," Bob said. Jeremy looked at the stakes he'd put in last month and read what he'd carved on the closest one, a tree stump four feet high: *Post No. 2 McHenry's Load 500 ft downstream to Post No. 1 Aug 17 1898 Jeremy Britain.* In the distance was Post number one. It was true, his claim wouldn't be recognized until he'd registered it and it was true, he could come back next year. As he packed up, he remembered Mr. Fraser's comment when he first saw the stakes, "*Load?* Why are you calling it *Load?* You mean L-O-D-E, Son. A lode is a source of minerals." But it had been too late to change the spelling and besides, Jeremy liked the weightiness of *load;* it reminded him of his tea tins.

The snow changed to slush as the morning wore on, but the peaks around them sparkled white. In the meadow where they exchanged the north-flowing stream for the south-flowing, it was apparent that this snow would not melt again until spring.

At camp they found Ben and Gassman packing up as well. "Oh good!" Ben announced when he saw them. "We were hoping you'd come in. Everyone else has gone back to the main camp. We're out of grub —"

"So are we," said Bob.

"— and we need to get down river."

"No pass, eh?" Rimmer commented.

"Need you ask?" Gassman sneered. "There never was a pass or if there was, Mac's been changing his description! He's bossed us this whole trip with his stupid notions!" He picked up a crate, stomped to the river and put it in the canoe.

"Tempers a bit high?" Bob asked, watching after him.

"Just a bit," said Ben. "Everyone's at the tense, silent stage. I hope they stay there. Silent, I mean."

Mac had known about rafts too, Jeremy thought, and look what happened. He was the only one to let his feet get really bad. The only one to have a toothache.

Jeremy took his pack to the canoe and when he returned said to Ben, "Shall I hump down this load?" He pointed to a pile of boxes next to some moosehide and bones.

"Nah, leave it. It's just garbage." Ben laughed. "We'll be a lot lighter going down than we were coming up. Take the canvas off the latrine, though."

As Gassman, Bob and Rimmer paddled downstream, Jeremy looked back at the campsite. The blackened fire pit dominated the clearing, surrounded by squares of flat brown grass where the tents had stood. Behind the clearing were the stumps of trees they'd cut for firewood. The last things he noticed, before the canoe swept around a bend, were the piles of garbage and stacked wood. I can use that wood next summer, he consoled himself. And the latrine.

Hours later, they pulled up exhausted on the bank by the cache camp. If he'd been asked beforehand, Jeremy would have said that going downriver would be as easy as eating pie, but the constant paddling or poling through rapids and shallows and deadwood brought back the pain and fatigue of their ascent.

The others greeted them as they stiffly unfolded themselves. Mr. Fraser strode over, rubbing his hands. "Good to see you! You're the last in! We couldn't have waited much longer!"

"We practically had to haul the kid out by his earlobes." Bob punched Jeremy lightly on the shoulder.

You did not, Jeremy thought, not really, but he just smiled as he lifted his pack out of the canoe.

After a meagre dinner of moosemeat and bean stew, they sat

around the fire drinking weak, sugarless tea and discussing how long it would take to get to Selkirk.

John Larson changed the subject. His face grew florid as he sneered, "So much for your fabled pass, MacLeod! What a wasted summer! We should be studied by a head doctor for allowing you to con us!"

Jeremy shrank into his jacket as Mac leapt to his feet. "Take that back, Larson! I did not con you! You all came willingly! You all agreed! So you didn't find the pass! That doesn't mean it's not here!"

Larson had risen also. He was a big, blond forthright man whose face reddened with the least exertion, physical or mental. He and Mac glowered at each other.

Mr. Fraser said, "Mac's right, John. We did all come willingly. We knew there was a chance it would be a wild goose chase."

But Mac's been so convincing, Jeremy thought, remembering how he'd insisted he knew all about rafting. He'd insisted the pass was here, insisted they were in the right area. Then he recalled Soapy Smith's gang convincing men that an unknown thief had stolen their wallets, and that their telegraph office was hooked up, outright lies. Mac hadn't lied, Jeremy didn't think, but wasn't his insistence a kind of con? Maybe not as bad as Soapy's gang, not deliberate lies, but lies to himself? And what about the rest of them, believing him — wanting him to be right? People believing the telegraph office worked just because it was there? Hearing his name jerked him back.

"Jeremy's been the smart one," Charlie Osborne was saying. "He stayed put and did the hard work that prospecting requires. How much gold you taking out, boy?"

"A tea tin and a half." Jeremy watched Mac stomp away from the fire. Larson poured out his dregs of tea and slowly sat down. Wilson glanced sideways at him.

"That's a lot," Rogers said. "Should be worth a fair sum."

Do you expect me to share it? Jeremy didn't say, but looked around the circle of faces. "I'm registering my claim in Selkirk and coming back in the spring." He didn't need to say this either, but it made him feel more certain that the gold was his.

"Machinery's the way of the future for these deposits." Bob rode off on his favourite topic. "If the assay results prove out, dredging could be profitable."

"This country is inaccessible to machinery," Charlie Osborne pointed out. Rogers nodded. They'd said earlier that they couldn't wait to get back to Oakland and civilization.

Mac returned and sat down. "It won't always be inaccessible." With his usual speed, he'd recovered his ebullience. "With a consortium and investment money, we'll get a road up here, take out that gold and find the pass! I know it's here, we just didn't get far enough!"

Jeremy smiled. Gassman snorted, a laugh or a sneer, or both. Mr. Fraser pursed his lips and raised his eyebrows. Larson stalked off, muttering. Jeremy thought, if Mac's part of a scheme, I'll remember not to be. His ideas aren't as good as he thinks they are.

"Well, boys," Frank Fuller stated, "we've been in Klondike, part of the gold rush. We've had some adventures to tell our grandchildren."

"True," agreed Mr. Fraser. "It's been just like the old days, tramping about the country away from the hustle and bustle of civilization, just us and our wits dealing with nature."

"The last great frontier," Bob offered contemplatively.

"The last wilderness," John Wilson nodded.

"Won't be long before man's got this tamed too," said James Miller. "Once the railroad's through, wilderness turns into fields or towns or mines soon enough. Didn't take long in Iowa."

"When I come back," Jeremy realized, "I can take the train!"

"Well, boys," Mr. Fraser stood up and stretched, "I'm turning in. We've still got miles to cross and we need to get an early start."

It took them a week to reach the Yukon River and Fort Selkirk. Even the activity they saw on the Pelly — the number of travellers, campers, cabins, even some men haying on a benchland — did not prepare them for the changes at the Fort. There were over a dozen new buildings — eleven grouped around a parade ground to the east — and a steamer tied up to a new dock. The store had an addition. People streamed back and forth and roundabout creating a general hum and bustle. Jeremy sat and stared until Ben ordered him to close his mouth in case a fly flew in.

They beached their canoes and, leaving Fuller to look after them, headed to the buildings, the men hopeful of mail, Jeremy to register his claim. He carried his tea tins in a canvas bag in case the Registrar was also the Assayer. The mail was kept in the store so Jeremy went on alone to the new government building. It smelled of green wood and sawdust. There were some Mounties and a crowd of men in uniforms Jeremy didn't recognize, but he saw *Yukon Field Force* stitched on a passing shoulder.

He went up to the man behind the counter. "Is this where I register a claim?" he asked.

"Yes." The man slowly looked up from his sheath of papers. He blinked, then frowned at Jeremy. "How old are you?"

"Fifteen. In a few weeks."

"You have to be eighteen to qualify for a free miner's certificate."

"I don't expect one for free. I'll pay."

"Of course you will," the man retorted severely. "When you're older. Everybody pays. A free miner is anyone over eighteen or a joint stock company." He inked his pen and returned to his papers.

Jeremy watched the floor planks until he reached the door to avoid catching laughter on any of the uniforms' faces. He knew he was blushing. *I'll pay* reverberated in his brain. Then anguish joined humiliation: if he couldn't register his claim it would be unprotected. Anyone could work it. Anyone over eighteen could register it.

Mr. Fraser and the others leaned against the store wall, reading letters. Jeremy dragged himself over. As he reached them, Mr. Fraser folded his last letter with satisfaction. "Everything's fine at home and my son made the rugby team. At least everything was fine on April 21st. I'd be happier if there were a more recent letter." He saw Jeremy. "Why the long face?" he asked.

Jeremy slowly set down his heavy sack. "I can't register a claim until I'm eighteen."

"Oh for goodness sake! Of course you can't! You're a minor!" He clapped Jeremy on his shoulder.

Bob said, "Where have our brains been? Did that not occur to any of us?"

"I guess not." Rimmer put his letter in his pocket. "Ben, you should have thought of it, you're the lawyer!"

"It's probably because we've been thinking of you as an adult, not a child," Ben offered, with a mixed smile of sympathy and chagrin.

"You've been working like a man the whole trip," Mac added. "Especially on your claim. Yep, we just thought of you as a man."

"That's it," agreed Wilson.

The others nodded along with him and Mac, and Jeremy felt elated, until he remembered the problem. "But I have to wait three more years to register my claim."

"I'll register it," said Mr. Fraser.

"Thanks Sir, but —" Jeremy searched for polite phrasing. "That's very nice of you but — does that mean you'll own it?"

"Technically yes," said Ben, sounding lawyerly. "But he can hold it in trust for you and waive any rights to its contents."

"I'll draw up a contract that you make all decisions, including when you work it." Mr. Fraser rubbed his hands together as if everything had been accomplished.

"Well, thanks." Jeremy smiled with relief. Then he frowned as another problem occurred to him. "Does not being eighteen mean I can't sell the gold either? I was going to sell it and give you all some because you didn't find any." He paused, testing the last sentence as it hung in the air. It was true. That's what he wanted to do, he just hadn't known it before. "I wouldn't have any gold if it weren't for you," he finished.

"Technically you can sell the gold by yourself —" Ben began, and Mr. Fraser took over, "— but it'll raise fewer questions if I do it for you. We'll wait until Vancouver."

"Oh," Jeremy's voice leaked disappointment. "I hoped I could do it here. Soapy Smith's gang might steal it in Skagway and I want to know how much it's worth!"

Bob smiled. "I'm curious too. It depends on the purity. You do have that great glob of amalgam in there, but I'd say it's worth at least four or five thousand dollars."

"That much!" Jeremy breathed.

Gassman said, "It's a very fine offer to share it with us, but you should keep it. You worked hard for it." The other men nodded. Gassman continued, "You're not going to go back to selling papers on the street, are you? You have to think about what you're going to do."

"He's going to school," Mr. Fraser said firmly. "It's a condition of my registering his claim."

"School!" Jeremy snorted. "I'm going to work my claim!"

"A prospector needs maths and geology and chemistry and surveying," Bob said.

"Oh, a prospecting school?" Jeremy thought he might be interested.

"Hullo there, Fraser!" It was Mr. J.R. Perry, who'd come up to build sawmills. From the look of the new buildings, he'd been successful. He and Mr. Fraser pumped hands and clasped elbows and decided to get caught up over a cup of coffee. Jeremy, Bob, Ben and Charlie Osborne tagged along; the rest of the men drifted off to other tasks.

After they'd apprised Mr. Perry of their summer, Bob asked, "What's been going on in the world? We heard they're building a railway over the summit."

"Ah yes, the White Pass and Yukon Railway. Track's laid on the Skagway side already, they're determined to have it running next year. Every man who gave up on the gold rush has a job on it."

"Did they have any problem with Soapy Smith's gang?" Jeremy asked.

Mr. Perry looked surprised. "You really haven't had any news, have you? Frank Reid killed Smith in July —"

"What? How?" Jeremy interrupted.

"There was a shootout. Reid was deputized to form a citizens' committee to get rid of Smith and his gang and they all met at the wharf one morning. As I said, Reid shot and killed Smith, but unfortunately Reid took a bullet of Smith's in the thigh and succumbed the following week. The rest of the gang shipped out. Skagway's as safe as Fort Selkirk now." Mr. Perry sipped his coffee.

"Wow!" Jeremy breathed.

"Real dime novel stuff," Ben said. "You were right about Smith, Jer. Deputy and citizens' committee sounds at least quasi-legal."

Mr. Perry turned to Mr. Fraser. "If you didn't know that, you probably don't know what happened to your friend, Major Walsh?"

"I assume he's busy being District Commissioner," Mr. Fraser retorted.

Mr. Perry shook his head. "Ogilvie, the Surveyor, is Commissioner now. Walsh got himself right in the middle of a scandal and was recalled in August."

"Recalled!" Mr. Fraser continued in his sternest tone, "I've known Walsh for years! He's always been upstanding! A little impetuous perhaps, but of the highest moral rectitude!"

Mr. Perry nodded. "Many agree. Some think his brother got him in his pickle and Walsh took the blame for him. Some think he's just out of his depth and did too many favours for friends."

"What happened?" Jeremy asked, thinking, good thing he hadn't gone to Dawson with Major Walsh.

"Walsh ruled that Dominion Creek — a really rich creek — was not to be staked until July 11 and that everyone had to have permits. Then he let his brother and his cook go there three days early and at the last moment he declared no permits necessary. You can imagine the miners' fury! There's to be a Royal Commission to investigate. Walsh really riled Sam Steele too, he used Mounties as his personal servants. As if he thought he was still in the Force."

"Bad judgements," Mr. Fraser mused. "I can see it, he always was a one man show, not an administrator. But he did nothing deliberately underhanded, I'd stake my reputation on that!"

"It's been a zoo up here all summer," Mr. Perry continued. "Some estimate thirty thousand people in Dawson alone. Practically impossible to manage. Steele and Ogilvie are working twenty-hour days." He shook his head. "You couldn't pay me enough to do their jobs!"

They'd finished their coffee and stood up to go. Mr. Perry clapped Mr. Fraser on the shoulder. "Now, James, your crew's going out, eh?" His smile teased all of them. "You'll get down south and find yourselves pining for this country. Why not put in a full year and become sourdoughs instead of cheechakos?"

"We don't have enough supplies," said Bob.

"A lot of us have families and businesses," Osborne elaborated. "It's been a great year, one I'll never forget, but I'm looking forward to some city comforts."

"I'm coming back in the spring, Mr. Perry," Jeremy announced. "I'll look you up then, but before that I'm going buy a bicycle and learn to ride it."

"We're not finished here yet," Mr. Fraser interposed. "We still have to get down to Skagway and catch a steamer. That reminds me, Perry, we have some dogs across the river. Could you sell them for us?"

"Probably."

"Can't we take them with us?" Jeremy asked.

"No," said Mr. Fraser. "They're not city dogs."

"Can't we even take Captain and Leo?"

"No. They'll be best here."

They'd left Sue, the mare, when her work was done; now they were leaving the dogs without so much as *thank you*. The dogs had been good to him. He had a flash of Collie placing his chin on his thigh the night he'd had to sleep in the stable-tent. It seemed so long ago now. Poor old Collie. Poor Blackie. Poor Hank.

"Be sure to sell them to someone who'll treat them well," Jeremy told Mr. Perry. He added, "Please," to soften his instruction.

"I'll do my best," Mr. Perry said. "I'll be in Skagway in a couple of weeks. If you haven't left yet, I'll see you there."

Skagway, Jeremy thought, stepping out into the late afternoon sun. Now as safe as Fort Selkirk. He wouldn't have to worry about his gold. Or himself. How long would it take him to believe that?

27

How it all Ended

Wed. September 21st

Froze hard last night & snowed. Got credit cashed & bought horse $30.00. Charlie Osborne started with another man for Frisco via Dalton Trail, lost fry pan & turned back.

Sat. 24th

Rained through night. Started about 2 p.m. taking boat up river 3 miles to get across. Got Cattleman named Stone to swim our horse across Yukon but rope broke in mid stream & horse was drowned. We went across & camped for night.

Sunday 25th Sept. 1898

Very fine day. Bought a mule for $30.00. Sent our sleeping bags back to Selkirk; too heavy. Ben & Rimmer put me aboard Steamer James Domville which was on a bar about a mile below our camp & they took mule & light load over trail to Five Finger Rapids while I with most of stuff took passage for there. Steamer only got off bar about 6 p.m. & lay to all night. Met Charles Milne of Vancouver. Meals $1.50 each & could not get a room so slept on deck, chilly.

Monday 26th Sept. 1898

Steamer started at 6 a.m. & went about 5 miles & got on another bar where she stuck for about 24 hrs. Steamer Ora came along just after noon, going down, stopped & tried to help but Captain would not do what they wanted so they went on. Mismanagement of Steamer kept us there too long.

Jeremy leaned on the railing next to Mr. Fraser and asked, "Would Prospector's School teach this hydraulicking that Bob told me about?"

"Probably. And they're developing new mining technologies all the time."

"What if they won't take me at the school?"

"Then you go to high school until you've satisfied their requirements."

"Maybe I don't read well enough," Jeremy continued to worry.

"When we get to Vancouver we'll set up an interview with them." Mr. Fraser turned to him. "You'll stay with my family until we get things sorted out. We can always accommodate another boy."

Fine for Mr. Fraser to say; Jeremy felt a flutter of nerves. What if his sons didn't like him? What if Mrs. Fraser didn't? Well, he'd go to school and buy a bicycle, he wouldn't have to hang around Mr. Fraser's house all the time. He'd look for Cowlick Sunday. Jeremy pushed away from the railing and grinned.

Tuesday 27th

Got off bar in morning & worked along by line till p.m. then ran nicely for some time. Ran out of wood & passengers went ashore & cut some twice. Mail Steamer Flora passed us going up but we passed her again.

Wed. 28th Sept. 1898

Were tied up all night but got off this morning & got to Rink Rapids about 11 a.m. Had to go ashore & cut wood & repair wheel then passengers took her line & helped her over the rapids. We reached saw mill near Five Finger Rapids about 4 p.m. where I got off. Met Charlie Osborne & partner who had started to go over Dalton Trail but got afraid & took steamer here. Found Ben & Rimmer here with mule. Slept in Arctic Express Company's building & nearly froze. Hard frost.

Thursday 29th Sept. 1898

Dalton & party crossed first then I took boat & got Ben & Rimmer & mule over safely. Loaded up & started about 11 a.m. carrying small packs ourselves to lighten mule. Found horse on trail which we caught & put our packs on & took with us. Made about 12 miles & camped. Cold night.

"You've grown, Laddie," Rimmer observed. "You're as tall as James now."

Jeremy, surprised, caught up with Mr. Fraser, who was leading the new horse. When he looked over, it was not at Mr. Fraser's shoulder, as it had been when they'd walked out of Skagway, but at the top of his ear, rather, where his ear probably was under his parka hood. He'd be fifteen in a few weeks, that was practically grown-up. Except for registering claims.

"Do you still have your nice alto?" Ben asked and launched into *Greensleeves.*

Jeremy hummed, then sang a verse with him.

"No alto anymore," Ben diagnosed, "but a nice tenor. And soon you'll be six feet tall, like me."

"We didn't sing all summer," Jeremy observed.

"No," Ben said, in a dry tone. "We worked." Then he glanced at Jeremy and smiled. "You could join my choir if you want to sing.

Choral singing is really satisfying team work."

He could join that, could he? Hmm. As long as the choir didn't hold practices when he was at school.

Sat 8th Oct 1898
Late start & only made about 20 miles. Struck Dalton's Post & N.W. Police Camp on Elsili River about 1:30 p.m. Got information & grub. Passed through an Indian Village. Slight snow last night & cloudy today. Went about 6 miles & camped

Jeremy didn't feel three inches taller, but the pants he'd bought in Fort Selkirk in June were above his ankles now, as had been the pants he'd discarded then. It hadn't occurred to him last February that he'd keep growing, but he remembered how hungry he'd been the whole time in Klondike — oh so what, he was always hungry!

Mainly he thought about the people he'd met, like the pretty girl in the red dress he'd never really talked to, like the Robinson's crew who just took poor dead Collie and maybe would have taken their boat too. Like Major Walsh, who hadn't lived up to Mr. Fraser's standards — had he, Jeremy? Would he be able to? — like the really scary Soapy Smith, who was dead yay — oh sorry, God — like those men who had the whisky and he'd got drunk, what were their names?

He thought about the people he hadn't met on the trail, like Cowlick Sunday. Yep, he really had hoped, if he, Jeremy, came to the gold rush, Cowlick would too and they'd meet again, just like Mr. Fraser and Mac or Mr. Fraser and Walsh or Mr. Perry with the sawmills. That man was everywhere, too bad he wasn't Cowlick.

Wed 12th
Had travelled about 6 hours when we struck a camp of 7 men & 5 horses near Salmon River. They told us we could not get horse

feed for 15 miles so we camped there. We were short of grub but they helped us out, very decent fellows. Rained last night.

Perhaps Jeremy had thousands of dollars — well, at least a thousand dollars — of Klondike gold. When he wasn't at Prospector's School, he could spend some of it looking for Cowlick! Maybe he was still on his apprentice farm in Sooke. His farmers might know where he'd gone, if he had gone. Jeremy could put an ad in the paper, *Looking For Cowlick Sunday, pls reply Box* — . Everybody liked Cowlick. He'd bet the Fraser boys would like Cowlick even if they didn't like him, Jeremy.

Saturday 15th October 1898

Left our horses to be driven to pasture by Swedes. Crossed on ferry to Chilcat & portaged to Haines Mission & took mail steamer for Skagway where we had to catch larger steamer. Arrived about midnight & took beds at Rainier Hotel.

The crew took double rooms; Jeremy shared with Mr. Fraser. Their room had a bathtub, but both fell into their beds and slept so soundly neither knew if the other snored.

In the morning, Mr. Fraser had the first bath; he declared it the next thing to heaven. When Jeremy sank into his bath, he knew it *was* heaven. No more pails of melted snow, no more cold rivers, no more splashing in creek water.

When his bath had cooled and he was also driven out by hunger, he dried himself, then towelled the steam off the mirror. Yes, he needed a haircut; shaggy hair dripped onto his shoulders. Yes, he did look different, his nose *was* bigger. He rubbed the fuzzy hair on his upper lip, then tilted his head to check his cheeks and jawline: were those a few hairs? Yes. Yay? Yay. He really was going to have a beard like the men!

Jeremy and Mr. Fraser met the others in the dining room.

"Look at our bouquet of flowers!" Mr. Fraser declared. Jeremy recalled his first bath on the trail: *the rose in the bouquet.*

Ben had shaved off his beard, like Mr. Fraser, leaving only a trim moustache and a swath of white skin where his suntan ended. Bob and Mac had trimmed their beards. Rimmer had created a swirling moustachio; Bob asked if he were shopping for wax after breakfast.

And breakfast: eggs — fresh, not powdered — bacon, sausages — yum — potatoes — real, not evaporated — fried tomatoes, and oh my, oranges! "That was best meal of my whole life!" Jeremy announced.

"What do you mean?" Rimmer faked an injured tone. "I thought my stews and pies were really good!"

"And my beans," said Bob, play-sulking.

"They were, they were," Jeremy replied. "But do you think I could have another order of this breakfast?"

Everyone laughed at him, and he grinned back.

After breakfast, Jeremy left the hotel to see for himself if Skagway was really as safe as Mr. Perry had said.

Gleaming new railway tracks stretched the length of Broadway's muddy middle. As in Fort Selkirk, many more buildings edged the streets, but he could still glimpse tents on Skagway's outskirts. The parade of people and pack animals seemed not to have lessened.

Jeremy breathed deeply: the tang of salt in the damp air was the same. And, he realized — it smelled like home. He breathed deeply again. Add snow over all this mud, Jeremy thought, and it could be last February. He walked down to the saloon where he'd sold the *Vancouver World.* No newsboy stood there now, but he could hear from inside the rising, falling babble of voices. Jeremy shivered and pulled his tuque over his ears. Must be the coldest corner in town.

Across the street, the "Telegraph Office" seemed bright with another business; the original sign hung askew. Skinny dogs still skulked and fought and prowled through garbage, growling at him, or looking hopeful of handouts. Too bad horrible Soapy Smith hadn't finished his adopt-a-dog plan before he got shot.

"Where's the cemetery?" he asked a passing man. The man gaped at him. "Soapy Smith's grave?"

The man, who had a scraggly beard and raggedy clothes, searched his mind. "Few blocks that way?"

"Thanks." Jeremy set off.

He found a new cemetery with some graves marked by hasty crosses. A number of them dated the deaths to April 3, 1898. At first Jeremy wondered if Soapy Smith had gone on a rampage that day, then he remembered Dr. Grant's report of the avalanche on the Chilkoot trail. But there really was only one grave he was interested in; finally he found it.

Jefferson R. Smith
Died
July 8, 1898
Aged 38 years

It really was true! Jeremy didn't look for Frank Reid's grave, but he mentally thanked him for his deed.

Sunday 16th

Dull & threatening rain. Met J.R. Perry, Cope Garland & other acquaintances. Ben & I went to church in a.m. to Y.M.C.A. heard a Baptist. In Evening to Presbyterian service.

Jeremy sang all the hymns. Even the ones he didn't know.

On the way back to the hotel, he asked Mr. Fraser, "Does your family have a dog?"

"No. But the boys might be ready for one this year."

How does Mr. Fraser do that — let a big smile take over his eyes and not turn up his lips? Jeremy figured he'd have to study the technique. And practise.

Monday 17th
Rained all night. Took passage on Steamer Rosalie for Vancouver, boarded at noon, called at Dyea.

Meals were included in the price of the ticket. Jeremy ate.

Afterward, he found Ben, Bob, Mac and Rimmer leaning on the stern railing, looking back up Lynn Canal. "Will I see you in Vancouver?"

"You sure will, kid." Ben punched Jeremy's shoulder. "None of us live very far from the Frasers. And you're going to join my choir, right?" Jeremy nodded.

"We'll have gold rush reunions," said Bob. "Show up with two buckets of water for your bath."

"Reminds me," added Mac, "we still have half a case of soap."

"Oh you —" Jeremy smacked his tongue.

"The only one you might not see for a while is me," said Rimmer. "I have to check on things in Colorado, straighten them out about this war with Spain. I expect letters, kid. Once a week at least. James will have my address."

"Will you write back?"

"Count on it." Rimmer twirled his waxed moustache ends and wiggled his eyebrows.

Later, Jeremy found Mr. Fraser reading a newspaper in the lounge. "In Fort Selkirk, you said your son made the rugby team. Which one?"

"Team? Or son?"

"Son."

"Ross. My eldest." He turned back to the paper.

Jeremy sat down. What's rugby? He'd never seen rugby. Didn't know it had a team. Well, onward, what else could he do? A bicycle, school, choir and finding Cowlick. A dog perhaps. And he had his gold. Didn't sound so bad. Then, next year —

Saturday 22nd October 1898
Beautiful day, clear warm & not windy. Arrived in Vancouver about 4 p.m. & found all my folks well. Very glad to get home & see them after an absence of 8 1/2 months.

Afterword

Between February and October 1898, my grandfather and some of his friends joined thousands of others in the trek up the White Pass to the gold rush. But halfway to the Klondike, my grandfather's group veered away from the Yukon River, and pursued a route not taken by most of the other gold seekers. Over the entire trip, my grandfather kept a daily journal of brief entries in which he recorded what he and the crew were doing, but he never recorded the reasons for trekking where they did. It is difficult to tell from the journal what they accomplished, if anything, and why they undertook this unusual journey.

Even after the arduous trip in search of gold, the North and the goldbug continued to lure my grandfather: within three years he had moved his family to Atlin, in northwestern British Columbia, where he was Gold Commissioner from 1902 to 1922. He died fifteen years before I was born. By the time I was an adult, his children, my uncles and my mother had died as well, and I had not heard any family stories about his trip.

I have my grandfather's journal probably because my mother was the only girl in the family and cleaning up after a death fell to her. Like the family Bible, the journal has been around my entire life, but it was only after many years that I finally decided to open it. I was surprised to find that it contains a complete storyline: they went, they trekked, they returned. What it does not offer is a motive for the trip, a rationale to appease my curiosity, to explain *why* they went. Over the years of my intermittent re-readings of the journal, my curiosity grew as to why my grandfather had decided to venture up the relatively unexplored region around the Macmillan River, and not down the Yukon River to the Klondike. What, I wondered, was special about the area they explored and what information did he and his friends have that perhaps was not generally available. Mainly, however, I wondered what the trip would have been like: if they had taken me, how would I have managed?

Goldrush Orphan has grown out of my attempts to answer my questions about the trip. The storyline follows the journal record, and the entries at the beginning of each chapter are authentically my grandfather's. Because he wrote in the conventions of his time some abbreviations are different from today's. For example, he used *co'y* instead of *co.* for *company,* and *&c* instead of *etc.* for *et cetera.*

I created Jeremy so that he — and I — could have an imaginary place to exist within the factual trip. The motives, the rationale, and the explanations for the trip are my own, made plausible from my research on the Klondike gold rush.

NOTES

1. The Klondike gold rush was the largest outburst of mass hysteria in Canadian history. It was fueled by a number of events: a world-wide depression that had continued for most of the 1890s; accelerated communication by daily newspapers and telegraph (at least compared to the living memories of that generation); mass transit by railway and steamship; an increasingly urbanized population with an average annual salary of $600 and no organized government relief for the poor and unemployed; a sense that the only remaining frontier was the North; and a desire for adventure in a generation that saw itself as having finished the push westward to the edge of the continent.

2. In the 1880s and 1890s, there were many orphans like Jeremy, children whose parents could not look after them, for any number of reasons, such as the family having too many children, financial hardship, geographic dislocation from extended family or unwanted pregnancies. Orphans (including the abandoned or those whose families needed help) were cared for by church-run institutions, and apprenticed at ages today's generation would think too young. Children were expected to work at an early age and education was not so valued as it is now. In 1898, Jeremy's situation would not have been unusual. The alternative to orphanages and apprenticeships was a life of hardship on the streets.

3. The British Columbia Protestant Orphanage was built in 1893 at the corner of Cook and Hillside Streets in Victoria. (It is today the Cridge Centre for the Family.) Prior to 1894, when the new building was occupied, the orphanage had an earlier site on Raeside. There is a touching article in the *Victoria Times-Colonist*, Sunday, August 20, 1995, by J.F. (Sandy) Carmichael, who spent a year in the orphanage during the Depression of the 1930s and remembered it fondly.

4. My grandfather's diary is actually quite short. When I photocopied it and then transcribed it onto the computer, the document printed out at 30 single-spaced pages. My grandfather made entries every day — I like to think he did this to share his experiences with his wife and sons when he returned home. I have included only certain selections; to have included the entire journal would have slowed down the story. Jeremy and the Robinson crew are fictional, and therefore they are not mentioned in my grandfather's entries. Smith, his gang — Reverend Bowers, Yeah Mow and Syd — McHenry and E.A. Hegg, the photographer, were real people of the time. They are not mentioned in the journal, but I included them in my story. Everyone else in the story, such as Walsh, Steele, Perry, the Cle Elm and Anamosa crews, is mentioned in the journal. Because Hegg took his team of goats through the White Pass at the same time as my grandfather's crew, and Smith was then consolidating his control over Skagway, I took the liberty of including them.

5. Jefferson (Soapy) Smith was a real person. In 1897, he and his gang moved to Skagway from the Colorado silver mines. There, he had developed a scam in which he sold bars of soap for $5 to people who hoped to get one of the bars they'd seen wrapped in a $50 bill, hence his nickname Soapy. By 1898, Smith's gang ran Skagway. Many citizens were misled about his true nature because of Smith's acts of apparent community-mindedness, such as his adopt-a-dog program, his church-building and his prevention of a lynching. Others, however, recognized him as the dangerous scoundrel he turned out to be, and his gang as a motley collection of ruffians. On July 8, 1898, Frank Reid, a quasi-legal deputy who had the support of most of the community, engaged in a gunfight with Smith, who died of a gunshot wound. His gang left town in a hurry, only hours ahead of the law. Unfortunately, Smith also managed to shoot Reid, the bullet lodging in his thigh. Reid died a few days later. Both men were buried in the Skagway cemetery where their graves can still be viewed.

6. Robert J. McHenry lived in the Welland Canal area of what is now Ontario. He was accused of being William Townsend, the leader of a gang of murderers who had killed a number of people, including a policeman. He was tried twice in the 1850s and acquitted both times. There is also mention of a McHenry who, in the 1880s, after the Dease Lake (British Columbia) gold rush, came out of the Macmillan River area with 40 pounds of gold (Keele, Joseph, 1908, cited in Samuel R. Holloway's *Yukon*

Gold, Outcrop, 1985). It is possible that the trial and the Dease Lake references involve the same person. I presumed so in order to provide a reason for Fraser's crew to be prospecting in the North Macmillan area. Since no reason is given in the journal, this one seemed plausible.

7. On Ogilvie's map, included in *The Klondike Official Guide* (Toronto: Hunter Rose, 1898), the area between the Macmillan and Peel Rivers is only vaguely mapped and the rivers appear closer together than they really are. Today, one would not think that the next river north from the North Macmillan could possibly be the Peel. However, James Fraser, working from Ogilvie's map, seemed to have made this assumption.

8. During my research, I learned to be skeptical of primary sources. My grandfather's journal refers to James Walsh as Major, but by the time Walsh had left the North West Mounted Police in the 1880s, he was Inspector, and by the time Fraser bumped into Walsh on the gold rush trail, he was about to take up duties as Yukon District Commissioner. I assume that Fraser continued to call Walsh "Major" because this was the ex-Mountie's most familiar designation, especially since the two men's time in Winnipeg coincided during the 1880s. (Walsh was the North West Mounted Policeman in the Cypress Hills area whom Sitting Bull trusted. Walsh persuaded Sitting Bull to return with his people to the United States where the Chief was killed by authorities in 1890.)

Similarly, Fraser's journal refers to *Captain* Strickland, whereas *Inspector* Strickland was in charge of the North West Mounted Police detachment at the summit of the White and Chilkoot Passes during the mass migration of 1897/1898 to the Klondike. I have no idea why my grandfather demoted the Inspector, but it has contributed to my skeptical view of single primary sources.

9. When the Klondike Gold Rush is mentioned more than one hundred years after the event, popular imagination calls up various images: black and white photographs of the stark human chain struggling up the almost vertical slope of the Chilkoot Pass; swollen, putrefying carcasses in Dead Horse Gulch; North West Mounted Policemen checking people and supplies through the border at the top of the snowy passes; boat-building at Lake Bennett and the dash of thousands down the Yukon River; wild Dawson City where hard-drinking "girls" cleaned out the fortunes of prospectors in from the creeks; a boom of gold, gold, gold — and then a sudden bust.

Most people who participated in the dash for gold in 1897 and '98 did not strike it rich. An estimated 60,000 to 100,000 men, women and children, speaking a babel of different languages, climbed the Chilkoot and White Passes or attempted the overland route from Edmonton or steamed up the Yukon River from the coast of Alaska. Fewer than half that many reached the Klondike area and Bonanza Creek; about 4,000 grew wealthy and fewer than 100 remained so after the gold rush finished.

10. Today we tend to speak of "the Klondike" or of "someone going to the Klondike." During the gold rush of 1898, people usually omitted the article "the," saying that they were going "to Klondike."

ABOUT THE AUTHOR

Sandy Frances Duncan's family has lived in British Columbia since the 1890s when her grandfather, James Fraser, moved west with his family. After earning a Master of Arts degree in Psychology from the University of British Columbia, Duncan worked as a psychologist for nine years before beginning to write fiction. She is an award-winning author of ten published books, including *The Toothpaste Genie* (Scholastic), *Cariboo Runaway* (Pacific Edge Publishing) and *Listen to Me, Grace Kelly* (Kids Can Press). She has contributed to a number of anthologies including *Dropped Threads: What We Aren't Told* (Vintage/Random House), *West by Northwest* (Polestar), *Language in Her Eye* (Coach House Press), *Celebrating Canadian Women* (Fitzhenry & Whiteside) and *Vancouver Short Stories* (UBC Press). Her interest in the Klondike grew out of her grandfather's journal which he kept on his journey into the Yukon in search of gold in 1898, and led her to research the Klondike and gold rush period extensively, with tours to many of the sites on her grandfather's journey. She presently lives on Gabriola, one of British Columbia's Gulf Islands.